LOST and FOUND

Trish Marie Dawson

Lost and Found

Copyright © Trish Marie Dawson 2013

First Edition

ISBN-13: 978-0615784168
ISBN-10: 061578416X

Pretty Little Weeds
PUBLISHING

For Shane.

IHYFM was my baby.

You've helped make my baby's baby possible. Love you.

LOST and FOUND

PROLOGUE

The warm wind whipped around my face, tugging strands of hair out of my pony-tail and carrying the dry scent of summer with it. I sat cross-legged in the dirt, twisting a single yellow rose bud in between my fingers. Inhaling deeply, I leaned into the grassy mound with my right hand, and stretched my left arm back and forth. It wasn't completely healed yet, neither was the pain in my shin. Winchester had done a meticulous job of sewing the eight inch long gash up. It had healed nicely on the outside, but the slashed muscle was taking much longer to recover. I worried the limp in my gait would never go away, but considering how badly banged up the accident had left me, it could've been much worse.

The wind changed direction and pushed at my back, causing the pale blue gauzy top I wore to flutter around my waist and a familiar male smell came with it. *Connor*. I smiled over my shoulder at him and he sat down in the grass beside me. His jeans brushed against my thin, cotton shorts and he playfully banged our knees together.

"Hey baby, thought you might be here." He said after tenderly kissing my cheek.

"It's a good spot, isn't it?" I rested my head on his shoulder and looked down at the yellow rose. Even though it hadn't fully opened, its fragrant essence fanned out around it, gracing nature with its aroma as only a rose can. Most of the potted roses had burned with the lodge but a few were salvageable. It took several weeks longer than usual for one particular rose bush to bloom and I held the first bud in my hand.

"It's perfect. You know he would love it here, right?" Connor said quietly.

I nodded.

The lake opened up in front of us, contrasting perfectly with the dark pine trees in the background and the tips of the mountains even further away. He put an arm around my shoulder and hugged me tightly. "Kris made an early dinner for everyone but come back whenever you're ready, okay?" I nodded again and smiled at him as he stood and walked away. I watched the breeze push against his shirt, flattening it to his upper body. He had let his hair grow out and the long, wispy dark waves reached just below his ears. At first he complained about the growing length of his hair, but with my assurance that it only made him sexier, he vowed not to cut it. I sighed heavily as he headed back toward the cabins where the others would be waiting. Skip and Winchester. Jacks and Ana...with the small bulge that was showing in her lower abdomen. Kris and Connor. My friends. My family.

A small, fuzzy rabbit hopped out from behind a tree but quickly dashed back under cover when it saw me. I smiled, happy that life had started anew...in the forest, at least. It had taken a while, but even our deer returned to the lake, sometimes coming as close as the cabin steps to say hello. She had filled out, losing her juvenile markings and was spotted most regularly by Kris, who spent at least two hours of each day hiking the trails around the lodge with the dog. In a way, I suppose the deer was a part of the family too.

I carefully dug my painted toes into the soft dirt and wild grass, trying not to badly mess up the pedicure that Kris had given me the day before, while the earth cooled my warm feet and I noticed movement in the sky. A sleek white bird flew in low over the water and dragged an elegant foot along the surface. Zoey raised her head and quietly huffed at the aviary display that rippled the lake water from the center out. Before the water's edge, the bird lifted with the breeze and floated into a nearby tree, timing its landing with rehearsed perfection.

"Fin." I sighed. "We miss you."

I looked at the mound of dirt encircled with dozens of smooth, round stones to my right and laid the flower delicately on top.

"*I hope you find me again in the next life.*" I whispered, as I rested my hand on his grave. "*The first yellow rose is for you.*"

CHAPTER one

There was barely a chance to gasp before I was pitched violently off the side of the bike and gravity had its way with me; swiftly pulling me down to the street with a sickening thud. After my body rolled to a stop, I was aware that I was face-down with my cheek resting on the hot pavement, my arm twisted underneath me, my legs spread out wide and motionless. The motorcycle helmet had come off and made wobbly turns on the ground as it wildly spun on its top away from me. When my mouth opened to exhale what little air remained in my lungs, jagged pieces of loose gravel scraped against my lower jaw. *I literally kissed the pavement.* For some reason the thought was funny - as well as the empty helmet spinning off toward the edge of the highway. I had to giggle despite the pain radiating slowly through my body. *This is going to hurt later.*

"Riley!" Connor slid along the ground coming to a stop at my side, landing hard on his knees as he gently placed one of his gloved hands on my back. "Don't move…just stay still," he said softly.

Oh, don't worry. I'm not going anywhere. I giggled harder until I had to suck air in to breathe and then it wasn't so funny anymore. My right side took the brunt of the fall and everything from my shoulder to my ankle screamed in painful protest. As Connor fumbled with his helmet and tossed it to the ground hard enough to make it bounce twice, I managed to pull my pinned arm out from under me, which helped alleviate some of the pressure on my right shoulder. Even though he put his hands on my back to keep me still, I shifted my legs until I could bend both knees and raise my feet up off the ground. I must have looked like I was trying to swim on the side of the highway. Yeah, it hurt…a lot, but my legs worked and I didn't think my back was broken so I attempted to roll over onto my side. Once I got there, all I could think about was how blue the sky was.

Lying flat on my back, I was finally able to fill my lungs with air again. After exhaling noisily, I happened to look to my right just in time to see my black *Scorpion* helmet slowly roll off the side of the highway and down the steep rocky slope. *Damn, I liked that one.*

"Can you sit up?" Even though his voice was low and calm, Connor's bright blue eyes revealed his fear.

"I think…I'm okay. Just got the wind knocked out of me. Give me a second." I gave him a reassuring smile but inwardly loathed the idea of standing up.

"Okay. Okay, take your time." Connor's voice dipped lower, as if he was talking to an injured animal.

"Connor, I'm fine. We were only going what - less than thirty miles per hour?" I tried not to wince while bending my knees.

"It was still a bad fall, Riley." His furrowed brows were almost completely lost beneath dark waves of long hair. A thin layer of sweat coated his upper lip and his cheeks were flushed a bright pink color. He was gorgeous.

"Okay, help me up."

I reached out and let him grip my arm with one hand while he gently pushed against my lower back, helping me into a sitting position. Every single muscle in my body groaned.

"You alright?" Connor looked me up and down as he ran a hand over my body, softly probing my bones and joints until he rested it on my thigh. I nodded at him while concentrating on the effort it took to breathe deeply.

"Damn. Look at the bike."

I grimaced at the shiny machine as it lay on its side, a good twenty feet from me. A small puddle of liquid had formed beneath it and even though I knew nothing about bikes, I knew *that* was not a good sign.

Connor seemed to relax slightly and chuckled, "Yeah, you scraped the hell out of it." He looked down at me with a smile, leaning forward close enough to gently brush his lips against mine. "Know what happened?"

"Huh?" I asked.

He laughed softly. "Do you know what happened, why you tipped?"

"Oh, I have no idea. One minute I was on it, the next…well, I wasn't."

As I smiled up at him, a familiar stab of pain shot through my left shoulder blade. I was beyond thankful that I fell to the right, and not the left. My shoulder was still healing from the car accident earlier in the year; it couldn't take more damage so soon.

"We might have to leave this here. It's a good thing you wiped out close to the shoulder." Connor stood and walked over to the bike, nudging at it with his foot. It didn't move.

"Is it bad?" I grimaced as he knelt and dipped one of his fingers into the puddle that had spread to the front tire then rubbed them slowly together.

"Um, how about you ride back with me?"

I lowered my head back onto the pavement with a sigh. I was not gifted with the ability to ride a motorcycle, though I loved the thrill of it. This was the second one I had seemingly totaled in less than a week. My plan was shot if I couldn't figure this out.

"Maybe you could just help me lift it, and-"

Connor cut my suggestion off by swiping his hand through the air quickly. "No. You're riding with me and that's final. Here, put this on."

He swooped down to pick his helmet up off the ground and pulled it over my head without saying another word. I glared at him through the face shield while he tugged the chinstrap tight. After moving my head up and down and to the side, he rapped his knuckles on the top of the helmet with a grin.

"Think you're all secure, babe."

Inside the helmet, my voice was mumbled slightly when I responded, "Yeah, that's what I thought last time. Look how that turned out."

We turned down the lodge driveway twenty minutes later, just as the sun began touching the tips of the trees off the western horizon. I hugged Connor tightly as the tires crunched over the dirt road. We passed the burnt remains of the main building and followed the small pathway around the back lawn. Giant pine trees loomed all around us, blocking out most of the direct sunlight.

The sprinkler system was one of the amenities we had lost during Matt's arson attempt of late spring. The lawn was the first thing to brown and fill with weeds, but I didn't mind. There was something unnatural about perfectly cut grass in the mountains, anyway. As we neared the cabin trail, I noticed all the dandelions growing freely in the lawn and smiled. I preferred them to the previously intricate green carpet any day.

Connor pulled his bike to a stop at the head of the trail and helped me hop off the back. He noticed my limp was more pronounced than usual but let me walk the trail down to the cabins on my own, holding my hand in his as we stepped quietly.

Zoey was the first to greet us. She bounded off the front steps of cabin number six and ran toward us at full speed with her long, pink tongue hanging out the side of her mouth and her busy tail wagging furiously from side to side.

"Whoa, girl... No jumping." I tried to bend over to rub her head but my body quickly protested by sending a painful spasm up my right side.

"Zoey, come here." Connor patted his leg and the dog moved to him for some behind-the-ear scratching.

"You head up to the cabin, I'll meet you there. I'm going to get Winchester, okay?" Connor said over his shoulder as he walked toward the two-story structure that Winchester shared with Skip, our lodge patriarch.

I groaned with half-hearted irritation. "I don't need Win, I told you - I'm *fine*."

"You are *not* fine. And stop complaining - go inside and lay down. We'll be right there, okay?"

And with that, Connor turned his back to me and walked up the small dirt pathway that would take him to the middle cabin. I cursed at his backside, no matter how enticing his behind looked in his tight jeans, and limped the short distance alone to the last cabin on the trail; lucky number seven. Without Connor standing at my side, I let myself wince with each step until I made it to the porch. My body was aching all over, more than I wanted to admit to Connor. What was the point of getting him worried? There wasn't much to do about it anyway.

My head had barely settled onto the couch cushion when I heard the scrape of the dog's nails on the wooden porch and the two men talking out front, as they hurried through the doorway. Winchester took one look at me and his eyes widened slightly before his eyes narrowed into a disparaging squint.

"Now, look. Before you get all pissed at me…it was *totally* an accident and I'm not that hurt - not really." I raised myself up onto my elbows as if to prove my point, but my breath hitched with the pain in my side and I gave up, flopping back down into the cushions with a hiss.

"Riley. You have to stop trying to kill yourself."

Winchester's crisp white tee creased across his abdomen as he sat down on the coffee table next to me and opened up the large first aid kit he brought with him. He had become our resident nurse. From mending simple things, cleaning and bandaging cuts to the more serious chores that included attempting to stitch up gashes and holes. This would be the third time he had worked on me in as many months. He called me his most popular patient.

"Connor said you crashed. Landed hard and rolled on the pavement," he said with a pause as he took my jaw carefully in one of his smooth hands so he could tilt my face to the side. I was sure I had a glorious case of road rash on my right cheek based on the intense burn that radiated off my skin. He narrowed his eyes more before he continued talking, "…and he said your helmet came off as you went down." He let go of my chin and leaned closely to stare into both of my pupils.

"Oh, stop it, Win. You're no doctor. Just clean me up and be on your way."

It came out sounding a bit harsher than I meant it. A muscle in Winchester's jaw twitched before he quickly backed away from me.

"Right." He glared at me long enough to make me feel bad. And I already felt like crap.

"Sorry, I know you are the closest thing we have to a doctor. I didn't mean it that way. I'm just irritated; you know…that I wiped out…*again*." I sighed and leaned deeper into the pillow, flexing my left shoulder a few times.

The delicate features of his face softened and he patted my hand before reaching into his bag. He poured over several medical books all summer. Without his help, I'm sure I would never have survived the car crash that killed half of our group just a few months before. I watched him pull out small bottles of liquid, lots of gauze and packets of antibiotic ointments. He soaked some of the cotton pads and began cleaning my face; rubbing the dirt and gravel out of my skin as gently as he could. It took all of my self-control not to thrash below his touch. The cleaning process was more painful than the actual crash.

After removing my heavy denim jacket and jeans, leaving me wearing only my tank top and white cotton boy shorts, he thoroughly examined my back, neck, shoulders and arms, finding only one other scrape that ran along the inside of my right wrist. My legs were badly bruised but otherwise unscathed.

After nearly a half hour of bandaging, my skin smelled of antiseptic as I was helped upstairs to rest but with strict orders to not fall asleep right away. Winchester was worried about me having a concussion, though I doubted seriously that I did. I vaguely remember flipping over an embankment in Matt's truck and the issues I had for weeks from the concussion.

I lay beneath the thin sheet listening to the wind rustle the curtains while Connor showered. He left the bathroom door open, so the strong ocean fragrance of his body wash quickly filled the room. I would never tire of his smell. The anticipation of him cuddling up next to me in bed, smelling so delicious almost made me forget I had pillows completely surrounding my body, serving as props for my sore limbs.

He came out of the small and steamy room wrapped only in a towel. The tease.

"You suck." It was a simple statement, but he stopped and gaped at me as if I had just finished screaming a long string of curse words at him.

"What did you say?"

He was still staring at me, his eyes wide, his hair plastered to his head, water dripping from his ears onto his shoulders. The towel was low enough for me to see his hipbones and that oh, so pleasant happy trail of soft, dark hair that led down south.

"I said *you suck*. You come out of the shower practically naked, smelling all delicious and I'm expected to just lie here, ignoring you? *You suck*." I stuck my lower lip out in a pout.

Connor blinked and laughed before glancing at the open bedroom door. "I'm sure I could think of a few ways to keep you awake. But, Winchester is bringing the others by any minute. That could be awkward." He winked at me and pulled his towel off in a swift move, flipping it at the foot of the bed.

I gawked at the perfect curves of his naked backside while he fumbled around in the dresser, pulling out various pieces of clothing. By the time he was dressed, wearing clean jeans, and a tight black t-shirt, I was absolutely seething at the fact that I couldn't launch myself across the room at him and drag him beneath the sheets.

෯ৰৢ

After the others took turns coming in and out of the room to spend time with Riley, Winchester finally gave her the go ahead to sleep a quarter past midnight. But Connor stayed up well into the early morning hours watching her carefully; leaning close to her face to make sure her breathing sounded normal. His elbows were sore from the way he propped himself up to keep an eye on her but he ignored it. A couple of times he stroked the bandage on the right side of her face that covered most of her cheek and jaw.

When his arms couldn't hold him up anymore, he fluffed his pillows so he was angled up enough to see her face while he rested on his side. He kept playing the accident over in his mind. It drove him crazy that he didn't know what went wrong. One minute she was fine riding ahead of him on Sunrise Highway with the ends of her long, blonde hair streaming out behind her. He looked away for just a second. Just a second... And she was flying off the bike, toward the guardrail. His stomach knotted at the memory of seeing her sprawled out on the pavement, not moving.

He rolled onto his back and draped am arm over his face, blocking out the subtle glow of moonlight that streamed in through the open windows. This plan of hers was stupid. He needed to figure out a way to convince her to change her mind. At this rate, she was going to kill herself before they even got to Los Angeles.

CHAPTER two

The strong smell of caffeinated coffee woke me. For one brief moment, I forgot about the beating my body took the day before until I tried to push up off the bed just like any other morning. My weak arms shook from the weight of my upper body and I fell back onto the mattress with a groan. My entire body felt like one gigantic bruise. There wasn't any one place that didn't hurt. Even brushing my hair off my forehead caused a painful tingle along my scalp.

After settling back against the mound of pillows that were propped around me the night before, I angled my body in a way where I could watch Connor. He must have been up late if my clumsy stirring didn't wake him. His mouth was parted slightly so I could hear his breathing as he inhaled and exhaled in his sleep. I watched his body rise and fall a few more times until Kris quietly came to the open doorway with a tray in her hands.

I brought my hand up quickly to keep her quiet before I whispered, "*Sshh. He's asleep.*"

She nodded and set the tray down on top of the dresser and crossed the room. Her thick hair was just below her shoulders now and the length seemed to be pulling some of her frizzy curls out a bit. She had about one million more freckles splattered across her face than she did when I met her. After a careful hug, she reached up and gingerly touched the bandage on the side of my face. I had only known her for a few months but she was family; the little sister I never had. And maybe even the daughter I had lost.

A few sips of the French roast were all it took to wake up fully, but it posed a problem too. I gestured to the bathroom and Kris helped me shuffle out from under the sheets so I could walk the short distance from the bed to the small room in the corner. Even though the pain was intense - I had to pee.

Despite her protesting looks, she finally caved and helped me hobble out of the room and down the stairs to the main part of the cabin where I was greeted by my little lab/cocker spaniel mix that survived the world's deadliest virus with me. Zoey was all that was left of my previous life. I rubbed the top of her head vigorously until Kris pulled her away. The two of them had bonded tremendously over the last few months. Kris was seventeen now, having celebrated her birthday two weeks ago but she still rolled around with the dog just as a small child would and dropped everything to play fetch with Zoey.

"Thanks for the coffee," I said with a smile. I felt the tug of the bandage pull on my skin and tried to hide the wince from Kris.

"Sure. But if Connor wakes up freaking out that you're not there and finds out you went down the stairs without his help, it was all you. I will plead the fifth," she laughed.

"Don't worry, I can handle Connor." I smiled as Kris rolled her eyes.

"Are you hungry? Cause I was planning on making pancakes."

My stomach clenched at the mention of food. "Yes, I'm starving."

The kitchen stool proved too hard to climb up onto, so I opted for the couch again. At least there, I could prop the pillows around me and carry on an upright conversation with Kris. She had just poured the batter for the first pancake onto the griddle when there was a knock at the front door and Zoey rushed over to greet Winchester. He opened the door and poked his head inside but his smile faded when he saw me lounging on the couch.

"You should be upstairs, in bed!" He tried to look upset, but the scowl on his groomed face was comical and I couldn't help but smile at him.

"Mornin' Win. Don't worry; I had help getting down the stairs. If I lay in bed all day, I'll be even sorer, won't I?"

"Where's Connor? I'll yell at him for getting you out of bed." He took a seat on the massive reclaimed tree trunk that served as the coffee table and leaned forward to touch my bandage.

"It's not me you'll be yelling at," Connor's husky morning voice said from the top of the stairway as he took the steps down, two at a time.

I tried not to stare at him, but I did as he was wearing only his boxers. And they hung from his hips so low that even Winchester blushed. Connor padded across the room, ignoring the dog that leapt at his legs and stopped directly behind the couch with his arms crossed, glaring down at me. I smiled, but still had a hard time keeping my eyes on his face, so eventually I had to turn away. Winchester raised his eyebrow, but said nothing as he began to peel back the bandage above my jaw.

"Ouch." I flinched as the tape was pulled from my skin.

Connor towered behind me as Winchester dabbed at the healing scrape with clean gauze. After he put more ointment and a fresh bandage on my face, he leaned back to inspect his work. Apparently satisfied, he moved on to my wrist to repeat the process.

Kris lightened the mood by serving us all a steaming plate of pancakes. Connor was either unaware he was mostly naked, or was too stubborn to return upstairs to dress as he sat at the kitchen island on a stool to eat. I stole a few glances in his direction but our gazes never met. He was pissed at me and let everyone in the room know it. *He's so damn overprotective*, my mind raced.

We were just finishing up breakfast when Zoey rushed out the front door and returned moments later with Jacks and Skip in tow. I had seen both of them the night before, but Jacks gawked at me when he got a closer look at the bruises that bloomed colorfully overnight, covering my arms, legs and face in every color of blue and green imaginable.

"Shit, girl. You look like hell," he said as he leaned in to kiss the top of my head.

"Thank you so much, you're too kind," I muttered as I swiped a hand across his arm.

"Good morning, honey, how you feeling today?" Skip asked, as he too leaned down and kissed my hair.

"Actually, I'm a little sore," I paused to steal a glance at Connor, who was still pouting on his stool. "But, I think I'll be fine."

"Now's as good a time as any to talk about this plan you have, honey." Skip looked at each of the men before getting a nod from Connor to continue.

"I'm still going." I stared into my lap. If it was an ambush they had planned, it wouldn't work.

"Yeah, but honey, this is your second accident on a motorcycle, you honestly think you can make it all the way to L.A. on a bike you don't know how to ride?"

Skip sat on the edge of the couch waiting for my answer while Winchester silently packed up the items he had used from his first aid kit. The box was the size of a large briefcase and he set it down on the coffee table before getting up to clean his plate in the kitchen. Even Kris refused to look at me as she bustled about the kitchen. It seemed no one was coming to my defense.

I concentrated on making my face as rigid as possible before pushing away from the cushions and standing. I forced the wobble in my legs to stop as I took a step away from the couch. Skip and Connor both stood, unsure of where I planned on going. Winchester sent a sideways glance at Jacks before quickly looking down at the floor.

"If none of you are man enough to go with me, I'll go on my own. Even if that means I'll have to take a damn Vespa."

With that, I turned and walked slowly away from the group taking a great deal of satisfaction from the shocked looks I caught before rounding the corner to take the steps up to the second floor. It hurt but I made it to the upper landing without falling or bursting into tears. My thoughts ran wild as I turned the shower on and stuck my hand under the water stream, waiting for it to warm. *What's wrong with them? Why am I the only one that cares about what happened to Mariah? I knew in my heart that the nightmares and constant wondering would never stop till I had answers.*

∿∞∿

"But I'm not sure. Not really," Kris said while she sat on the edge of the bed.

"Yeah, but there are way too many similarities for it to be just coincidence, Kris, you were the first one to say so." I watched her paint my toenails a bright orange color.

"What are you going to do once you get there? I mean, how will you know where to look? It's been months. They could be anywhere by now." She paused to look up at me, before putting the finishing touches on my big toe.

"I think we need to try. Mariah could be there still. What Matt and the others did…if she's still there, I can't live with that." I looked hard at Kris while she set the nail polish bottle on the side table.

"If you're going, I should go with you." She avoided looking at me.

"That's totally out of the question. You already told me what we need to know." I shifted so that I could swing my legs over the side of the bed.

For a minute, we just stared at each other. I had never pulled the parent-card out with Kris; she wasn't my child, but she was only seventeen and I didn't want to put her in a situation that could be dangerous.

"Look," I sighed, "…this isn't something any of us can figure out till we get there. I just have to know, I have to know if Mariah is still in L.A. and if the men that took her are the same ones that hurt you."

Kris traced the scar that ran the length of her jaw with one finger and slowly let her hand trail down her neck to where the second scar was. They faded some over the summer but both were still noticeable. She had finally shared with me her story a few weeks back, about the two men that abducted her after she set out on her own when her parents died from the virus. They beat her up and dragged her to a nearby building where they kept her locked up for hours before trying to rape her at knifepoint. She had a pocketknife of her own wedged inside her boot and was able to get away thanks to a great deal of luck. Not long after that is when Jacks found her hiding out at a gas station on the southern outskirts of Los Angeles, bloody and scared. It was an experience no teenager should have to go through. I didn't want her to return there and have to relive the nightmare.

"You still think anyone traveling up and down the west coast would try and go through L.A.?" she asked.

I nodded. "Yes, I do. You said the parked traffic was bad and that could be a problem, which is why I thought taking a bike would be best. If you lived anywhere near there and survived this," I waved my hand around the room, "…many people would probably look for others there. You did." I watched her nod slowly.

"Yeah. I guess you're right. And if others do pass through there, I bet those jerks are still doing the same thing…waiting and grabbing who they can." She shifted on the bed so she was facing me. She opened her mouth to speak but clamped it shut and looked down at her hands.

"What is it, Kris? It's okay," I spoke softly.

"Um…did you mean what you said about getting a scooter?" She blinked up at me, a bit embarrassed.

"You mean, downstairs?" I laughed loudly but stopped when I realized Kris was looking at me nervously. "Yes, I guess I did. Learning how to stay on a motorcycle is proving to be harder than I thought. Why?"

"Well, because I know how to ride a scooter, my best friend had one. So I could definitely go with you then." She stared at me, gauging my reaction.

"Kris…even if we did that - took a couple of scooters, it's a long drive. And what if we *do* find those guys…or more like them?"

Her brown eyes looked up at me, pleading for me to say yes. "Just think about it, okay? I could help, I know I could."

She got up, snatched the nail polish from the bedside table, and hurried out of the room before I could object again. The only thing girly about Kris was the fact that she enjoyed painting her nails, and everyone else's around her. Connor let her paint his toes once, but that was after several beers and a full on dare from Jacks that he wouldn't walk around with painted toes for a week. He lasted almost a month before I told him his pink toes were clashing with my orange ones.

After I leaned back onto the bed, I let my thoughts take over. *She's right. She could help us; she's not a kid anymore. Maybe I should let her come.* I dangled my legs over the edge of the mattress and swayed my feet from side to side until the pull on my bruised lower back became too uncomfortable. When I sat up, Connor was standing in the doorway, watching me.

"How much did you hear?" I asked.

"Enough."

"And…?" I waited for him to answer but instead he walked across the room and sat down next to me.

"And, I think if you're sure you want to do this, I'll go with you. But not until you're better and we've got a solid plan. Okay?" His blue eyes sparkled as they bore into mine.

I nodded and let my eyes fill with tears as he pulled me against his chest. After burrowing my face into his shirt while he stroked my hair, the clean and fresh scent that was Connor, filled my nose. I was grateful for the millionth time, that it was he, who pulled me out of the San Diego Bay, back in January.

ം∼ഔ

The waves pull away from the shore leaving frothy bubbles along the wet sand and return abruptly, depositing fresh seaweed and broken seashells onto the beach before the ebb of the ocean pulls the waves back again. Even though the sun is partially obscured by the clouds, there is no mistaking the summer feel of the day. It smells of salt and coconut lotion...and goldfish crackers.

"Mommy, look! Look what I found!" Dean skids to a stop at my feet, dripping cold water onto my toes and holds his cupped hands up to my face.

"Eww, what is it?" I ask, while catching a glimpse of something slimy in his little hand.

"Gel-fish! Mommy, it's a gel-fish!" He grins at me as I push myself up to my knees to get a better look at what he has.

"Do you mean jelly-fish?" I ask with a smile, sure that it must be something else in his hand but when I peel back his short fingers I see that he is indeed holding a sandy piece of jelly-fish.

"Oh, Dean! Where'd you find this? It stays in the water; jellyfish can sting you. Go put it back, baby."

I turn him around and pat his bottom as he scurries toward the shore to deposit the chunk of jelly into the next wave. I don't have the heart to tell him it's no longer alive. I wave at Shannon as she jumps through the waves a few yards to our right, diving under the big ones and floating on her back when the water calms. As I look up and down the beach, I smile at the families playing in the surf.

Eventually Dean comes bounding back up the sand and plops down on the towel next to me. Another mischievous smile lights up his face.

I sigh before asking with a crooked grin, "So, what do you have now, my little biologist?"

He tilts his head to the side, as if challenging me to wrestle his three-year-old hand open. I try not to cave in too quickly but my curiosity has my full attention, so I tickle his side until his fingers splay open on his lap revealing a large chunk of bloody flesh. I

25

recoil from his hand in horror. I would know those blue eyes anywhere and I start screaming.... Because he's holding his sister's face in his hands.

↝∽⊱

The strangled sound of my voice pierced through the night air, loud enough to wake the whole house. Kris came stumbling into the bedroom in her over-sized sleep shirt just as Connor shook me awake, ripping me out of my nightmare. At first, I struggled against him as my body shook but he refused to let go, even after my hot tears soaked into his shirt. Feeling the sudden urge to throw up, I scrambled away from him and barely made it to the toilet in time to release my dinner.

"Is she okay?" I heard Kris's shaky voice in the next room while I rinsed my still raw face off with cold water from the tap.

"Just a bad dream, she'll be okay. Go back to bed kiddo, it's alright."

Connor's answer was enough to send Kris stumbling groggily back to her room. His sleepy voice was fully loaded with hints of his Irish heritage. I loved to hear his accent; it was rare on account of all the time he spent in the States over the last twenty years.

"I'm sorry," I mumbled when I finally left the solitary confinement of the bathroom.

"Babe, don't apologize for having a bad dream. I've had a lot of them myself, lately."

He pulled the covers back and scooted to the side, leaving enough room for me to climb under the sheets and cuddle up against him. I tried to relax and concentrate on the curves of Connor's body as his chest rested against my back, his legs tucked up close behind my thighs.

Zoey huffed softly from down the hall, no doubt from Kris's room where she was not only allowed, but also encouraged to sleep on the bed every night. I shifted slightly, feeling comfort in the heaviness of Connor's arm draped securely around me. We sighed against each other silently and then something on the other side of the room caught my eye. My heart skipped a beat just before I squeezed my eyes tightly shut. A dark shadow was standing in the corner. *It's not real, it's not real,* I said to myself over and over. But I knew better. The same figure had visited me every night for a week. It wanted something, but I wasn't brave enough yet to find out what that was.

CHAPTER three

"You're up early," Kris said softly.

I turned around in time to see her pass through the doorway with the dog. After greeting Zoey with a vigorous ear-rub, she hit the porch deck running, her nails clicking on the weathered wood all the way down the stairs. Little flurries of dirt clouded around her legs as she disappeared in a rush behind the building to her favorite potty spot.

"I couldn't sleep much last night." I turned around and leaned my back against the deck railing.

"I know me neither." Kris looked tired and irritable.

"Sorry if I woke you."

"No, no, you didn't. I was already awake actually." She sat down on one of the colorful Adirondack chairs with a loud sigh.

"We're all having bad dreams, aren't we?" I grabbed at my loose hair and pulled it back into a messy knot so the slight breeze would stop blowing it into my face.

"Yeah. Sucks." Kris hugged her knees to her chest and stared out into the woods in front of our cabin.

"Hey," I approached her and put my hand on top of her head, rustling her dark hair until she playfully swatted my hand away, "...how about some pancakes? We still have chocolate chips, remember?"

"Deal!" She jumped up from her chair and I smiled as she rushed around me, back into the cabin.

Movement in the woods caught my attention and I turned in a half-circle, straining to see between the overgrown shrubs and trees that started on the other side of the small trail that linked the cabins together. My eyes settled on the trunk of a massive pine as I struggled to focus on the dark cloud behind it. My breathing stopped in my throat as the shape of a man began to form. I bristled as he stared out from the woods, looking at the cabins....looking at *me*. Everything stilled; the breeze stopped, the birds quieted, and all that could be heard was the thudding of my own heart.

But it couldn't be...*could it*? The tall and dark figure slowly lifted a hand and waved once at me as I took a step forward, peering harder into the darkness of the quiet forest until I was certain without a doubt that I was seeing *him*. Fin.

క్ర

As soon as I recognized him, he was gone. The man behind the tree became a normal shadow again. As I spun around to flee into the cabin, I crashed face-first into Connor's bare chest.

"Hey! Where are you off to in such a hurry?" He dragged a hand through his sleep-messed hair but his goofy grin fell when he looked down at my face.

"Oh God...I saw...I saw..." I couldn't say Fin's name out loud. I had helped put his body into the ground just a few months before. It didn't make sense - seeing him hiding in the trees.

After glancing over my shoulder, the woods appeared just as they always did. Connor must have sensed my anxiety because he looked up and down the trail with concern. Eventually satisfied that we were in fact alone, he put his arm around my shoulders before guiding me back to the door. I noticed him staring off into the woods before we left the porch with his brow furrowed, but he said nothing. Neither of us did. Neither of us had to.

Though no one had mentioned it, we all knew we weren't alone at the lodge. It wasn't talked about but it was there - the strange sounds in the night...the shadows that lurked...the whispers and the screams. We all woke up from our nightmares only to find that monsters were hiding in the shadows, waiting for something...waiting for us. It made it nearly impossible for anyone to get a good night of sleep. It was starting to show on our faces, just as it showed on Connor's as he turned me away from the woods to follow me back into the cabin.

Kris had already covered the counter space with the ingredients for breakfast, including freshly cut orange slices sitting in a large bowl. The kitchen was quickly filling with the aroma of citrus, cinnamon and vanilla. We had recently raided a few backyards and small orchards for fresh food. Most of the citrus trees in the greenhouse were burned earlier in the year. We didn't speak of that day often; it was the day that Fin died. And Matt too, though no one actually missed him and his delinquent friends.

I tried to push thoughts of Fin out of my mind while I poured the batter Kris had mixed onto the grill. When it bubbled around the edges, I flipped the pancake and blinked at the heat that radiated off the stovetop. Lost in a daydream of the past, I ignored the playful banter between Connor and Kris from the nearby living room and didn't notice the sound of the golf-cart until it pulled to a stop in front of the cabin.

Kris's loud squeal of delight brought me crashing back to reality and I flipped a pancake off the grill moments before it began to burn. So, the happy couple had finally returned from their baby-shopping spree from the day before. While Connor and Kris met Jacks and Ana outside, I cut up a few more oranges and doubled the pancake mixture. Figured I might as well make breakfast a family affair.

ဆုတ်

Jacks sauntered into the cabin looking a bit tired but otherwise happy. He was going to be a dad after-all, but spending hours combing through the dead city streets of San Diego to hit up the right baby shops with his pregnant girlfriend in tow was not his ideal way to spend a beautiful cloud-free day in July. What Ana wanted though, she seemed to get. And get a lot they did.

After breakfast, Jacks convinced everyone to take turns unloading bags and boxes of baby clothes and nursery essentials from the bed of his truck while Ana shouted out commands. I was the only one exempt from this duty since Jacks frowned at my still fresh road-rash injuries and officially dubbed me a spectator. It had been a week already and I was more than able to help, but inwardly happy I got passed over so easily.

Rather than simply standing around staring at the others as they bustled around the full truck, I decided to follow Ana back to the cabin she shared next to mine with Jacks, to help unload the multitude of supplies she would soon find unnecessary. *Five nursery lamps...really?* Who needed that many lights in a baby's room? Or two boxes - *BOXES* of baby blankets. Ana was soon going to find out how much laundry a little person created, unless her plan was to throw out everything that got dirty. Knowing her prissy personality, I didn't doubt that as a possibility.

Watching her hobble up and down steps was my newfound guilty pleasure. Once she started showing she couldn't hide the pregnancy anymore. And I suspected it was because she was nervous about who the baby's father was. It wasn't my place to know, so I didn't ask. But I hoped that Jacks had. Not that it mattered much; he was sold on the idea of becoming a parent and if the math fit for him, so be it. She claimed to be somewhere around the end of her second trimester, which meant the ever-increasing swell of her stomach was becoming a daily spectator event, much to her displeasure.

Ana's usual tight-clothed, high-heeled fashion sense had been replaced with one that would rival any hippie's wardrobe. In fact, she dressed more like me...minus the jeans. She hated anything that was tight around her stomach or chest, which meant no more skinny jeans and push-up bras. Oh, the joys of pregnancy. Her dangly jewelry didn't go away though or the solid coat of makeup she wore daily. How she kept a constant supply of foundation on hand, I had no idea.

"So, do you want me to unpack the clothes...maybe hang them up in the closet?" I stood at the foot of the stairs, holding a bag of multi-colored socks not much bigger than my thumb and baby jumpers in my arms.

"No, no, no. I'll do it. Jacks has to put the dresser together first. I want the clothes in there." She grabbed the bag from me and wobbled up the stairs to the second floor. I tried not to laugh at the view.

"What about the blankets...you want those upstairs too?" I called after her. I figured I'd be safe with blankets.

"No, not *yet*! Those go in the dresser *too*," her voice trailed off as she walked down the hall into the spare bedroom turned nursery but I still caught what she said next, *"...honestly, I'm surrounded by idiots!"*

I counted to ten before taking a deep breath and trying to sound as if I hadn't heard her. "Hey, maybe I'll just go next-door and make lunch for everyone?" I needed an excuse to escape. It was still an hour before noon, but Ana was making it impossible to help. As was her usual way.

"Fine, whatever!" she hollered down the stairs.

Kris was parking the golf-cart in front of the cabin when I stepped back outside. The hot rays of the sun warmed my shoulders immediately. I made a mental note to put my bikini on after lunch and take a quick swim in the lake before I got too caught up in Ana's crazy decorating. With my bandages off, I was finally allowed back in the water.

Poor Kris was already caught in Ana's net. She was unloading more bags and small containers out of the back of the cart and smiled up at me as I approached. It was fun for her - planning for a baby. Half the group was beyond excited. Those of us that had already been parents were torn with conflicting emotions though. I know we were devastated, but we would never admit that out loud. I was happy for Ana and Jacks, truly I was. But her pregnancy was a constant reminder of my own lost children. On the inside, I was loathing the day Ana's baby cried for the first time.

I stood with my hands thrust into the pockets of my jean shorts and took in the view around me. The lodge was a lovely place. Even though we had lost the main building and the greenhouse, the rest of the property was still beautiful. The lake was perfect for the hot summer days and there was more than enough room for everyone to have their own space. I should have felt happy, because I had Connor. But it was becoming harder and harder to shrug off the survivor guilt and the depression. It was on Connor's face too. The dark rings below our eyes never seemed to go away. The longing for the innocent lives we had lost - it was slowly consuming us.

Each flick of the small waves exhaled a cool breeze that paired nicely with the refreshing temperature of the lake water. I drifted aimlessly atop a full-length inflatable float with my eyes closed, enjoying the penetrating heat of the early afternoon sunshine. My left elbow dangled slightly over the side of the small raft so that every other wave slapped against it softly. It was strangely comforting and relaxing. Other than my backside, which was an inch or two under the water line, my left arm was the only part of me that was thoroughly wet.

A subtle shift in the waves made me open my eyes and despite the glare of the sun on the water, I caught a glimpse of something dark floating toward me on my right. When I lifted my head up to get a better look, whatever it was quickly sank below the surface. After trying to sit up, the flimsy float bowed beneath me, dipping me lower into the lake. Panicking, my legs had nowhere to go but back into the water as I stared into the darkness beneath me, waiting for whatever I saw to surface again.

I could see Zoey where she lay stretched out on her side at the end of the dock, snoozing in the sun; it wasn't the dog swimming in the water. As the current shifted below me, a strangled sound pushed its way up my throat and escaped out of my mouth just as I pictured the shark from *Jaws*. This is absurd because I knew there wasn't a shark in the lake, but my imagination was taking no prisoners and held firmly to the thought that I was seconds away from being torn to pieces by razor-sharp teeth. All of a sudden, a set of hands burst out of the water and grabbed my arm, pulling me into the lake with a loud splash.

I kicked and fought off my attacker under the water and forced myself back up for air. Once I gulped in enough oxygen to breathe, a face surfaced just in front of mine. Bright blue eyes peered at me mischievously beneath a full head of dark hair.

"Bastard! You almost gave me a heart attack!" I screamed at Connor and splashed his laughing face with water. Zoey lifted her head up slightly to gaze at us before stretching and rolling onto her back. She returned to napping with her front legs pointing up at the sky.

"I'm sorry," Connor choked out the words between laughs and watery coughs, "I'm sorry...you just looked too comfortable...I *had* to mess with ya." He reached forward and grabbed my upper arms, tugging me into his chest.

"Relaxing was the point, jackass!" I struggled in his strong grip but my slight frame was no match against his long and lean one. I let my mouth fill with water and spit it at him, enjoying his shocked expression.

"Did you just spit *in my face*?" He pulled me tighter into him, sliding an arm around my waist, effectively pinning my chest to his. His fingers began a rhythmic prodding up and down my side and hip.

I squealed with laughter as he tickled me mercilessly while our bodies slid together and bobbed up and down in the water. I tried several times to dunk him, but couldn't push myself far enough away from his grip to get the proper leverage.

The sun beat down on the top of my head, warming my scalp. As I felt his hand move slowly over my hip and tug on the string of my bikini bottoms, I narrowed my eyes at him. "What are you doing?" I gasped as he answered by pulling the material free, tossing it onto the empty float drifting a few feet from us.

"It was in my way."

I lost myself in the sugary-lemon taste of his tongue as he crushed his mouth to mine while his hands expertly roamed around my body. Breaking free just long enough to take a deep breath, Connor pulled me through the water toward the raft and lifted it above our heads, depositing the plastic inflatable behind us, between our bodies and the shore.

"That won't stop anyone from seeing much if they look hard enough." I giggled as his mouth sucked and nibbled my earlobe, slowly working its way down my neck.

"I don't care who sees us. I want you. *Now*."

His eyes lit up with lust as he pulled me close. Somehow, I missed the moment when he slipped out of his shorts and was pleasantly shocked when our hips met…skin to skin.

"You have a very naughty streak, Kevan O'Connor." I purred into his ear while kicking my feet steadily in an attempt to keep my head above water.

Connor bristled against me and instantly released my waist, using both his hands to cup my face. I ignored the wind that rolled along the top of the lake and let my arms fall from his shoulders as I floated in front of him…mesmerized by his gaze. Drops of water fell from his long, dark lashes as his watery-blue eyes bore into mine.

"Say that again." The need in his voice was husky - *sexy*.

I tried to cock my head to the side but he held my face firmly in place. Our feet and legs bumped into each other as we were jounced around like human buoys in the middle of the lake.

"You're very naughty," I said with a smile.

"No..." he shook his head slowly and as he did the look of playful lust dissolved and turned into more of a desperate plea. He took a deep breath and searched my face with his gaze before he whispered, *"My name - say it again. Please."*

With one hand, I reached up to gently stroke his lower lip with my index finger and whispered back, *"Kevan O'Connor."*

Our mouths met again, as well as our hips, and we pushed and rubbed against one another, hungrily drinking in the taste and feel of each other until the need to become one was unbearable. Forgetting everything, including where we were, I lifted one leg, hooked it around Connor's waist, and used my arms to steady myself in the water as he gripped my left hip with one hand and slowly eased into me. Instinctually, I tightened around him, moaning at the fullness of him inside me. We rocked against each other, riding the gentle waves of the lake, using our arms to float as best as we could, slowly building up to the overwhelming sensation our bodies were craving.

"God, Riley..." Connor moaned, quickening the pace of each thrust, reaching deeper.

"Yes, oh yes..." I murmured against his cheek before crushing my lips to his.

When I tilted my head back, my hair floated in the water as spasm after spasm tore through the muscles in my groin and vibrated erratically through my thighs. Connor pushed harder into me before convulsing and biting down on his lower lip to keep from crying out. I pulled his face to mine as his body shook and tugged gently on his lower lip with my teeth.

"Oh my God, woman," he panted against my open mouth.

I wiggled my hips against his, refusing to release him. He was still hard inside me and I wanted to enjoy the sensation as long as he would let me.

"You have to stop grinding like that, Riley," his voice cracked slightly, *"...or I swear to God I'll come again."*

I flexed my pelvis rhythmically against him. "Promise?"

CHAPTER four

The swim back to the dock was grueling. My arms and legs were spent; my muscles jerked uncontrollably from our lovemaking session in the middle of the lake. We had treaded the water for nearly an hour while having sex and after spent a considerable amount of time trying to locate Connor's shorts, which we eventually spotted floating a good hundred feet from the middle of the lake.

Several times my head would dip below the water line and I would panic, thinking I might drown only thirty feet from dry land. My only solace was that Connor struggled to swim just as much as I did. When we reached the end of the dock both of us gripped the wooden pillars with relief, ignoring the slimy feel of the wet wood beneath our hands.

"Damn. That was harder than I thought it would be." I leaned my forehead on my arm while Connor rolled over onto his back and floated beside me.

"No joke. You wore me out, woman," he laughed into the warm afternoon breeze.

I smiled against my arm for a moment before taking the opportunity to sneak up on Connor and push him under the water. He came back up sputtering and cursing with a boyish grin on his face. I had already swum a good ten feet from him by the time he surfaced, in an attempt to stay clear of his wandering hands. Only a few more seconds of swimming and my feet would be able to touch the ground. I didn't make it in time.

One of Connor's hands reached out and grabbed the back of my bikini top, pulling the ties out in one deft movement. I had to scramble out of the lake topless, stumbling over smooth stones the size of lemons and broken twigs while Connor laughed behind me, dangling my wet bikini top from his hand.

When I made it to soft dirt, I spun around to face him with my arms crossed protectively around my chest. With a wicked smile on his face, he spun the fabric around on his finger. I set my mouth into a fake pout as I struggled to hold the laughter in.

"I suppose I'll have to walk back to the cabin half-naked." I lifted an eyebrow at him as he clumsily made his own way out of the lake, still twirling my yellow bikini in the air above his head. He stopped ankle-deep in the water after the implication of my words sank in. The bikini top slid off his stilled finger and settled into the crook of his elbow.

His smile faltered slightly as he said, "You wouldn't dare."

"Is that a challenge?" I lowered my arms from my chest to prop my hands on my hips. Feeling the fading sunshine on my nipples, I tossed my hair back over my shoulders and widened my stance. A smile played at the corner of my mouth as Connor's face fell. He glanced up and down the lake and stared hard at the cabins before rushing toward me.

"Jesus, *here*. Put it back on before someone sees you." He tossed the top at me but I let it fall to the rocky sand at my feet.

Instead of bending down to pick it up, I turned from him and ran to the trail that connected the main part of the lodge to the cabins as fast as my wobbly legs would allow, aware that my breasts swayed with each stride. Connor yelled and cursed behind me, closing the gap between us in just a few seconds.

"Riley! *Damn it!*"

I squealed when his strong arms wrapped around me from behind and lifted me off the ground. He turned around so that his back was to the cabins and set me down carefully, splaying his fingers over my naked breasts.

"I want to be the only one to see these beauties. Put your top on!" he said playfully before tossing the bikini at me again and quickly leaning down to bite my shoulder.

I positioned the small triangles around my front and turned so that he could tie the strings together, laughing the whole time his fingers trembled against my skin. Zoey ran up beside us, barking and wagging her tail vigorously, interested in joining whatever game we were playing.

"What happened to the naughty Connor?" I asked breathlessly as he snuggly tied my top together and snapped the wet bikini string against my back.

"You want naughty? Just wait till I get you inside…behind *closed* doors."

Zoey barked excitedly at our feet as Connor bent down and threw me over his shoulder, ignoring my protest. "We'll need a babysitter for the dog because the cabin is all *ours* for the rest of the night. By the time I'm through with you, you'll know my naughty side," he said over my loud squeals and giggles.

ೕ∞ᴄ

I arched my back up to meet his fingers, enjoying the feel of his rough skin on my body as his touch brought out moans of pleasure from some unknown place deep inside of me. He sat straddled over my hips, his throbbing erection resting just below my navel. I ached to touch him but my hands were pinned securely above me.

In the full moon of the night, I was able to make out each angle of his defined chest and the washboard effect of his muscular abs. The feel of his whiskered chin dragging over my collarbone and the roughness of him across my nipples made me gasp in anticipation. The coarse stubble tickled my skin and even though I felt the sensation everywhere, the heat of my groin reached near-nuclear temperatures.

With one of his hands still holding mine together tightly, he shifted so that he could rest on his side. With his free fingers, he continued to explore my trembling body. He drew lazy circles along the edge of my ribcage, leaning forward to flick his tongue over my erect nipples. Every time his mouth touched me, my breath hitched. I squirmed beneath him as his hand trailed further down, over my stomach and hipbones. He gently pushed my legs apart so that he could run his fingers up and down my inner thighs, teasing me until I moaned.

"Please…I want you, now," I pleaded.

"Soon…soon."

He released my hands and immediately I dug my fingers into his hair while his mouth trailed feathery kisses down the curve of my waist, over my abdomen and along the inside of my thigh. I lifted my hips in submission as his tongue explored the heat between my legs, softly flicking and probing.

In the moonlight, the gold in his hair shimmered as his head moved beneath my navel and I gripped his wide shoulders with my hands, digging into his flesh with my nails.

"Oh my God, don't stop..." I moaned, "...please don't stop."

I gasped when his lips vibrated against my clitoris as he said, "Don't worry, I'm just getting started, baby."

Moments later my body lurched with wave after wave of intense pleasure as he brought me up and over the peak of a glorious orgasm with only his mouth. I was still basking in the glow of my climax when he moved his body over mine, nudging my legs further apart as he lowered his hips.

"Fin..." I groaned into his mouth as our lips and groins crashed together at the same time.

ഐഓ

Covered in sweat, I bolted upright in bed. Connor's arm was draped heavily across my midsection and slid into my lap after I moved. *That did not just happen,* I thought to myself. *I did not just have a sex dream about Fin! What the hell?* But I had, my body remembered it in every way. My heart rate was racing for the Olympic Gold and sweat glistened every inch of my skin.

I swiped at my upper lip and forehead in frustration; irritated and embarrassed by the warm moisture between my legs that proved my body enjoyed the dream just as much as my mind had. Connor lay on his stomach in his favorite position next to me, his arm still resting limply in my lap. My cheeks flush as I recalled some of the things I did with Fin in the dream...or more importantly, some of things he did to *me*. Part of me wanted to shake Connor awake and let the dream spew from my mouth - an instant admission to absolve me of any further guilt. But that would do neither of us any good. Instead, I slithered slowly out from under Connor's arm and crawled silently out of bed. No man wanted to hear about his lover dreaming about someone else.

After pulling on the first few articles of clothing I could find in the pale moonlight, I quietly left the room, stealing a glance over my shoulder at the dark-haired, divine being that was asleep on the sheets. I wasn't sure if the guilt I felt was rational or not, but it hurt regardless.

∽◦≪

The dirt felt cool under my bare feet as I walked up the shadowy trail. Shoes weren't necessary. I knew the path well, even in the dead of night. I stopped in front of the first cabin and the sounds and smells that emanated from Fin's place not that long ago flooded through me. It wasn't fair that he died, not after surviving the virus. I hated Matt for taking him from us, from *me*. The glass windows were unlit of course, and with the curtains closed, it looked as if the building was frozen in sleep.

With an angry sigh, I turned away from the cabin and continued up the path, passing the entrance to the lake dock until the dirt merged with the weed-filled grass. Even without the full moon to guide me along the way, I knew exactly where I was going. It was a place I visited almost every day. I slowed my pace to avoid stepping on anything sharp as I weaved in and out of a handful of tall pine trees, keeping the lake on my left and the dense forest to my right as I slowly ascended. By the time I reached the small outlook that faced the lake, I was slightly out of breath, more from nerves than the exercise.

I sat down next to the mound of dirt surrounded by stones with a soft grunt. Since I was wearing only my cut off jean shorts and Connor's t-shirt, the late night summer air felt refreshing and cool. The moon reflected off the watery surface of the lake below in such a way that it reminded me of a ginormous diamond. After shifting in the dirt, I rested my right hand on the grave next to me.

"Fin…I have to let you go," I said softly.

A bird squawked somewhere in the distance and I listened to the soft creaking of the pine tree limbs above me as they groaned from the breeze. It was a beautiful night a perfect night.

"I'm seeing you and dreaming about you now…can't you just let me be?" I whispered to the night. After burying my face into my

hands, I leaned forward onto my bent knees and let the tears come freely. I cried until my body shook with sadness, until I had cried myself dry.

"I have to say goodbye, Fin. I have to leave for a while…*I have to let you go.*" I sniffled into my arm before wiping my face on Connor's thin shirt.

"Don't go…stay…" A husky voice drifted on the breeze and I peered up nervously from my knees.

"Connor?" I asked the empty night.

"Stay with me…please stay…"

The voice was closer and coming from the trees behind me. A twig snapped nearby and I scrambled to my feet, facing the darkness of the woods. The moon couldn't touch the forest floor, not with the tree canopy as full as it was but I peered into the trees anyway, hoping to see something - anything. Eventually I did.

The leaves rustled at the base of a pine and as I watched, a dark mist formed into the shape of a body. I gaped at the shadow as it continued quickly to change until it had morphed into that of a man. I had barely registered what my eyes had seen when it flew across the forest floor and slammed into me. It passed right *through* me, filling my body momentarily with added energy. My flesh broke out in goose bumps and the force knocked me ungraciously backwards, onto my ass.

I sat on the ground struggling to catch my breath in the cool air, clamping onto my lower lip with my teeth to keep myself from screaming out loud. Fin. I had felt him, tasted him even. I sensed every part of him as he passed through me. With my hands splayed out in the weeds on either side of my hips, my body shook with fear and something else, something worse - longing.

I didn't walk, I *ran* back to the cabin. Once inside I bolted the door and washed my face and hands in the kitchen sink. I had to get the dirt off, as if that would wash Fin from me. I could still taste him in my mouth - still feel his hands on my skin. It wasn't the shock of having Fin's ghost pass through my body and soul that had me rattled, it was the fact that I finally knew up on the hill how much I missed him. How much he missed me.

With my hands gripping the edge of the sink, I stared out at the calm lake through the kitchen window until the shakes were gone. Until my breath no longer hitched and my heart rate returned to its normal beat. Only then could I make the short journey up the stairs to the man that was sleeping in my bed. The living and breathing man that loved me.

&3ez&

She sat with one leg tucked under her while the other dangled over the edge of the pier, her perfect toes hovering just inches above the water. Connor stood on the dirt trail and listened to her laugh. It was a loud, carefree and honest sound. He only heard this laugh from her when she thought they were alone…her and Fin.

He shoved his hands deep into his pockets and watched from a distance as Fin stretched out beside her, resting his palms on the wooden planks of the dock behind him as he leaned toward Riley, saying something that made her face the sky and laugh again. She shoved him, playfully. Fin retaliated by tickling her side until she squealed. They were flirting. With Connor right there. As if, he didn't exist at all.

When Fin bumped shoulders with Riley so he could whisper into her ear, he couldn't take it anymore. He yanked his fists from his jeans and stomped toward the pier with every intention of punching the shit out of Fin's face. He'd show that asshole who Riley belonged to, even if meant breaking every bone in his hands.

They must have heard him coming but they ignored him and he made it halfway down the pier before it happened. A pain ripped through his chest as the air left his lungs, almost as if he had been kicked in the gut. He skidded to a stop, flailing wildly at the railing to his right until the worn wood found his fingertips. He could almost feel the splinters digging into his skin as he gripped it for support while his mouth hung open in shock. He couldn't take his eyes off of her. She was kissing Fin. Actually kissing the bastard!

When his breath returned, he yelled out a string of curses with so much force that his voice cracked. This infuriated him further so he screamed even louder at them. Damn bastard! Fucker! I'm going to beat every ounce of life out of your body! *And still, they ignored him. Even as Connor ran full speed down the pier, they simply stood and began walking hand in hand toward him, seemingly oblivious to the fury on his face as he closed the gap in less than three seconds. He swung at Fin's head and pivoted wildly as his fist met with nothing but air. Fin wrapped his arm around Riley's waist as they passed, tucking his fingers down inside her shorts while she giggled.*

Connor felt nothing but rage as he swung at Fin's head, again and again and again. Missing every time. As Fin and Riley walked away he followed just behind them, punching, swinging, kicking and cursing but nothing happened. It was as if Connor wasn't there at all. By the time they reached the trail, he was exhausted. All he could do was watch as Fin pulled Riley into his arms and kissed her neck, her jaw, her mouth. As Fin's hand roamed over the front of Riley's shirt Connor snapped. He lunged himself forward but instead of slamming into Fin he went right through him, and ended up flat on his face in the dirt.

Their feet moved by his head as he rolled onto his side, crying out for Riley. Screaming at Fin's back as they walked up the steps of Fin's cabin. She's mine…mine! *The dust from the trail stuck to his face as tears flowed down his cheeks. Watching her walk away from him in the arms of another man tore his heart into pieces. It broke him completely.* Riley. Please don't leave me…Riley…

"Connor, wake up. It's me, I'm here. Wake up."

Right after climbing back under the covers Connor began to kick the sheets and moan my name in his sleep. With one hand on his chest, I used the other to push back sweaty clumps of dark hair off his forehead.

"Connor," I said softly, "Please wake up, it's me, Riley."

He bolted upright, bringing both hands to his chest and gripped my wrist so tightly it was almost painful. I pushed his hair back from his face again before lightly kissing his cheek. His entire body was slick with sweat.

"Riley?" his stammered as he wrapped his hands around my arm, pulling it back into his chest.

"Yes, I'm here. It's okay. You had a bad dream."

My knees groaned from the pressure of sitting on my feet but I didn't dare move until Connor was fully awake. As he slowly blinked the sleep away, I continued to touch his face, soothing him as best as I could. The nightmares were getting worse for both of us.

"Don't leave me," he whispered.

"What? I'm not going anywhere," I said softly.

"Mine. You're mine, right?"

I hesitated long enough for Connor to notice and our eyes met in the darkness. "Yes, Connor. I'm yours." His face relaxed slightly before he slumped back against his pillow, pulling me down with him so that I rested on his bare chest.

"Mine," he said one final time before drifting back into sleep.

When the sun peeked over the treetops and hit our cabin with its warmth, I was still awake with my head on Connor's chest. I spent the first half hour of the new day staring at the fine, brown hair on one of his arms until he finally stirred.

"Morning," he said gruffly.

He stretched beneath me and I rolled off of him, onto my stomach. Three days of dark stubble filled the lower half of his face and down the front of his throat making it nearly impossible for me to focus on any coherent thought. The man oozed sex, *especially* first thing in the morning. I fought off my usual morning instinct of kissing every inch of his face and pushed myself into a sitting position next to his hip.

"Good morning," I said softly.

Even the way he arched his brow at me was sexy so I stared down at my hands while he shifted onto his side to face me.

"What is it?" he asked as he dragged a hand through his sleep-tousled hair.

"Do you remember your dream last night?" I chewed on my lower lip while he stared at me.

"My dream?"

"Was more like a nightmare."

"Did I wake you?" He sat up with a grunt and trailed one of his long fingers down the inside of my knee.

"Um. No, but you said something when you woke up." I shifted so we were facing each other. Connor dropped his hand onto the sheet and sighed deeply.

"Was it kinky?" he asked with a playful expression.

I swatted at his thigh and laughed. "No! I said you were having a nightmare."

"Oh yeah. Okay. Well, what did I say?" He smiled sleepily at me.

"You said not to leave you and asked if I was…yours." I watched the corners of his mouth tighten and his eyes fell from my gaze.

"Huh. What did you say?" he asked.

He wasn't looking at me, so I lifted my hand to his face and rubbed his lower lip with my thumb. That got his attention. His bright blue eyes lit up with desire as I continued to caress his mouth with my finger.

"What do you think I said? That I was, of course."

Our mouths met with a sense of urgency. Connor kissed my breath away, not letting go of me until we were both panting. Clothes were ripped off and tossed to the floor, hands groped madly and mouths sucked on supple flesh until our bodies molded together as one. I pushed away all memories from the night before as Connor slid inside me and roughly pulled my hips against his repeatedly until my legs shook in anticipation of what was to come. We needed each other. Completely.

*This was it; he knew it was. The last time Connor would hold Riley in his arms before everything changed. She wanted to leave so he had no choice but to go with her. Something in his gut told him that this trip to lower Los Angeles was a mistake. He would never say it out loud to the others, but Mariah wasn't worth it…**nothing** was worth losing Riley.*

CHAPTER five

The bedroom door flew open with such force that both Connor and I jumped from the mattress with our eyes still closed. Kris bounded into the room and squealed, covering her face with both hands.

"Oh my GOD! I did NOT have to see that!"

"What? What's wrong?" I rubbed at my eyes briskly.

"You're naked, both of you!" she screamed through her fingers.

I glanced down at my body and looked over at Connor, who stood at the foot of the bed, groggy and confused. We didn't have a stitch of clothing on.

After snatching the top sheet from the bed and wrapping it around my body, I gestured for Connor to put something on, and before he pulled his jeans up and over his thighs, he winked at me. I was mortified. And he thought it was funny. *Men.*

"Sorry, Kris," Connor said as he closed the top button of his pants.

"Hurry up! You have to see this!" she mumbled, refusing to take her hands from her face.

"See what? What's wrong?" I asked again.

"You can take your hands down now, Kris. We aren't naked anymore," Connor said with a chuckle.

She peered at me first, and sighed heavily when she saw me wrapped in only the sheet. "No, like, you have to get dressed, you know - in clothes. Meet me downstairs! And hurry!"

I watched her back as she rushed out of the room and listened to her sneakered feet running down the stairs.

"What's that all about?" Connor asked as he tugged a shirt off the chair beside the bed.

"No idea," I mumbled, picking up my outfit from the night before.

We were dressed but still tugging on our shoes as we took the stairs down to the main level. Zoey rushed me, nudging my knees with her snout. "Good morning to you too, girl." The kitchen smelled faintly of oranges and oatmeal. We missed breakfast.

"Come on, come on!" Kris hissed from the front door. She was standing with her fingers curled around the knob, excitement hitching her voice up an octave.

"What *is* it, Kris?"

She only smiled at me and opened the door, leading us out into the fresh mountain air. Connor and I had fallen back to sleep after our early morning escapades. It was mid-day already. The sun stretched out across the sky, high above our heads, warming my head and shoulders instantly.

After we were outside, Kris shut the cabin door, leaving Zoey inside. Confused, the dog stood up, placing her paws against the glass and gave us a single 'woof'. Her large brown eyes peered at me as her tongue lolled out the side of her mouth. She was silenced by Kris, who seemed to be getting more excited by the second.

"Zoey can't come?" I asked.

"No, not this time. She's probably safer here," Kris answered with a giggle.

Connor lifted an eyebrow at me in concern and rolled his eyes after I shrugged my shoulders. We followed Kris off the porch and across the dirt path that ended not far from our cabin steps. She walked right into the woods, just passing by the tree where I saw Fin materialize into thin air the day before. If we fell too far behind her, Kris would beckon us to hurry with her arm, not stopping or turning around to face us, but watching the trees in front of her carefully.

"Kris, seriously…tell us what's going on," I paused to lean against a thick pine tree after nearly ten minutes of walking through the scratchy brush and as Connor stopped behind me, he took the opportunity to run his hands up the back of my shirt.

"Stop!" I hissed playfully into his ear when he leaned forward for a kiss. Connor stuck his lower lip out in a pout, but released my bra strap without snapping it.

Anxiety filled her voice as Kris spoke over her shoulder, "We're almost there, come on!"

I groaned and pushed myself from the tree, falling back in line behind Kris, Connor taking up the rear. Not long after that, I realized where we were. There was nothing in this part of the woods - nothing but the meadow.

Every twig beneath my shoe crunched and it seemed like the woods echoed with the sound; even the dead leaves that crumbled under my step sounded like fireworks as we slowed to an almost painfully slow walk. The smell of pine and sap drifted all around us, making my nose twitch. Kris lifted her hand up, signaling for us to be quiet, so we were. Only our footsteps and breathing could be heard. It was obvious she wanted to sneak up on something - or someone.

Just before we reached the circular patch of land that opened up to the size of a football field, she bent down behind the brush, signaling us to do the same. When I half squatted and half crawled beside her, she parted the bush, giving me a clean view of the meadow. Kris clamped her hand over my mouth but it did little to stifle the gasp.

"Oh my--," I muttered against my smashed lips.

"Sshh! You'll scare them off!" Kris whispered against my cheek.

"Thay alwedy know wrrr hrrr," I answered.

"Huh?"

I swatted Kris's hand off my mouth and rubbed at my lips. "I said they already know we're here. Look at them."

Connor was kneeling in the dirt on my right, staring wide-eyed into the field with a boyish expression. The youthful look took at least ten years off his handsome features, and paired with the longer hairstyle he was sporting, he could have passed for twenty-something. When he smiled, the laugh lines around his eyes and mouth that I loved so much crinkled, betraying his age.

We turned to stare out above the brush together in awe, with Kris huddled on the other side of me, quiet as a mouse. It was clear she didn't have experience with the situation but she was excited...we all were.

Horses.

∽∾

I approached the palomino mare first since she seemed to be the most curious of the pair. They did their best to ignore us while we hid behind the tree line; flicking their ears and glancing sideways across the field, but once I stood and left the safety of the trees, they stopped grazing and turned to face me.

Ragged pieces of what was left of the golden-colored horse's halter hung from around her neck. She was without a headpiece and had no bit in her mouth. The ends of the material were chewed, as if she or the other mare had gnawed at the straps in an attempt to remove them. The bay, copper-red in color, stood only in her mangled coat. There weren't any signs on her thick hair that she had been harnessed recently. Her back twitched as I reached out to stroke her friend, as if she was preparing herself to bolt or charge.

"Ssshhh, girl. Easy, now." I brought my palm up for the palomino to smell, feeling the hot air of her breath as she sniffed hesitantly at my hand. With the other, I reached up and stroked the side of her neck, reaching slowly up toward her ears, scratching gently at her matted and dirty coat. When I brought my hand away, it was brown from grime.

"Look at you, pretty girl. You need a bath and a good brushing, dontcha?" I cooed at her.

The bay stomped her right front foot down on the grass, but the palomino didn't budge, in fact she looked down at my feet and bent her head forward, giving me permission to rub my hand up between her eyes. She had a white blaze that ran the length of her face in the shape of a narrow hourglass, with darker browns around her muzzle and nostrils. At one time, she was probably properly cared for, but it was obvious it had been many months since anyone had tended to either of the horses. Both were covered in dried mud that flaked off their legs, and burs and stickers filled their tails and manes. It didn't appear that either was starving but they could stand to put on some weight. Though filthy and on the thin side, they were still beautiful.

"You made a new friend," Connor said quietly from behind me. I nodded silently, afraid to disturb the mighty horse that was relaxed beneath my hands.

The bay didn't approve of his presence at all and stomped again in the soft dirt, shaking her long and tangled mane until it flew up around her head. She grunted and whinnied in protest and I saw Connor back away from the corner of my eye as the palomino stiffened against my palm.

She bolted away from me just as the bay charged in my direction. With only twenty feet or so between us, there was nowhere to hide - nowhere to run. My last thought before we collided was, *Oh man, this is gonna leave a mark.*

❧

The bay rushed at me, stopping just short of my chest and slammed both feet into the ground before me in warning. She snorted in my face and whinnied so forcefully that her spittle sprayed across my forehead. Afraid to lift my hand and wipe at it, I tried to ignore the warm and gooey trickle that dripped off my left eyebrow.

When she realized I wasn't going to challenge her, she sidestepped toward the nervous palomino, putting her wider frame between us, watching me carefully. Eventually I couldn't stand the feeling of her spit dribbling down my face and slowly wiped the substance from my skin, transferring my wet hand to my jeans, rubbing my palm clean.

The three of us stood there, watching each other until my knees creaked. Eventually the bay turned her side to me, flicked her tail in the air and began grazing the grass once again. She looked up often, and seemed satisfied to see me standing in the same spot, but my legs were beginning to cramp. When I decided to sit down, I did so slowly, keeping my eyes on the large horse with the reddish-brown coat.

She ignored me completely for five minutes, before turning in my direction. I scrambled to my feet a second before she reached me, preparing for the worst. The palomino followed close behind her, making soft snorts through her nose. She didn't seem happy either.

"It's okay," I said quietly, watching the horse's brown eyes size me up.

She flicked her ears back and forth, and muscles trembled under her skin from her neck down her sides. She was afraid of me.

"Good girl," I said quietly, "It's okay, girl. It's okay. I won't hurt you." I risked bringing my hand up for her to smell and she sniffed it forcefully. I left my palm up, hoping she would allow me to stroke her, and when she lowered her head slightly I gently placed my fingers between her eyes, caressing the flat space tenderly.

I looked over my shoulder at Connor who had retreated and was once again standing next to Kris, a smile spread out wide across my face. They gave me a little wave, but made no attempt to join me in the middle of the meadow.

"That's a good girl…" I murmured.

The bay shifted her weight between her front feet, breathing loudly through her nostrils as I stroked her and she stepped forward, closing the space between us. Her lowered head was just in front of me and I brought my other hand up so I could rub both sides of her neck. Everything was going well until with a sudden dip, the mare's head lowered before rising against my chest with a massive shove. I was off my feet and on my back instantly, the air exploding from my lungs in one forceful exhale.

Somewhere in the distance was Connor's voice, booming through the forest but it echoed off the trees and only made the ringing in my ears worse. Afraid the horse might trample me, I struggled to lift up on my elbows and raise my head so I knew which way to roll. Struggling to suck oxygen back into my nearly collapsed lungs, I looked up not to find the horse's hooves in my face, but her ass. She stood with her rear facing me, swishing her tail calmly from side to side, and grazing again. When the air finally came, my throat made an ugly sound as I gulped it down. And I laughed.

"Well played," I said between gulps. She didn't bother to turn to look at me she had made her point. I wasn't in charge of her.

"Jesus, you okay?" Connor's hands were on my shoulders, and though he was a male and a protective one at that, I couldn't help but find it funny that he made no attempt to put himself between me and the horses behind.

"Okay. Just…got the wind…knocked out of me." I sucked in more air and let Connor pull me up to my feet. My ribs weren't broken, but they hurt just as badly.

The palomino grazed her way toward us and stopped to sniff Connor's hair. He bristled as she muzzled against his face, stepping around him to smell his clothes.

"I think she likes you," I laughed at his wide-eyed expression.

"R-right. Let's hope she's not just picking out a good place to bite off a chunk of flesh," he said stoically as the palomino worked her way around the two of us. With a jump, I laughed when she snorted into my hair, sending the loose strands flying about from the heavy gusts of her breathing.

The bay stood watching her friend inspect us with interest. I doubted she truly wanted to injure us, or she would have already, but trusting - she was not. When I clicked my tongue at her, she whinnied and approached cautiously, stomping each of her feet almost as a reminder of what they could do to me if she chose to kick them against my head.

Connor tugged at my wrist as I stepped forward to meet her, but I shrugged him off. "It's okay. She needs to know we're friendly, besides, I don't think she wants to hurt us," I said over my shoulder at him.

"Riley, she just flattened you out. That didn't hurt enough?"

With a sigh, I glanced over my shoulder and smiled faintly at him. "Haven't you been around horses at all? You're from Ireland!"

"Not everyone from bloody Ireland rides horses!" he hissed back. His expression changed from irritation to concern as he looked beyond me and I turned around to find the bay's face inches from my own.

She smelled of dirt, grass, and old manure. Tentatively, I reached up again, placed my palm on the blaze between her eyes, and cautiously rubbed the coarse hair until she shifted.

"Riley...don't," Connor said quietly behind me.

I stepped along the side of the horse, running my hand under her tangled mane, across her shoulders and along her back. I patted her gently, returning my hand to her neck, scratching beneath her hair. The palomino was still inspecting Connor's hair and I smiled at him while he patted at the creature's neck.

"See?" I said, as the bay flicked her ears and turned into my scratching hand, "I told you, she just needs time to get to know us, is all."

When the bay turned around to stare at me, I could see the pain and fear that was imprinted in all our gazes. She was scared and just as lost as the rest of us.

"Don't worry girl, we'll take care of you." She sighed and snorted in response, bending down to finish her grazing while I alternated between pats and rubs up and down her side. An idea blurted from my mouth before I had the chance to properly consider it.

"Connor?"

"Yeah?"

"Can you ride?"

CHAPTER six

"You're crazy! I mean, certifiable, Riley. You can't be serious!" Connor stood with his feet firmly planted in the weedy grass, staring at me in disbelief. The shoulders of his shirt were covered in damps spots where the palomino had nibbled and nuzzled him. He was lucky the friendly horse hadn't grazed across his head, and trimmed his hair to the roots in the process.

"Think about it, Connor. The horses are pretty much all-terrain. We wouldn't need to worry about fuel or traffic; it makes sense, you know it does!" I stood as tall as my narrow frame would allow with my arms crossed at my chest, willing my face to look determined.

"I think you're nuts, Riley. Damn crazy," he mumbled into his hands as he dragged them down his face.

"Not to interject, but maybe she has a point," Winchester said. He stood next to the golden mare, his palm resting on her side. "I mean, at least Riley won't be crashing any bikes, right?" I was the only one that laughed.

The horses had eagerly followed us back to the lodge along the remnants of what used to be a trail leading to the main building. There was no stable on the property, but along the recreation building, was a wooden railing with posts that ran deep into the ground. It was the only place we could think of to keep the horses, but there was no way to contain them.

The bay mare was pretending to ignore us as she nibbled at the plants and grasses that bordered the trail and the main lawn, but I caught her peering up at me every time I glanced in her direction. Her large, brown eyes seemed hesitant, but willing to trust us. When we made eye contact, she would swish her tail and look back down at the ground to continue her grazing.

"Wait. Just wait," said Jacks, "Look, I've seen Riley ride, I know she can do it. But Riley," he turned to look at me, "Are you saying you want to ride a horse from the mountains of San Diego all the way to the city streets of Los Angeles? I mean, Connor's right…that's just crazy, babe." He put his hands up in the air and looked uncomfortable about picking sides. I tried hard not to glare at him.

"What the heck do you think people did before cars were invented? The bikes will only get us so far and plus, horses are quieter. People would hear us coming from miles away if we took bikes." I propped a fist on my hip and pointed at Connor. "Besides, you said you could ride! Why does this idea bother you so much?"

"I said I *could* ride! Not that I particularly enjoyed doing it for days at a time! This would be a lot of work, Riley, a *lot* of work."

"I get that. But what else do we have to do? Is there something better on your schedule for this month?"

Connor and I glared at each other, neither of us willing to be the first to break. It was Skip that jumped in between us and put a hand on each of our shoulders. "Look kids, we don't need to figure this all out today, do we? We don't even know how to keep these beasts from wandering off. Let's just take this one day at a time. Let's go have a drink and relax for a bit. And for God's sake, someone's got to bathe them…I can't handle the stench for much longer." He crinkled his nose up to prove his point before walking past us, with an anxious Winchester in tow. Jacks shrugged at me and turned to follow the other two men as they made their way down the trail and back to the cabins.

Connor hadn't budged and Kris hadn't left her place next to the palomino, who seemed beyond pleased to have so much attention. The bay was still grazing, seemingly uninterested in the men that had left the group.

"Kris," I said over my shoulder, still looking at Connor's pissed expression, "Wanna go for a drive with me; pick up some horse supplies?"

"Yeah! But what about them, do we leave them here?"

"There's rope in the utility closet inside the rec room. I'll get it," I said, finally tearing my eyes from Connor and his flushed cheeks to stomp up the nearby steps.

He was still standing in the same place when I came back with the rope. "This should work, if they'll let me tie them to the post, that is," I said, half under my breath. It was the first time I had ever tied a horse to anything, so I did my best at making the knot secure, without making the loop around their necks too loose. The palomino was completely pliant, allowing me to lead her to the railing and secure her rope to it without as much as a whinny. She resumed grazing at the base of one of the posts, as if she belonged there.

The bay was a different story. She allowed me to loop the rope around her head, but she didn't budge when I tried to lead her to the post. After five minutes of gentle tugging and murmured reassurances, she slowly made her way toward the fencing, loudly protesting with snorts, whinnies, and shakes of her head. Once I was close enough to tie her off, I wasted no time securing her rope to the log-style railing for fear that she might realize what I was doing and bolt - with me still holding onto the rope. An image flashed through my mind of me being dragged down the lodge road, gravel filling my mouth and nose and tearing the flesh from my face.

"Now what?" Connor asked, not bothering to hide the irritation in his voice.

"Now...we find a ranch that has stables and pick up some supplies." I turned from him, beckoning Kris to follow and marched down the trail to the cabins, not bothering to glance behind me to see if Connor was following or not.

After grabbing up the keys to the Jeep, Kris and I returned to the front of the lodge and climbed into the dusty vehicle. We left Connor brooding inside the cabin, alone. Even the dog seemed hesitant to stay with him, so she sat on Kris's lap as we drove down the long and gravelly driveway, turning South on the highway. Plenty of people had owned horses in the area; it was just a matter of finding what we needed and bringing it back.

We struck gold with the first ranch-style property we pulled into. The smell of decay had peaked in June; the heat of summer seemed to dry out the corpses that were in town. The stink there was mostly trapped inside houses, so the smell wasn't as pungent. But the countryside was different on account of all the dead livestock.

Regardless of the rot, the shadows never went away, not completely. It seemed that most of us were plagued by our dreams regardless of where we were, not by the ghosts left behind. Then again, none of us ventured out into previously populated areas of town unless we had to.

As Kris and I stood outside of a barn fit to house at least twenty horses, the only scent in the air was stale hay and dried flowers. And dirt. One of the barn doors was open and as we walked inside, a flutter of wings above us made me jump. A barn owl flew out of the rafters and out the door with a loud screech.

"Ouch," I said under my breath, grimacing at the bruises Kris was leaving in my arm.

"I'm sorry!" she said, releasing me. She gently rubbed at the spot where she had clamped on to me when the bird burst out of its nest.

"It's okay," I laughed, "It got me too."

The inside of the barn was poorly lit but after we stood still for a moment and let our eyes adjust, we could see well enough to look around the place. It took almost half an hour to find what I thought we needed. A few side pulls, extra rope, two shedding tools and an almost full gallon of horse shampoo. Kris found saddle blankets and carried them out to the Jeep.

"What about hay? Don't horses eat hay?" she asked as I dumped the supplies into the back seat. Zoey rushed in and out of the barn, nosing around the stable doors. I refused to look inside them. The smell of death lingered inside the stalls and I had no desire to see decaying horses.

"Uh, yeah. But, obviously these two were eating what they could find. Hey, look at that." I pointed to the side of the barn, at the truck that was parked in the weeds, a horse trailer fixed to the fifth wheel.

"The trailer?" Kris asked as I walked away from her.

"If it works, we could fill the back with hay. Maybe the horses will sleep in here till we figure out what to do with them."

"Can you drive that?"

"If there are keys...probably."

She stood with her arms crossed, leaning against the weathered wood wall of the barn as I inspected the vehicle. The horse-trailer was unlocked, and relatively clean on the inside. The truck was unlocked as well, but the keys weren't in plain sight.

"No keys," I said with a sigh, as I climbed back out of the driver seat.

"Now what? You going in the house?"

Kris didn't enter houses. She would climb fruit trees or scale fences to pick through over-grown gardens, but any time we needed supplies that we could only find indoors, she always waited in the car. She swore the ghost of a dead man had kissed her cheek once as she pilfered through a downstairs bathroom. She had run from the house screaming and crying, and vowed to leave the indoor gathering to the rest of us from that point on. I didn't blame her. I didn't much enjoy wandering through the houses of dead people either, stealing their canned foods, toilet paper and batteries.

"I'm not sure. Wasn't there a little office inside the barn?"

"Yeah, but it's like the size of a closet. I didn't see any keys in there either," she answered.

"We weren't looking for keys earlier, come on." The dry wind pushed against us as we rounded the corner of the building, causing dust to fly up in our faces.

"Yuck!" Kris spat as we rushed back inside the barn.

I swiped at my face with my shirtsleeve, rubbing the dirt off my lips. The wind had been picking up and the temperature was high during the day.

"Damn Santa Ana weather," I mumbled.

We trudged to the far side of the barn where a small room was tucked in the corner next to several large barrels. A few tools that I didn't know the names of hung from the walls, as well as a few framed pictures of prize-winning horses. Other than a small office chair and wobbly wooden desk, a four-drawer metal cabinet was the only other furniture in the room.

I sifted through the small wicker basket that sat atop the cabinet, finding loose keys, bolts and thumbtacks. No truck keys. Papers were strewn about the desk in lumps, as if someone had sifted through them. I pushed them aside into a pile, finding nothing but a bottle opener beneath the mess.

"Check the drawer," Kris said from behind me.

One thin drawer ran the length of the table and inside I found not only one set, but also two sets of keys, including a dusty *Playboy* magazine from the nineties. The cover had been flipped open enough times that the spine was completely pliant, bending freely. Soft wrinkles and bends covered every inch of the magazine, but it was otherwise in great condition.

"Someone must have liked this edition," I said with a laugh, raising it up for Kris to see the blonde model on the front, expertly hiding her private areas with her long hair and hands. The disgusted look on Kris's face made me laugh harder and I tossed the magazine back into the desk, pushing the drawer shut. The *Playboy* would be sealed in there, forever. However long forever ended up being.

We were covered in dust and smelled like old hay and horse and not in a good way. Instead of getting used to the smell of the dead animals, my nose seemed to have a harder time processing the sickly-sweet odor of the barn the longer we stayed inside it.

As we walked toward the exit, the morbid side of my curiosity won and I went up on my toes to look over one of the stall gates. I flinched back in horror, covering my mouth with the back of my hand and nearly stumbled over a felled pitchfork.

"What? What is it?" Kris asked.

I shook my head from side to side, not sure of what I saw, but certain I didn't want to see it again. "I-I don't know."

Before I could reach out and stop her, Kris stepped forward and gripped the stall door, going up on her toes, just as I had, to peer over the side. "No, Kris - wait!" It was too late. She recoiled from the gate, covering her face with her hands.

"I want to go - I don't want to be in here anymore!" she said, taking no time to wait for me as she stumbled away from the stalls and back outside, into the fresh air.

Zoey stood from her resting spot beside one of the Jeep tires, watching us with a worried expression. She had also stopped going inside houses and structures she didn't know. Her canine senses couldn't take the rancid stimuli.

We leaned against the Jeep, staring at the barn with the single open door that almost resembled a mouth. So much death. Everything had died. Well, not *everything*.

"What do you think did that?" Kris whispered, wiping clear snot from her leaking nose.

I glanced at her before returning my attention back at the barn. "I don't know…some sort of large animal, I guess."

"Think it might still be around here, watching us or something?" Her eyes darted over the empty grass fields that surrounded the barn and up the hill that led to the main house.

"No. I doubt it, sweetie. Whatever…*did that*…well, it'll be long gone by now." I smiled reassuringly but did my own visual inspection of our surroundings before pushing off the Jeep and walking back to the trailer. I didn't want her to see my face. To see the doubt that I knew lingered there. The horse had been mauled to pieces; torn limb from limb and partially devoured. All except for the head - which sat picked clean on a bench facing the stall door. No sane animal had placed it there.

‰‰

"What are we going to name them?" Kris asked as she pulled handfuls of hay out of the back of the open horse trailer I had parked on the lodge lawn, dumping them into a pile on the grassy ground. Tufts of the dry strands stuck to the ends of her curled hair and across her shoulders, almost making her look as if the stuff had been dumped over her head.

"Hmmm. Well, you were the one who found them first, why don't you pick?" I smiled at her face as it split nearly in half from a grin she didn't display often enough.

"Okay. Lemme think," she murmured against the friendly palomino's neck as she greedily dove into the hay pile - muzzle first. "Well, this one is super sweet and her gold coat makes me think of sunshine. Is 'Sunny' too corny?" she asked me.

"I think that's perfect," I leaned across Kris's shoulder and scratched the palomino's ear, "I think you look like a Sunny. How's that sound to you?" I asked the horse. She twitched her ear, but didn't stop eating.

"And the bay? What should we name her?"

Kris crinkled up her nose at the larger and much darker-colored horse. "She doesn't like me."

"She doesn't like anyone…yet," I laughed.

"Okay. She needs a name that goes with her reddish-brown coat. Hmmm…something grown up and attitudy."

"Attitudy? Is that even a word?" I asked Kris.

"It is now," she laughed.

"What about Foxy?"

Kris squealed, making both horses jump. They glared up at the teen who was bouncing on her toes, clapping her hands softy, before quickly returning to their hay. "Foxy is perfect for her!"

"Foxy and Sunny it is!" I laughed at the giggly girl until she danced off to retrieve one of the shedding tools.

"Have fun brushing them, but be careful, ok? I'm going to check on Connor and see if he's still pissed off at me." I waved at Kris, who seemed to have found her happy place amongst the horses while I backed away toward the trail.

We could do this, the horses were already trained, I could tell. They were healthy; they were strong - why not ride them, instead of noisy and unreliable motorcycles? I didn't understand Connor's reservations about taking them to Los Angeles. Especially since he admitted he could actually ride a horse. On the drive back to the lodge in the truck, I decided to cut back on trying to convince him to take the horses and focus on making them healthy and happy first. He'd come around. Connor always did.

My thoughts had been so preoccupied with getting the trailer onto the property and not startling the horses that I had almost forgotten about the mutilated one we found in the barn. The gruesome scene came flooding back to me as I climbed the porch steps. Out of habit, I looked over my shoulder at the quiet woods. I wondered, not for the first time, what lived inside the gloomy shadows that flanked the tall pine trees. I just hoped whatever it was that had attacked, eaten and dismembered the stable horse was long gone and not in our woods, watching us; waiting for its moment to invade our little community.

I squared my shoulders at the tree line and muttered under my breath, "Not on my watch."

∽∾

Connor punched the closet door so hard three of his knuckle impressions were left in the painted particleboard. He flinched, staring at the caved-in spots with animosity, as if it was the doors fault his hand hurt, and not his own.

"Damn!" he cursed at the wood, rubbing over the raw parts of his hand with his other thumb.

She couldn't go, not on a horse, not all the way to Los Angeles. What if she was thrown or the horses got spooked and left them stranded in the middle of nowhere? What if he was thrown, his neck broken and not able to take care of her? With a sigh, he ran a finger over the amygdaliform of one of the indents, tracing the almond shaped hole carefully. She did this to him, riled him up inside; tortured his heart and clouded his mind. It was all her fault that he was falling apart at the seams. But he didn't mind, of course he didn't, because he loved her. And love was...well, messy.

She'd find a way to leave. Even if she started out on foot - he knew she would. Because Riley was the most stubborn woman, he had ever met. That damn heart of hers was going to get them both in trouble - or killed. And now Kris wanted to go.

"Damn it!" he yelled again into the empty bedroom.

He kicked at one of his boots and watched as it flung into the side of the bedframe and bounced to a stop below the open window. Still cursing under his breath, he strode over to the sill, brushing the sheer curtains aside in irritation and peered out into the woods, watching the shadows as they flicked in and out of the safety of the trees as sun shined down through their canopies. Before he turned away, he thought he saw a more solid shape take form but when he squinted to see it better, it shifted and blended in with the rest of the forest shadows.

"Great, now you're seeing things. Right. Just...brilliant," he muttered to himself as he stomped toward the bathroom, kicking the door open and cursing some more when it banged into the wall and swung back into him, catching his elbow painfully.

After splashing cool water on his face and staring at his rugged reflection in the mirror, he wondered what it was that Riley saw in him. His face looked gaunt; the dark circles under his eyes becoming more and more pronounced each week. He hadn't bothered to shave in more days than he could count on both hands - and his hair - what a mess that was.

"Oh my God, you look like shit. Complete and total shit," he hissed at himself.

He rummaged around in the sink cabinet pulling items off the shelves and dumping them onto the counter until he had everything out that he would need. He figured he had at least a good hour before Riley and Kris would be back from their horse supply trip. And he planned on looking less like a deranged serial killer-turned hippy by the time they returned.

"Bloody hell," he sighed. "I wouldn't listen to me either if I looked like this."

And with that comment lodged securely in his brain, he grabbed a fist-full of his dark curls and shoved the hair clippers underneath, snipping at least two inches off in one swipe. He grabbed another clump of hair and repeated the process over and over until the sink was full. After shaking his head to get the loose hairs off, he ran his hands through the shorter waves, trimming the back of his neck as carefully as he could. The clippings nearly filled the wastebasket after he dumped them. Next, he filled the sink with warm water and lathered his face and neck with shaving cream. When he was done shaving, his skin was smooth and soft. He even trimmed his eyebrows just enough to make them look a little less wild and jumped in the shower to wash all the hairs off.

He felt ten pounds lighter when he dried his body and climbed into clean jeans. Just as he was wrestling a thin t-shirt over his damp head, he heard Zoey bark from downstairs. Not bothering to pull on socks or shoes, he glanced at the oval mirror that hung above the dresser on his way out of the room. It wasn't that long ago where his job demanded a certain amount of attention aimed at keeping his looks agreeable. He had let himself go over the last several months.

He briefly smirked at the cleaner, younger-looking reflection. "Much better. Let her try and argue with that face."

CHAPTER seven

The instant I stepped into the cabin, I smelled him. The ocean fragrance of his body wash filled the entire lower level of the cabin so much so that I glanced around, thinking he was standing somewhere nearby. Zoey barked for him before padding off into the kitchen and nosily lapped up a generous amount of water before stretching out on the cool floor for a nap.

"Connor?" The room stayed empty but I heard the soft footfalls of his feet as he descended the stairs.

"Hey," he said to my back before I had a chance to turn around.

My mouth dropped open and my eyes glossed over. His shirt stuck to his chest, as if he had just pulled it onto his damp skin. His expression turned amusing as he strode up to me, pecked my cheek swiftly and continued on to the kitchen. *Ahh, I see how it is*, I thought, as I stared at his firm backside before it disappeared behind the island counter top. Zoey greeted him with a snort, and continued on with her nap.

Snapping my mouth shut and swallowing the lump in my throat, I stepped up to the counter as casually as I could manage and slid onto one of the stools to watch him bustle about.

"You cut your hair," I stated.

"Yup. It was time. Tea?" he asked as he held one of the colorful mugs out at me.

I shook my head and propped my elbows on the tile top. "No, I'm good."

With a shrug, he continued to move around the kitchen, preparing his drink, and ignoring me. Eventually the silence ate away at me and I released my lower lip from my teeth.

"You shaved, too."

He turned around and smiled, flashing his perfectly straight, white teeth. "That I did. You approve?"

"Sure."

I knew what he was doing. He was trying to charm me out of my anger with him. I sucked my lower lip in again and continued to nibble on it, thinking quietly to myself. My eyes couldn't stay on one part of his body for long, so I let them roam his figure, freely. With his back to me, I could stare unabashedly at his shoulders and the rounded muscles of his back and at the two indents above his ass that were visible beneath his shirt. The jeans he chose to wear hung low on his hips but hugged tightly to his legs, leaving not much for the imagination. Not that I didn't already know every inch of his naked form, but the outfit and his newly fresh look was a giant tease to every one of my senses.

Feeling uncomfortable on the wooden stool, I wiggled around, crossing and uncrossing my legs. Unable to find a position that worked, I gave up and walked over to the couch. My body was still sore from the bike crash and the scabs along my jaw seemed destined to stay awhile. But even with the wipeout a recent memory, my mind felt as if it had taken a beating.

"So," Connor said, blowing at the steam that rose from the top of his cup, "I take it you got what you needed for the horses?"

I nodded and leaned deeper into the plush cushions. "We got what we needed. But we won't be returning back to the same farm." I shivered at the mental picture of the severed horse head and tried to replace it with something less gruesome. It didn't work.

"Why? Was the place wiped out?"

"No. Something bad happened there. We'll find another place to rummage through next time," I answered, keeping my tone level and my gaze on the fireplace across from the table my feet rested on.

"Hasn't something *bad* happened everywhere?" he asked, clearly knowing I didn't want to talk, but pushing anyway.

"It was a different kind of bad. I'll talk to you about it later," I looked up at him, meeting his charmed appearance with a smile. Inside my mind, I chanted over and over: *Do not jump him, do not jump him*. But after he moved from the kitchen to the neighboring chair, sitting with one leg hooked casually over the other, sipping that damn cup and looking sexy as hell, all I could think about was ripping his clothes off.

Since I knew that was exactly what he wanted to happen, I rose instead and walked away from the sitting room, not speaking again until my hand was on the wooden staircase banister, "I need a shower, keep your eyes out for Kris, okay?"

ᦒᦒ

The cold water gave me goose bumps, but I still felt flushed. As I stood beneath the streaming water, my mind was full of thoughts ranging from borderline indecent as far as Connor was concerned, to graphic and gory horse parts and on to fear and frustration that too much time had already passed since I decided to look for Mariah. She was out there, lost somewhere in a dead city. Finding her had become an obsession and I knew why. *I* had sent them away. *I* had killed her brother. Sure, it was self-defense, but that didn't keep the guilt at bay.

Someone had to care about her and for whatever reason I didn't understand, that someone was *me*. It was illogical. It was border lining on stupidity. The thought that I would locate any trace of her in a city as large as Los Angeles was absurd, but - and I knew this to be true - if it was me out there, I would want someone to come and find me, or to at least try. Connor had to understand that, or I'd end up going alone.

Not that I couldn't go alone. It's not as if I didn't think about it, but that would create an unnecessary problem and probably a small war between Connor and me. A war I wasn't sure I'd win. If I stayed in San Diego, I would be unhappy. If I left for Los Angeles, Connor would be unhappy. It wasn't a matter of right vs. wrong, it was a matter of who won this round. As I scrubbed the smell of horse and dry hay off my skin with my lathered loofa, I repeated one sentence over and over again in my head until I truly began to believe it: *I will win this fight.*

‿∽◈∾‿

"Feeling better?" Connor placed a glass of an antique bronze-colored liquid in front of me as I slid onto the barstool. I intentionally came downstairs after my cold shower in just a loose top - no bra and a short pair of running shorts. It seemed that neither of us was above using our sex appeal on each other.

I let the water drip off the ends of my hair onto the floor underneath the stool. "What is this?" I sniffed at the glass and winced. "It's strong, whatever it is."

"Try it," he said, taking a sip from a matching glass. The muscles in his arms rippled as he effortlessly hoisted himself up onto the counter by the sink so he could sit and face me.

"Is it whiskey?" I sniffed again, leery of anything that didn't come from a longneck bottle. Connor could drink me under the table any day. I had learned that fact months ago. The drink was fragrant and confusing on my senses; oak, pears, chocolate, cloves and coffee flooded through my nasal membranes. "I've never smelled anything like it."

Connor chuckled and dragged a hand across his open mouth. "Oh, I'm sure you haven't. This is a very rare drink, my dear."

I leaned forward over the glass, inhaling its complex aroma once more. "But, it *is* a whiskey, right?"

He laughed again, leisurely sipping from his glass. "Taste it, and then I'll tell you what it is," he said with a wink.

Raising the tumbler to my lips, I let only a dribble of the liquid onto my tongue; almost sure I would hate it. The smoothness of it surprised me so I opened my mouth to let in more. With a slow swallow, the sweetness of it warmed my tongue before the bitter oak and chocolate hit the back of my mouth. Heat erupted inside my throat as the drink went down.

Peering up at Connor with one of my eyes squeezed shut I managed to squeak out a few words before coughing, "Yeah, that's good stuff."

He reached behind him and carefully grabbed a tall bottle with a faded red label and jumped off the counter before setting it down between us. I leaned forward to read the dusty label out loud. "*Glenfiddich, Rare Collection, 1937*…is that the year?"

"Yep." He laughed when my eyes widened and my mouth dropped open.

"Where'd you find it?"

"In one of the big houses on our last Julian trip. Jacks and I hit the jackpot in this dude's wine cellar. I brought back a few things. This bottle I planned to save for a special occasion but then I realized the man that owned it probably thought the same thing and yet, there it stayed, locked behind a glass cabinet door with a bunch of other rare shit. You know, I think only sixty-something bottles of this are out there. You can only find them in Auctions now." His eyes glazed over as he realized what he said. "I mean, before. Whatever, it's a rare whiskey, this is." He sipped from his glass again and pushed mine closer to my hand.

"It's not bad. But may I ask - why'd you pull it out now?"

"What? You're thinking I planned on getting you drunk enough to promise to stay here in the mountains with the rest of us. And not go riding into the sunset on the back of a horse you don't know, spending a week traveling to one of the most dangerous cities in the country?" The sharp edge to his voice betrayed the smile on his face.

"That's exactly what I was thinking," I said, sipping from my glass. I couldn't help but wince from the heat.

"And, I take it you came down here dressed like that in order to convince *me* to let you go?"

"Well, two for two. A smart one you are." I rose my tumbler up. His eyes roamed freely over my shirt, pausing over the material that was stretched across my breasts. "Is it working?" I asked with my most seductive smile.

"Maybe, I'll tell you later. We're about to have company." With a nod, he gestured outside and I turned to see the rest of the group walking up the trail to our cabin steps.

"I hope you plan on sharing your whiskey find with the others." I said with a laugh while Zoey met Winchester at the door, all tail wags and jumpy paws.

"Of course. Why wouldn't I?" Connor waved the group in and smirked as I crossed an arm casually over my breasts.

"I'll be right back," I said as I waved at the others. I took the stairs up two at a time, hoping the other men weren't staring at my backside as I ran from the room. My plan had backfired. *That's okay,* I thought, *there's always a Plan B. And Connor will eventually have to come upstairs and climb into bed with me.*

꙳

Connor was still drinking with the other men well past one in the morning. The rare bottle of *Glenfiddich* had been a treat for them, especially Skip, who wasn't much of a drinker but did enjoy the occasional snifter of whiskey. The bottle was gone in less than an hour and the men had moved on to another amber-colored liquid that I stayed clear of. By the time I dragged myself upstairs, I was more than ready for sleep.

When my head hit the pillow, the weight of my eyelids multiplied exponentially and rather than struggle to keep them open, I submitted to my body's call for sleep. My last conscious thought was about Connor and how I was going to convince him to get on one of the horses as soon as they were ready to ride.

It was the change in the air around the bed that roused me from a dreamless sleep. I heard the curtain from one of the windows drag across the windowsill and sensed its movement as it fluttered up against the glass. I lifted my head, my vision still blurry and smiled up at the face peering down at me.

"Connor…did you get enough to drink tonight?" I mumbled.

The face leaned forward slightly and I felt the mattress give a little as his elbows pressed into the bed. A chill ran along my cheek, travelling down the side of my face and crawled around to the back of my neck, lifting the small hairs that ran along my spine. The sensation made me shudder and I bolted upright and away from the man kneeling on the worn, wooden floor next to where I had been sleeping.

It wasn't Connor.

꙳

Connor stumbled up the stairs, half-laughing and half-grimacing as the drink he'd poured eagerly down his throat threatened to resurface with each step he took up to the second landing. For the first time since Fin, he was happily drunk, without a care in the world. And so was Winchester, who was sprawled out on the living room sofa, and Jacks, who was helped back to the cabin next door by Skip, where a pregnant Ana waited.

He giggled, not bothering to cover his mouth while he passed Kris's dark bedroom as the image of Ana came mind. She would be pissed to see Jacks indisposed and unable to wait on her. The tongue-lashing she would give the man would be epic and Connor was more than bummed that he would not be there to hear it.

After precariously weaving down the hallway, he finally made it to the room he shared with Riley. He was surprised to see a crack of light coming from the underside of the closed door and he pushed on it until the heavy wood creaked inward. Riley sat on the mattress, pillows clutched to her chest with her back pressed into the bedframe. She didn't look at him as he nosily entered their bedchambers, tugging at his shirt with one hand and the buttons of his jeans with the other.

"Hey baby...you waited for me?" he slurred his words as he kicked off his shoes before plopping down onto the side of the bed.

The shirt was fighting with him and he cursed as the material twisted under his arms and around his neck. He couldn't seem to get the damn thing off. "Whada fuck," he hissed, as the shirt snagged his lips and nose. With both arms awkwardly flailing in mid-air he began to giggle again. "Baaaaby, tink I's need help," he said. A full minute went by in silence as he continued to struggle against the tight fabric before he was free. He tossed the stretched out shirt onto the ground at his feet and noticed a wet stain down the front of it. "Huh."

Riley hadn't said a word since he came into the room. The thought that she was angry occurred to him but his head had begun to spin and the room was tilting and swaying with it.

"Fine. Ya win, baby. I give, mmkay?" His accent was strong, even to his drunk self and that made him giggle again.

When she finally did speak, her voice was flat, devoid of emotion. It didn't even sound like her and for a split second he panicked, thinking he had wandered into the wrong bedroom. "Connor. Be quiet."

He turned his head around to stare at her. Yeah, it was Riley. It was definitely Riley sitting next to him, wearing something strappy and shiny. With a grin, he lifted a hand and fumbled at her shoulder, teasing the spaghetti strap until it slid down her arm. Without a word, she simply shrugged his hand off her shoulder.

"Awww, babe, dannae be like dat." He was drunk but not so drunk that he didn't realize how horrible his speech was. Clearing his throat, he tried again to speak to her but only got a fleeting glance in his direction before she looked away from him again. Feeling slighted, he smirked at her profile and followed her gaze across the room to whatever it was that was more interesting than him.

"Holy fuck!" he shouted, pushing off the mattress so quickly that he lost his balance and had to flail his arms to keep from falling backwards.

In the far corner stood a man with his back facing them. He shifted his weight from one leg to the other, causing his body to sway from side to side. Blood soaked his shirt from the collar to the waist area and in the center, where his shoulder blades should have been, was a dark and fleshy hole. The back of the man's light hair was crusty from dried blood and grass. Connor didn't need to see the man's face to know exactly who he was. But it couldn't be. He was dead. Dead and buried on a hill not far from there, with a panoramic view of the lake.

The spinning in Connor's head took over and his body pitched forward. Just before he collapsed onto the ground, his eyes rolled back into his head and Fin's rugged voice spoke to him, "Connor...don't let her go, Connor. You can't let her leave us..."

CHAPTER eight

I rubbed at my arm with a scowl on my face so severe I was certain the horse knew exactly what I was thinking. Foxy stomped her right foot down into the dirt and kicked at it, spraying my boot with dusty residue. She turned around and stuck her ass in my face. Swished her tail at me twice and then casually walked over to the hay pile that Sunny was eagerly picking through.

"You okay?" Kris asked. Her eyes were wide and her mouth was drawn in a tight line.

"I'm fine. Damn horse is just stubborn. I'll try again later," I said with a huff while Kris helped pull me to my feet. I lifted my arm to find my elbow scraped and bloody. But it was my pride that had taken the biggest blow. *Three times.* The bay had thrown me three times.

It was mid-day and the sun beat relentlessly down onto my shoulders, turning my tan a shade darker. Gnats flew around my face and I swatted at them, cursing under my breath as one of the puny bugs flew up my nose.

Sunny was easy to saddle and even easier to mount. In fact, she seemed happy to have a rider. But Foxy proved to be more of a challenge. She allowed us to saddle her without a problem and even to lead her around the lodge lawn on her side pull. But the instant I put my foot into the stirrup, she changed. The first time she threw me, I hadn't even lowered my butt fully onto the saddle before being tossed off. I immediately tried again, only to have the bay lower her head, tossing me up and over the saddle horn. Both times, I landed on my backside somehow. But this last time she reared up and bucked when she realized I had a solid handful of her mane and wasn't letting go. My left foot slipped out of the stirrup and off the saddle I went, landing hard on my back just inches away from her stomping feet. She could have crushed me if she wanted or at the least, landed a few good solid blows before she stomped away, but she didn't. She was testing me. It was a battle of wills and I was intent on winning the next round.

"Let's take a break, let them eat, and hopefully try again when the sun's not so damn hot."

Kris nodded and carefully approached the horses, tying their leads onto the post by their hay pile. Foxy didn't look up at her, just continued to munch on the dried strands as if nothing out of the ordinary had happened that morning.

I was shaking clumps of grassy dirt from my ponytail when I heard Connor's voice, followed by Winchester's laugh. The trees had thinned out some from the heat of summer but I could still only see the tops of their heads as they followed the trail up. I briskly rubbed at my clothes, wiping at the dirt and scuffmarks left over from my falls. The last thing I needed was another argument with Connor about my safety. There was no way to hide my bloodied elbow, so I propped my hands on my hips as the men came into view, hoping neither would spot my injury.

Winchester waved in our direction and I nodded at him with a smile, raising my uninjured arm in a quick wave. Connor looked as if he had gone a few revolutions in a clothes dryer. His hair was pressed straight in funky places and curled in others. Even from a distance, it was easy to see which side of his face he had spent the last ten hours lying on. He was wearing the same jeans but a different top - the only tidy thing about his appearance.

As they got closer he smiled timidly, as if he was nervous or anxious to see me. "Well, good morning," I beamed, when the pair was within earshot.

"It's a perfect day," Winchester said. His hands were shoved deep into his jean pockets and he looked me up and down before a scowl settled on his face. "What have you ladies been doing up here all morning?"

"Cleaning the horses, can't you tell?" I answered. It wasn't exactly a lie. We *had* spent over an hour brushing the horses down with the shedding tools. And I had attempted to use the hoof pick to clean out the clods of dirt and mud packed onto the bottoms of their feet. Neither horse had enjoyed that very much. They must have sensed it was my first time grooming a horse and that I was nervous around their legs. Falling off a horse and landing on your backside was one thing - getting kicked in the head was another thing altogether. Thankfully, neither Sunny nor Foxy decided to see what my face felt like beneath their hooves.

Winchester nodded at me but the scowl didn't leave his face. "Being careful, I hope?"

I smiled, silently urging myself to keep from lecturing him that he was not my father. "Yep. All good here. So, I see you both survived the night. How you feeling?"

Connor groaned, the first sound he had made, and Winchester winced. "Let's just say this morning my stomach objected...*profusely*," Winchester said.

"I figured as much." I turned to look at Connor and softened my tone, "Sorry about leaving you on the floor. You passed out and all I could do was roll you around until you looked comfortable."

"I'm sorry 'bout that. You know, for coming to bed so drunk."

I shrugged eager to change the conversation. I wanted to talk to Connor, to see how much he remembered before his face kissed the hardwood floor the night before, but not in front of the others.

Lost in my own thoughts, I didn't notice the men stepping back from me until there was a good five feet between us. When I looked up at them with a frown, confused by their matching expressions of concern, something tapped me on the shoulder. As I turned my head to see what Kris wanted, a piece of rope dragged across my neck and I yelped. The stubborn bay stood just behind me with her head next to mine, her lead dangling against my back. She pushed her muzzle along the side of my face, rubbing my cheek. With a playful nip at my shirt, she turned around and walked back to her hay.

I stood frozen, dumbfounded at the bay's behavior. Unsure of what had changed between us, I simply stared at her as she nudged the hay around before munching on it. Kris stood next to Sunny the palomino, her eyes wide with a big smile spread on her face. *Did I just win this round?*

✦

Connor lounged in the Adirondack chair, his bare feet propped up on the deck railing as he watched a flock of white birds dive toward the surface of the lake through the tinted shield of his sunglasses. He knew the headache would eventually go away, though it didn't feel like it at the moment. There wasn't enough room in his skull to contain the throbbing of his hung-over brain.

Zoey lay curled at his feet, tuckered out from chasing a squirrel between the cabin and the tree line for nearly an hour. The squirrel was clearly having fun teasing the dog, and though it was amusing to see, the back and forth motion of the two just made the splitting feeling inside Connor's head worse so he hadn't watched to see who ended up winning the game of tag.

The night before was fuzzy; toasts and shots and swigs from whiskey bottles plagued him. An image of Riley, sitting in their bed, arms wrapped around a pillow, just wouldn't leave his thoughts. And something else. Something dark; something he was sure he didn't truly want to remember, niggled at the fibers in his brain, doing its best to force a path to the front of his memory. He struggled to push it away, thinking of the lake instead. The dog and the squirrel. Or the fact that he had to clip his toe nails soon. But the dark memory kept trying to come back. He rubbed briskly at his face and winced when the jostling hurt his head.

"You know, you keep wearing your jeans outside in this sun, your tanned feet will no longer match your white legs."

Connor shifted in his seat, turning his sore head just in time to see Riley settle into the chair beside him. "I thought you liked my legs?"

"Oh I do, but keep this sort of sunning up and it will look like you're wearing brown socks when you're naked." She laughed, and even though the sound of a mouse fart was enough to make him cringe in pain, her laughter didn't. It was a honey-sweet musical sound that never failed to warm his heart.

"Done with your horses?" he asked.

"For now." She smiled at him, but he noticed the pull at the edges of her mouth, as if her grin was forced. He waited until she *looked away, sighing heavily into the warm air. "We need to talk about last night," she said quietly.*

"Yeah, I figured as much."

"And...?" she asked him.

"You go first. Last night is a big blur for me."

Connor sat still in his seat, listening to Riley recount the events of the previous evening. Ending with how he wound up on their bedroom floor, half-naked and alone.

"Are you certain?" he asked, feeling a cool sweat break out on the exposed parts of his body.

"Yes. One hundred percent; it was him."

He nodded curtly, amazed that his head could actually hurt more as Riley's words registered. After sitting up and being careful to keep the direct sunlight out of his face, he looked over his shoulder at the girl he loved.

"So, how long has Fin been back?"

The sateen sheets were cool and slick, and smelled of fresh lily. The laundry fragrance paired nicely with the scent of our body wash. Connor's breath touched the back of my shoulder and I concentrated on the soft wisps of air that hit my skin with a slow and steady rhythm. The day had been a long one; full of horses, discussions, chores and thoughts. That was what I was tangled in - my thoughts. As I waded through the murky waters of my mind, I felt lost and alone in the gloomy shadows. Even with Connor's arm draped protectively around me, I knew he wouldn't be able to save me from myself, or from the shadows that took form late at night.

Though I couldn't see Fin, I felt him nearby. His essence was heavy - impossible to miss. And he wouldn't leave me alone. Every time I blinked, I was certain his face would appear before mine, with him hunched over, watching me in bed. Or standing in the far corner, his gunshot wound open and oozing sickly-colored blood. If he could hear my pleas for him to move on, my demands for him to leave me be - he wasn't listening.

With a shaky sigh I shifted, rolling onto my back and adjusting Connor's heavy arm below my naked breasts. He moved slightly, bumping his bent knee into my leg but he didn't wake. The haircut he had given himself suited him. Though his hair still had plenty of length, it didn't hide his features anymore. The straight angles of his nose and jawline were visible once again, as well as his eyes. I loved his hair long. He looked wild, rugged, and sexy. But his eyes were my favorite - the clear blue color stood out against his dark features, begging me to get lost in them. Drown in them. And every time he looked at me, I did just that. Now that his hair was shorter, I could see more of his eyes, without having to push his wavy locks out of the way.

I was still staring at his sleeping face when dawn began kissing the bedroom windows. No matter how hard I tried to will it away, the new day had started. The room seemed to expand as the shadows were forced back into their hiding places and the light of day took over. I stared at the ceiling, checking out the wooden beams and a cobweb the size of a Mini Cooper that I hadn't noticed before. It was dusty, tucked into the far corner of the room, just behind the bathroom door. I became fascinated with it as the room brightened, hoping to see a spider run out along the sagging strands, but nothing did. The spider that created it had been gone a long time.

When hazy sunbeams began hitting the floor and spraying across the foot of the bed, Connor stirred beside me, flexing his arm across my midsection. I waited for him to stretch before I leaned over and softly kissed his mouth.

His eyes fluttered open, and with his early morning voice laden with a touch of his rusty Celtic accent, he murmured, "Morning, sunshine."

"Good morning."

"How long have you been awake?"

"Awhile. I know you slept well, you snored."

His eyes widened before he scoffed, "I do not snore!"

"You keep telling yourself that," I giggled.

"Kris is up, I can smell coffee," he sighed.

I heard her rise and creep down the stairs a half hour before, but I wasn't ready for coffee, plus part of me hoped I would drift off into some sort of slumber. My body was sore and achy from the day before.

"I'm going to take the horses out for their first ride today…with Kris," I said.

"Really? You think they're ready for that?" Connor propped himself up on one elbow and looked down at me.

"I'm sure Sunny is, but Foxy...we'll see. We won't know if they are ready till we try."

"True. Want me to go with?" He twirled the ends of my hair around his finger.

"Not yet, but thanks." I looked over at him and smiled. He was different, less combative, more interested in what I was doing with the horses. I wondered if he was beginning to change his mind.

"You know, I have this problem," he said with a sly grin on his face.

"What problem is that?"

Connor's fingers found my hand and he tugged it below the sheets, between us. "That's an impressive bulge, Sir," I joked.

"I told you I have a problem. Mind fixing it for me?"

His mouth met mine, parting my lips, eagerly probing inside to dance with my tongue. The sheet slid down to my waist and Connor kicked it the rest of the way off, exposing our nude bodies. He nibbled at my neck and shoulder while walking his slender fingers down my abdomen. The freshness of his body wash and the salty musk of his skin twisted my stomach into knots and titillated every one of my nerve endings. He had only to touch me to awaken every sense in my body.

We both jumped when a knock vibrated off the bedroom door. I clutched the sheet to my chest and heard Connor groan as he rolled off of me.

"Riley, Connor…you awake? Breakfast is ready!" Kris's chipper voice said from behind the door.

"Sure, Kris…we'll be right down!" I replied.

"Okay, great!"

"Wait, what?" Connor complained. He pulled me onto him until I straddled his waist. "That's all I get, a few kisses and love pats?"

I ground my hips against his before rolling away from him and quickly sliding off the side of the bed. "Come on, let's eat. Kris and I have a big day planned."

He was up and off the mattress before I slid my underwear on. The cotton fabric made it to my knees before he grabbed me from behind and pushed himself firmly against me. "But…you said you would help me with this problem," he grumbled into my ear, playfully nipping at my lobe.

I swatted at his roaming hands, which were seeking a resting place between my thighs. "I can help you with your problem later…will you stop that!" I laughed as he leaned into me, nudging my backside with his erection. I placed my palms on his thighs in an attempt to free myself, but he was stronger - and faster. One of his free hands darted between my legs and I gasped as his fingers slid inside me. The pad of his thumb rubbed against my clitoris as he pushed two fingers in and out at a pace that rivaled my heartbeat.

"Connor," I gasped as he spun me around to face the bed, bending me forward, still rubbing - still probing. I braced myself against the foot of the bed as Connor delved deeper inside me with one hand and cupped my breast with the other. Unable to stop myself, I pushed against him, longing for the feel of his sex inside mine. My muscles tightened around his fingers as a moan escaped my mouth but instead of continuing, he eased out of me.

"No, don't stop," I pleaded.

Fingertips ran up my spine and I arched my back from the sensation. "Riley, I want you," he begged.

"Please…take me, Connor…I'm yours."

And take me, he did.

CHAPTER nine

With each step along the trail, sweat rolled down the sides of my face and neck, soaking a dirty ring into the collar of my sleeveless top. I looked over my shoulder at Kris, and noticed her shirt looked no better than my own. We had only been on the horses for two hours, and it was the hottest day of the month. The thermometers inside the cabins read at a steady ninety degrees but all of us swore it felt more like one hundred and ten. The air was so dry that our throats were sore; none of us could get enough water.

For over a week, Kris and I had been taking the horses out for a daily three - five hour hike along various trails in the Laguna Mountains, testing them on different terrain, including the hard packed asphalt of the highway. I was almost certain that Sunny, our friendly palomino with the soft and gentle, Hershey-kiss eyes, was a trail horse at one time in her life. The only thing that Foxy struggled with was being in the rear. She hated to be behind the other mare and would yank at the rope reins and sidestep on the pathway until I allowed her to trot her way to the front. Lucky for us, Sunny didn't seem to mind being passed up.

I almost cancelled the last trail ride of the week because of the intense, arid heat, but we were leaving soon and I wanted the horses to be able to take a few days off before we set out. It would be a long week of walking from east San Diego County to the outskirts of southern Los Angeles, and I wanted to make sure the horses could handle the random hot days just as much as us people.

Kris and I found a tandem saddle at a horse-boarding ranch not far from Julian a few days earlier, which would work perfectly for the two of us. Connor was going to ride Sunny. She took to him, so it worked out nicely for everyone. An added bonus was that Foxy didn't seem to mind having both Kris and I on her back, though it left less room for saddlebags. I figured that on some of the journey the three of us could walk beside the horses to give them a break when they needed it. And as long as we stopped along the way to pick up supplies, we wouldn't need to carry much with us.

The plan was set in motion. We had it all sorted, even marked out nicely on a map with a red pen. The only hitch would be the weather and timing our departure to go with other events happening at the lodge. Ana had a month or so left of her pregnancy, and I agreed to spend no more than a week in L.A. looking for Mariah. It didn't seem like much but I told myself if we didn't find her this time around, I could always go back. It would take almost a week to get there, another week to look around and a week to return. That left only a week's worth of time for unforeseen events.

My mind ran the journey details on a loop through my brain, and even though we had planned what we could, I attempted to think of every worst-case scenario possible. I was imagining what we would do if one of the horses became injured when Foxy jerked at the reins and stopped walking so instantly that I slammed forward into her neck. She stood rigid with her head held high and her ears forward as if she was listening to something in the distance.

"What is it, girl?" I asked quietly, while stroking the side of her neck.

She blinked and let out a soft grunt, but didn't take her eyes off the trail in front of us. When I glanced behind me, I saw Kris atop Sunny, scratching at her ears.

"What's up?" she asked me.

I shrugged and looked around us at the dry forest that had begun to encroach upon the trail. The only prints in the dirt were ours, from our hike through the area two days earlier. There was a stream that hadn't dried up yet, not far away, which was where I intended on taking us so the horses could get water, but it seemed as if Foxy was refusing to continue.

I tugged on her reins in an attempt to turn her but she stomped her front feet in the dirt, not taking her eyes off the winding trail. With a sigh, I yanked harder, hoping that whatever she had heard or sensed was too far away to be a threat, but still she didn't budge.

"Are we going back?" Kris asked. Sunny seemed irritable; she stomped at the dirt and shook her head so that her mane flew out around her.

"Well, that's what I was trying to--", I was interrupted by a high-pitched shriek that reverberated off the trees in a multi-tonal echo that made the hairs on my arms stand up. The cry seemed too loud to be human and cut off abruptly. It was *close*.

Both the horses bolted the way we had come, back along the trail. I leaned forward and hung on for dear life, one hand wrapped in the reins, gripping the saddle horn and the other fisted in the horse's mane. Two more times I heard the screeching cry of what sounded like a woman, off in the distant and I glanced over my shoulder only to make sure whatever had made the awful shriek wasn't following us. The horses galloped until the trail merged with the highway again, and they nearly tossed us into the uneven dirt shoulder when we tried to calm them down.

"What was that?" Kris asked, keeping her eyes on the tree line that ran parallel with the road.

"I don't know, and I'd rather not find out," I answered.

My arm hairs still stood upright and with both horses twitchy and unnerved, we made our way back to the lodge in silence, never taking our eyes from the trees. Something was definitely there, watching us. It was a different kind of darkness than the one we had all gotten used to since the city fell, tethering the dead to the living.

The outcry we heard boom out of the trees was from something alive - most definitely alive.

We arrived back at the lodge sweaty and dirty from the ride. As Kris led the two jittery mares to their post to tether them, I pulled the water hose from the side of the Recreation building, letting the water flow from the spout until the temperature cooled. One thing the horses both liked was being splashed with fresh water. With their saddles off, I hosed them down until clean streams ran off their flanks, and let them air dry. With the late afternoon heat, it didn't take long for the liquid to evaporate. With a huge bundle of hay in between them, the mares calmed down and focused on one thing: food.

"Shower?" I asked Kris, who looked just as exhausted as I felt.

She shook her head, "Bath."

We took the trail leading down to the cabin slowly, our inner thighs sore from riding, legs trembling slightly, arms held limply by our sides. My whole rear-end felt numb but that changed by the time we reached the cabin. Groaning and grumbling with each porch step, the two of us entered the place looking like the horses had dragged us through the mountains, not carried us on their backs.

Zoey jumped up on us the moment we walked in the door. I bent forward, letting the small dog lick my face partially clean. I scratched behind her ears until she flopped down and rolled over, displaying her tummy for a rub. It took every muscle in my back to right myself when I was finished with the dog, and even more muscles to climb the stairs to the second floor.

Kris was standing on the landing, leaning against the banister talking to Connor. She mumbled something about the scream that startled the horses and Connor snagged my arm as I tried to squeeze past him.

"Are you okay?" he asked, as a look of concern wrinkled his forehead.

"We're here, aren't we?" I smiled up at him and pecked his cheek with a quick kiss before vanishing into the bedroom. I left a trail of dirty clothes on the floor from the door to the bathroom, stripping them off and dumping them as I walked.

Connor followed me in after Kris excused herself to her room. "Babe, what happened out there? Kris looked a little freaked out," he said, while I stepped into the shower, pulling the curtain closed around me. I flinched when the water came on - cold as ice - but I was too tired to step back and let it warm. When I opened up my bottle of spearmint and eucalyptus body wash, the smell alone was enough to make me sway in the shower, but not until the curtain pulled back and Connor popped his head in did I realize he was talking to me the whole time.

"Did you hear anything I said?" he asked with a smile.

"Nope. I'm in shower heaven, babe. Sorry, I'm exhausted; that was a stressful ride, however short it was," I mumbled back at him, as I ran shampoo through my hair. I pulled out a leaf, blinked at it, and sleepily wondered to myself how it got there.

"Okay, I'll let you shower in peace. You look *hot* by the way," he said. With a wink, he released the shower curtain, letting it fall back in place and I watched as his shadow left the room.

The soap going down the drain was tinted beige from the dirt that covered my arms, neck and face, and no matter how hard I scrubbed, I still *smelled* like horse. When I was finally satisfied that I was clean, I stepped out and wrapped myself in a terry bath towel, twisting another one around my hair.

My intention was to get dressed and go downstairs for dinner but the bed beckoned me across the room and I collapsed face first onto it, burying my head in a pillow. Sleep took me instantly, and for the first time in weeks - I didn't dream.

Connor sat downstairs at the counter, rearranging plates and cups and silverware until Kris begged him to stop. She downed three glasses of water since coming downstairs after her shower. Riley was still upstairs, and he was growing impatient waiting for her to join them. He had prepared dinner himself: a mixed veggie salad - all from their makeshift greenhouse. The lettuce and cherry tomatoes looked especially inviting and Connor had the urge to lean down and lick at his plate. Just before he did so, Zoey barked once and Connor rose from the kitchen island to look out the front windows. Winchester was standing on the porch, holding something in his hands.

"Hey man, how goes it?" he asked the impeccably groomed man.

"Oh, good...good. I just thought I'd bring this over. I know Kris and Riley were mentioning chocolate the other day." Winchester handed over a square container and Connor peered below the dishcloth to see a cooling batch of brownies.

"Seriously?" he asked, his eyes widening.

"Yeah, it was easy...just substituted the eggs for applesauce. And we have plenty of that, right?" he laughed. That was true too, Riley had pureed a whole crate of apples they picked from a nearby orchard and packed the sauce up in jars. They would have applesauce through the entire winter.

Kris squealed when she overheard the word 'brownies' and joined Connor at the door. He noticed that Winchester blushed when Kris leaned through the doorway and kissed his cheek. He rubbed at the spot as if he wanted to clean his face.

"Well, thanks man. I'm sure when Riley comes down, she'll dive right in."

"Oh, sure. No problem. Okay, so I'm back to the cabin, I'm making pesto tonight for Jacks. I mean…for Jacks and Ana, Skip too, of course," Winchester laughed.

Connor nodded at him and smiled, watching as the other man left the porch and stepped back onto the trail to go next door. Damn, that dude is so weird, he thought.

CHAPTER ten

The room was pitch-black when I opened my eyes and scanned the space around me. For a moment, I had forgotten how I ended up on the bed in only a towel. My hair was splayed out around my arms, the waves tangled and wild. Connor wasn't in the bed with me.

After dressing in a loose fitting pale pink top with aquamarine stripes and a pair of cut-off jean shorts, I attempted to calm my untamed hair by running my fingers through it but gave up and twisted the whole mess into a low bun. I knew standing in the dark hallway that Kris wasn't in bed either. The door was open and her room was just as dark as mine had been before I flipped the pear-shaped table lamp on that sat atop my dresser. The face in the mirror was worn down. Over the weeks, the sun had given me a healthy glow; richly tanned and freckled but my eyes looked tired.

With my hand on the banister, I stood at the top of the stairs, listening for sounds of life from the first floor of the cabin. No one was talking, nothing was moving around; it was dead calm. Downstairs I found the rooms just as dark as upstairs had been, the only difference being that the porch light was on.

"Where'd everyone go?"

I whistled once - a long and low whistle that I used to call Zoey to me when we were out hiking and she got too far ahead on the trail. She didn't respond, so I knew she wasn't inside the cabin, or anywhere nearby for that matter.

After digging my slip-on canvas shoes out of the entry way closet, I opened the front door and stepped out onto the porch, breathing the evening in greedily. I hadn't realized how stuffy the cabin was until standing outside in the crisp air. It was the first time in weeks that I wasn't stuck to my clothes with sweat. The weather was changing - finally. Fall was just around the corner, teasing us with the sporadic weather changes and the hope that the heat would soon ebb away.

It was time.

I went to each cabin, knocking on the doors and peering inside to see if anyone was home. Not even Ana seemed to be lounging indoors - which was odd for her. She never ventured out into the evenings unless it was to come over to our cabin with Jacks. Once the drama queen, with a knack for demanding the spotlight, she had become quite the mountain hermit.

Where the hell did everyone go?

A sound at the top of the trail caught my attention and I jogged toward it, cursing myself for not bringing a flashlight. I heard it again; muffled conversation, coming from somewhere ahead of me. I continued jogging, noticing that the ache in my joints was almost gone from my spill off the motorcycle. The new skin along the side of my jaw was shiny, taut, and bright pink, but Winchester had taken great care to keep the scarring at a minimum and I was certain his efforts would work.

I stopped halfway up the trail, straining to hear the voices in the distance. Standing alone in the dark, I could hear the smaller creatures of the forest moving through the trees. Larger birds flapping their wings in the sky and the crunch of dried leaves as something that was most definitely larger than a rabbit paced behind the trees. It was *that* sound that got me running again and seconds later, a moving light filtered through the tree line in front of me. I didn't recognize it right away, not until I reached the head of the trail and saw the raging bonfire. Everyone from the group was sitting in a circle around the makeshift bonfire pit we built a few months before. The bouncing light was from the flames that shot up two feet into the air, throwing eerie shadows all over the lodge lawn and into the trees. The wind was blowing east, taking the scent away from me, which is why I hadn't smelled the fire immediately.

The low pine branches reached out toward me as I walked by, moving quickly off the dirt trail and onto the pebbled one. It was only a trick of light but I flinched anyway as the limbs jumped and bent and moved around like they were alive; as if they wanted to snatch me and run off somewhere deep into the woods.

"Hey!" Connor shouted my way, waving for me to join them.

"Hi." I smiled as I crossed the grass and sat down on the blanket that Connor and Kris had laid out for Zoey. She met me with a series of sniffs and tail wags, eager to have my attention as I sat next to her and rubbed her belly. She had been spending so much time with Kris that I missed her.

The horses stood nearby, secured to their fence post, pushing their muzzles through a small pile of hay. I smiled at their improved appearance; Kris was taking excellent care of the creatures. Other than their long and stringy manes, the horses looked healthy. They had even put on weight since we found them. The fire shadows crawled across their backsides, making it appear as if the two were swinging their rumps around to some unheard beat and the visual of them dancing made me giggle out loud.

Skip and Winchester were going back and forth, telling a story about their construction of the new greenhouse earlier in the year. Though the story was a funny one, I had heard it enough to have it memorized. I tuned the conversation out but kept a smile plastered to my face and just watched them. We had become quite the family over the last year. Most of us were scarred by then…emotionally and physically. I fingered my jawline, feeling the thin layer of new skin beneath my fingertip and glanced over at Kris. From the angle where I sat, I couldn't see the scars on her throat, but I knew they were there. At least mine weren't inflicted by another person - not directly, at least. She had to look at them every day, knowing that someone put them there. Sometimes I thought she was the strongest of all of us.

"What's going on in that mind of yours," Connor breathed into my ear.

I smiled silently with my face up for a kiss. After our lips parted, we pulled away from each other aware that the conversation had ended since everyone else sitting around the ring of fire had quieted down.

Skip laughed before taking a swig of something from a can, "I would say for you two to get a room but hasn't stopped you before."

Connor's eyes widened and he tossed an empty can at the older man. Beer, they were drinking beer. "You're just jealous, old man!" Connor shouted playfully over the popping of the fire. After the group had settled down from a series of chuckles, Ana pointed behind me to where the charred remains of the main lodge house stood.

"It feels different - doesn't it?" she asked quietly. None of us were sure who she was asking exactly but since she had pointed just over my shoulder, I was the one that eventually answered her.

"Do you mean the lodge?" I asked. The long and thick pleat of her hair shifted on her shoulder as she nodded. "What do you mean?"

"It's just...don't you feel it?" Her voice was quiet, barely audible over the roar of the bonfire.

Winchester smiled as he gazed over my shoulder. "Yeah, I do. Like the heaviness is gone."

"Exactly. That's what I mean. Like...like whatever was trapped there is gone now." Ana smiled shyly and shifted on her blanket, stretching her curvy legs out before her. Jacks brushed his knuckles up against her bare arm and then her pregnant belly and she smiled at him. It was a brief, loving exchange that the rest of us weren't privy to seeing on a regular basis.

I felt Connor squirm beside me and glanced over to see that his expression was unreadable. I wasn't sure if he was upset or tired. "What is it?" I whispered.

He shrugged, letting out a heavy sigh. "It might feel better up here but not in the cabin, that's for sure." He gulped down several swallows of his beer and tossed the can into the fire, causing the flames to sizzle around the metal.

"What do you mean?" Skip asked him.

Connor and I exchanged weary looks before his eyes flicked over to Kris, who sat quiet and motionless with her knees pulled up and her arms wrapped tightly around them. "I think it's getting worse," he said.

I didn't look at him. I could tell by Connor's voice that he wasn't thrilled to talk about the dreams we had been having or the dark shadows that hovered in the corners of our bedroom in the middle of the night. But as I looked from one person to the next, it was obvious that only Kris and I understood what he had implied.

"Haven't you seen him?" I asked the group.

Jacks raised an eyebrow and Winchester leaned forward, placing his slender elbows onto his knees. The slight movement made his camping chair squeak. "Who?" he asked slowly.

"Fin."

Ana inhaled sharply and Skip's mouth dropped open but Winchester simply held my gaze, his expression not changing one bit. "Just you, or are all of you seeing…Fin?"

I rolled my eyes and sighed dramatically. "I'm not losing my mind."

"You just took a hard fall, banged your head, remember?" He stood from his chair to drop his beer can into the fire. The flames licked hungrily at the can and spit with fury at the remnants of alcohol.

"It's not her head, Win," Connor grumbled. "And it's not just her…Kris and I have seen him too," he said.

"What?" I looked at Kris, still with her arms wrapped tightly around her legs. "For how long?" Instead of answering me, she tucked her face down between her knees, hiding like a young child.

"She's been having nightmares," Connor said flatly.

"Haven't we all?" Jacks grumbled. He stuck the toe of his boot into the fire and kicked at a log until it rolled over and embers burst into the air. The crackling sound made us all jump.

"Not just dreams. Riley and I have seen him in the cabin," Connor said.

"And in the woods," I added quietly.

"Well, shit. Here I was thinking that the fire sort of cleansed this place and now you tell me that ain't true at all?" Skip asked.

"I think he wants something from me," I said. Everyone turned to look at me, including Connor. His eyes locked with mine and when he spoke, his words dripped with irritation and concern.

"And what's *that*?"

"I don't know what he wants exactly, but there's only one thing I can think of to make him go away." I paused and looked away from Connor. I stared hard at the fire until the heat made my eyes water. "I have to leave this place."

With everyone talking at once, it was impossible for Connor to hear Riley's voice over the others but it was obvious her mind was made up. Nothing anyone else said made her resolve change. It was time to go to L.A. and she wanted to leave…tomorrow. It was the

last thing she said before she pushed up off the ground and walked away from the rest of us. Back to the cabin, she said, to finish packing. She and Kris had their small bags of clothing and supplies ready days ago, but the food was still stacked on the counters, waiting to be shoved into the saddlebags and packs that we were supposed to carry. It was all the two of them had talked about over the last week. Horses. Trails. Los Angeles. He was already tired from the journey and they hadn't even started it yet.

This was really happening. She was really leaving. It was a fool's errand and she knew it, but her eyes lit with passion and guilty determination when she spoke of her desire to find Mariah. Connor watched her figure disappear onto the forest trail and knew it wasn't Mariah she was doing this for. It was her amends for putting a bullet into her brother's skull.

Even though it was in self-defense, she had killed a man. She quite literally had blood on her hands. Her conscious wasn't built for murder. He hoped letting her act out her fantasy of locating the missing Mariah would give her the peace she so desperately sought.

Doubtful, he thought. Survival was a basic instinct for all of them. But finding peace...would any of them ever feel that again?

CHAPTER eleven

The tandem saddle creaked softly beneath our weight as Kris shifted behind me and Foxy lifted each of her front feet and stretched her long neck out. With a flick of her ears, her telltale sign that she was ready, I tightened my grip on the rope that served as her harness and backed away from the fence post.

Connor sat upon Sunny with a resigned look on his face. The gentle early morning breeze lifted his hair off the back of his neck, threatening to blow off the cowboy hat he wore as a joke. As soon as he mounted the straw-colored mare, I had a hard time taking my eyes off of him. We all wore jeans but his were a faded washed-out color that went perfectly with the pale blue of his eyes. The long-sleeve Henley shirt he wore was rolled up to his elbows, showing off the chiseled shape of his tanned forearms and a small tuft of dark and silky chest hair that peeked out above the top button. I knew the hair was silky since I helped lather him down in the shower earlier that morning. I replayed the events of our frantic lovemaking under the warm water spray and a smile stretched out my mouth. *Those strong hands. Those long fingers - damn, what he could do with them.*

"Riley?"

I was snapped back from my wet daydream as Winchester placed his slender hand lightly on top of my left knee. After clearing my throat, I pulled the brim of my hat down to hide the blush that spread across my cheeks.

"Sorry, Win," I said with a nervous smile, as if he could read my very thoughts.

"Riley, just one thing - be safe. Don't try to be a hero and do something stupid, okay? We need you...*all* of you to come back." My smile faltered a bit when I saw the tears building up in his eyes. The summer sun had streaked parts of his brown hair a natural blonde and if it weren't for his OCD compulsion to stay constantly clean and groomed, he could almost pass for a beach bum. *Almost.*

"Win, I'll be fine. We all will. Hopefully we'll be back soon with Mariah, or at the very least...with answers."

Kris put a petite hand on top of her matching cowboy hat and leaned over to give Win a quick kiss on the cheek, followed by a little wave to the others. We already said our goodbyes, but they followed us up to the horses anyway, even Ana as pregnant as she was. Before I had mounted Foxy, she wrapped a string of blue and brown braids around my wrist and tied them in a knot. A single charm hung from the roped bracelet - a small silver heart. "Make sure you find your way home," she said quietly.

Goodbyes have never really been my thing, so I nudged Foxy with my heels and pulled on the bone-white harness rope until she turned to our right - away from the group. With a final wave and smile, we left them behind with the knowledge that it was possible and maybe even likely, that we would never see their smiling faces again.

As if Mother Nature herself approved of our departure, the wind came in from the west and pushed against our backs, urging us east toward the highway. I looked back only once to send a final wave at the small huddled group of people that had become my family. But more importantly, to send what I hoped was a silent and final goodbye to Fin.

After the lodge was out of view and the highway was laid out before us, something a rusty red color stood behind a crooked pine tree. It didn't move as the horses clopped down the drive and even though we were a good fifty feet away, I saw that it was a tall and lanky fox. With his head hung low, his snout seemed impossibly long. It was half-starved with an expression of longing that I knew all too well. It occurred to me then, that what we heard screeching in the woods was probably the lone and desperate pleas of that very creature.

$\wp\infty\wp$

The sun beat directly down onto the ground, with not even one cloud between the earth and the solar rays to give us a reprieve. By late morning, we had stripped out of our layers and down to our undershirts. The cowboy hats that Connor had given us kept the sun off our faces and necks but I was constantly swiping at my brow to keep the sweat out of my eyes. We followed the highway north until we reached Julian, where we stopped and raided a general store for buckets and water for the horses. When they had their fill, we turned west and followed the winding highway toward Ramona, walking the horses on the soft shoulder where possible. Mile long chunks of Highway 78 were empty of all vehicles but then there would be random clusters of stalled cars and trucks clogging up the road. The horses were able to maneuver around the metal clusters easily and I took every opportunity for the first half of the day to remind Connor about how sensible it was, bringing the horses instead of riding motorcycles.

Sometimes we would talk about the scenery - the rolling hills covered with trees that would open up to flat expanses of over grown land that had all but eaten up a random house or two. Or we would talk about how warm it was and joke about how much sunscreen we would end up using by days end. But mostly we were quiet, nervous as we traveled through parts of town we weren't familiar with. We rode for hours through countryside that was unnaturally still and quiet. And then there was the butterfly.

As we approached a tight bend in the narrow highway, I marveled at the oak trees that crowded the shoulder of the road; they outlasted most of humanity and the reality that the three of us were truly alone hit me like a punch to the gut. As my breath shuddered in and out, movement to my right caught my attention just as tears were beginning to sting my eyes. A Monarch butterfly fluttered past my head and landed on the strap of my tank top. He sat there perched atop my shoulder, his delicate orange and brown wings moving slowly against the tame breeze of mid-day. When the golden sunshine hit his body just right, he shimmered as if dipped in fairy dust.

After a full minute passed, I felt Kris squeeze my waist. She spoke softly into my right ear, "Oh my God, did you know there's a butterfly on your shoulder?"

I tried to keep my body as still as possible while I laughed, despite the steady jarring from the horse. For the past hour, Kris had her ear buds in. I almost thought she had fallen asleep behind me listening to her music.

"It's been there for a bit now, just hanging out I guess," I said. I drew a deep breath in to steady my nerves and calm the sob that so desperately wanted to escape and concentrated instead on the magnificent insect that hitched a ride.

"It's so beautiful," Kris whispered. She waved her hand at Connor, gesturing for him to ride up beside us and when he was parallel with Foxy, Kris pointed at my shoulder.

"So, you have a freeloader, huh?" His laugh echoed down the empty road and bounced off the passing oaks. The sound was throaty and honest. I took in the sight of him sitting on top of the mare, comfortable in the saddle with the reins loosely held in one hand, his other resting on the saddle horn. He looked as if he the two of them trotted off a movie poster.

"You look like a natural," I said with a smile.

"Tell that to my *ass* later," he grunted.

For the next hour or so, the Monarch rested on my shoulder, and not until we were out in the open again with only empty fields on either side of us did it take flight into the wind. He was migrating too, south into Mexico where his kind would be waiting for him. All three of us watched as the tiny butterfly filled the sky with hope, fluttering erratically off into the distance with only one thing on its mind - to *live*.

Our first night of the trek was spent on the western outskirts of Ramona. We unharnessed the horses and secured them inside an empty barn off of Horizon View Drive, a road that forked off San Pasqual Valley. We were elevated with a view, which meant we would hear or see any traffic moving on the highway. The evening air was warm enough to set our modest camp up outside, but Kris ended up sleeping in the barn with the horses.

"To keep them company," she had said.

The first night wasn't full of conversation, like I imagined it would have been. Going through the town of Ramona had unnerved all of us, including the horses. The normally calm Sunny nearly bucked Connor off twice as we passed through the various car wrecks and cluttered intersections. Death still loitered in the air there - it was a smell that lingered in our memories, just as much as it did the bodies of the dead. And they were all over the streets. Some hung from blasted out windows of houses, some lay decomposed on front lawns and others were trapped inside their cars - burned to a crisp. The military had not been kind to the town of Ramona. And that feeling of being watched was all over; it came from every corner and every window. We may have been the only living things passing through, but we were *not* alone.

Connor made a small campfire and we sat around it while he heated up a can of beans. Kris had made cornbread before we left and it was supposed to last us at least two meals. The bread was gone before the beans were.

Less than two hours after dark, Kris waddled off into the barn and Connor and I set our sleeping bags next to each other in the softest patch of grass we could find. Under normal circumstances, the star-filled night and open air would have been romantic but we were tired and sore from the day's ride. Not to mention wary of every sound and shift in the shadows.

Connor's voice, heavy with exhaustion and his Irish accent, spoke softly beside me, "You do realize from this point on, we will be walking through towns. We aren't in the solitude or safety of the mountains anymore. We won't be alone. At least, not totally."

I didn't look at him but nodded and said just as quietly, "I know."

"Alright then," he said with a sigh. I felt him roll over onto his side and shortly after that, his fingers ran along my braid and lingered on the ends of my hair. "We should get some sleep and start off first thing in the morning."

"Okay."

"I like this place, you know? That old barn and this view. It's like a picture. I could live somewhere like this."

"Yeah?"

"Good night, Riley" he whispered, leaning down to kiss my lips.

"Night," I sighed against his mouth and felt him pull away, stretching out along the top of his sleeping bag. Neither of us said it, but we knew it would be a long and restless night.

Just an hour or so before dawn, Kris emerged from her slumber, a shadowy figure against the dark red paint of the barn. I listened to her shuffle slowly toward the cold campfire and heard the subtle clink of metal against metal. I turned my head to the side to watch her work. Within a few minutes, the aroma of coffee grounds permeated the air and caused an involuntary groan to escape my mouth. Kris's shadow jumped in the darkness as I pushed myself up into a sitting position. My back and hips were sore from the hard ground and my neck was painfully stiff.

"Uhg…thirty-something year olds should not be sleeping on the ground," I complained.

She chuckled and tossed a small package at me. It landed in my lap and I fingered the plastic-wrapped rectangle. It was a granola bar - our main source of breakfast for the next week.

"Thanks, but I think I'll take coffee first," I muttered as I crawled toward the small pit. We had it lit within five minutes, and Kris set the small coffee percolator on top of the foldable rack that Connor had perched above the firewood the night before. Everything we brought was compact and light, except for the food.

With steaming coffee in our hands, Kris and I whispered over our small tin cups about the day. *How far were we going? What roads were we taking? What was the weather going to be like? Where would we stop to water the horses?* We were discussing who was going to navigate the map for the day when Connor's sleepy voice startled us.

"Mornin' ladies…did ya save some for me?" He was sitting upright, stretching much like I had when I woke. Looking just as stiff and haggard as I felt.

"Of course, Kris made you a cup." I stood and took the few steps to his bed, handing him his coffee with a wink. Bright streaks of purples and oranges were stretching out along the sky toward us from the east like skeletal fingers. Dawn had arrived.

"How'd you sleep?" I squatted down beside him.

"I feel like someone took a bat to my balls." He winced, sipping the hot liquid too quickly.

I laughed out loud, enjoying the sound of my voice as it boomed outward into the open space around us. "You should have gone with us on more trail rides before we left," I said, still giggling.

"Damn…I could really use a giant bag of ice to sit on right now."

"Don't be a baby," I teased, ruffling his already mussed up hair with my hand, "Come sit by the fire and warm up. We were just planning out the day."

Connor smacked at my backside as I walked away, making me yelp. The sharp sound was followed by a whinny from the horses. It was the first time we heard them since Kris had left the barn.

"Did you give them some hay?" I asked her.

"Yeah and water too. They'll be busy for a while."

Connor had found a gallon of water in a nearby shed just before we settled down for the evening, but the horses would drink that in no time. Water was our number one priority. Any time we stopped, we searched for it. Fortunately, many people had stocked up on jugs and water bottles in their haste to evacuate and since those people didn't get far, supplies were easy to find. At least at first.

⤙∞⤚

We dismounted the horses and stood next to each other - shoulder to shoulder on the hot pavement in awe. After six or so hours on the road, two short breaks for the horses and a meager lunch of olives, crackers and applesauce packets, we made it just inside the town of San Pasqual. We planned on making it to the border of Escondido before night fell, but standing on the highway with Connor holding his horse reins, and me holding Foxy's, we knew that wasn't going to happen.

The highway was gone. A huge circular hole at least half a mile wide replaced it. The crater was full of blasted chunks of concrete, asphalt, glass and twisted metal - cars. We stood in silence a few feet from the drop off looking at the blast zone until the horses got anxious and pulled on their leads.

"What the hell did this?" Connor asked.

"I-I don't know," I answered.

"It's amazing," Kris said under her breath. Both Connor and I shot curious glances in her direction. "Well, I mean, it is. I don't think a normal explosion did this, do you?" She stared, unblinking at the destruction and then jumped back, startling Foxy.

Her hands flew up to her mouth and her eyes widened. "Oh no," she gasped.

"What?" I reached out to grip her shoulder, but she shook me off and pointed a shaky finger directly below us. I followed it, looking at the blocks of busted-up road, bumpers and blown out tires until my eyes found what she was pointing at.

Bodies. Or what was left of them. Buried beneath the rubble were hundreds, thousands of dead people. A strangled sound came out of my mouth and just before my knees buckled, I felt Connor's arm slide around my waist.

"I think we've seen enough, ladies," he said quietly. His other arm was draped protectively around Kris's sagging shoulders. As he turned us away from the crater, I followed the inside curve of it back up toward the road with my eyes and caught the image of an infant carrier lying on its side covered in black dust. It wasn't empty.

I purged the watery remains of my lunch all over Connor's brand new boots.

CHAPTER twelve

It took us two hours to find a way around the crater. Eventually we had to double back and knock down a few property fences to make a wide berth back and around. Dusty, thirsty and frazzled, we decided to camp early. After finding the highway again and following the road back uphill we stopped at a nursery and let the horses loose to graze over the overgrown plants.

"There're some houses across the street. I'll bring back whatever water I can." Connor walked off, looking eager to be on his own legs again. It took several trips but he brought back enough water to fill one of plastic bins we found. As the horses drank, we wandered around the grounds until we saw enough. Most of the foliage was dead, but some of it had grown wild in places creating a secret garden, just for us.

"I'm not hungry," I said, as Connor handed me a small plate of food. My appetite was lost hours before, when I realized there were too many bodies in the wreckage of the crater to all be from the cars. They must have been gathered there at that spot for a reason when something awful happened.

"Riley, this is just the beginning. You can't *not* eat after you see something disturbing or you won't eat at all on this suicide mission of yours," Connor grumbled.

I snatched the plate away from him and made sure he saw how angry I was at his comment. The campfire shadows danced across his face as he leaned away from me.

"I know that," I snapped. "Something was wrong back there. Seeing all those bodies under that debris…don't you get it? Those people were taken out on purpose. Excuse me if that thought makes my stomach lurch."

He raised his hands up in surrender but said nothing. Kris pushed her food around on her plate but no matter how much she rearranged it, she wasn't fooling anyone. She hadn't eaten a morsel either.

"Sorry," I said quietly.

I stared into the flames till my eyes stung, trying to remember a time when my heart didn't ache for my children or when I actually felt safe. My mind was blank. Something wet hit my cheek and slid down onto my shoulder with a plop. I recoiled from it and turned in time to see Connor bite down on his lower lip. He was trying not to laugh out loud.

"What the hell was that?" With a nimble flick of the wrist, something flew off Connor's flat camping spoon and lodged in my hair. "Connor!"

He let his laugh out and Kris joined him as I picked the instant mashed potatoes out of my hair. "I can't believe you!" I squealed. The wet flakes stuck to my strands like glue. "I'll never get this out!" Another plop landed on my arm. "Oh, that's *it*!" I said with feigned shock.

Using my fingers, I scooped the small heap of potatoes off my plate and threw the entire handful at Connor's face. His laugh silenced immediately. I thought he was angry and my smile faltered as I sat still, waiting for a string of curse words or something equally upsetting to fly out of his mouth. Even Kris had fallen silent in nervous anticipation of what Connor was going to do. I barely had a chance to stand before he was up and launching himself at me. With a wicked grin, he tackled me into the dirt and began rubbing his face across mine in an attempt to kiss mashed potatoes all over my mouth.

Kris dropped her own uneaten plate of food to the ground as she laughed at the spectacle before her of the two of us wrestling noisily around her feet - covered in food. It was almost worth waking up with dried flakes of the instant stuff caked in my hair.

"Day two, are you ready?" I whispered in Foxy's ear as Kris adjusted the tandem saddle. The trusting mare blinked slowly at me.

"Feels good," Kris said at my shoulder. I watched as she tugged at the straps then hooked her foot in one of the stirrups and swung her leg up and over the saddle like a pro. I still had to bounce a bit before I could raise myself up onto the horse. My body was not as young and limber as it used to be.

Once on top of the horse, Connor handed Kris her backpack and tickled my knee. "Looks like you got all of dinner out of your hair," he laughed.

I playfully kicked at him as he skittered away and I watched his muscles ripple as he lifted himself up onto Sunny. The horse took a step backwards, adjusting herself with his weight and snorted loudly, which was her routine. She was not a morning horse.

"Ready?" I asked Connor as he wiggled around in his saddle.

"Yep. Lead the way, trail master," he joked.

"Ha ha, very funny," I quipped back.

I had one of his long sleeve tops on over my tank to shield the early morning breeze from my skin. But less than an hour after we left the nursery, I had to pull the sleeves up. An hour after that and I removed it completely. By noon, I would have preferred to strip down naked but a sunburn on my breasts was less appealing than sweating through my clothes.

"Let's stop here," I said, turning sideways to glance at Connor.

He was off his horse before Kris and I even made it to the shoulder of the road. There were less and less grassy areas to walk the horses since we were nearing the center of Escondido. It was high noon and we were hot and thirsty.

Kris and I dismounted and led Foxy off to the side of the road under the shade of a large pepper tree. While the horses nibbled at the grass, searching for goodies, Kris pulled out two apples to give them as treats.

"You know, you keep giving those apples to the horses and we won't have any for ourselves," Connor said. He plopped down in the shade with his pack in between his knees as he rummaged around for his water canteen. The front of his shirt was soaked in a V-shaped sweat pattern.

"We should look for citrus trees now that we're in the City again. Maybe we'll get lucky and find a yard with an orange tree or something." I sat down heavily next to Connor and let him brush his fingers across my cheek before sipping from my own water canteen.

"Lemme see that for a minute." Connor gestured to the map that Kris pulled out of her pack. After she handed it over to him, she fell back onto the dry grass with a mouthful of granola clusters.

"Why couldn't we hole up somewhere by the beach," she complained in between swallows. "At least then we'd have the ocean to go to when it got hot."

"Suggestion noted," I laughed. It wasn't that bad of an idea, actually, but most of the shoreline was heavily developed which meant we risked running into living people we couldn't trust and dead people we couldn't flee.

Connor was ignoring us. He was busy studying the map with interest. "So, if we turn off the main road here and follow this for a few miles, it will take us straight to Highway 15. We can follow that north for a while."

"I thought the idea was to stay off the freeway for as long as possible?" I asked.

"Well, look," he pointed to the map, "We'll save a lot of miles taking this section of highway north. We can always leave it for a frontage road when the horses need a break, too."

"Okay. So, where should we stop tonight?"

The two of us mulled over the map until we picked our spot. We'd most likely be camping out beneath the stars again, just west of central Escondido. That second day was the hardest to get back on the horses after lunch. Two nights of little sleep had strained us all, even the horses were more nervous than usual.

As we walked through the broken streets of south Escondido, I made a point to not look at the buttoned up houses and to not turn and follow the shrill sound of the wind as it picked up speed and rushed by our heads carrying the screams of the dead. Just as I had felt wandering through downtown San Diego so many months before, I knew something or someone, was watching us carefully.

Connor wiggled his toes in the cool night air, rotating his ankles until they popped softly. It felt good to have his feet out of his boots for a bit. Riley had fallen asleep almost immediately after she put her head down. Same with Kris. But he couldn't sleep. Someone was following them, and he wasn't sure if he should tell the girls or not. So far, the only advantage to taking up the rear on most of their journey was being able to look behind him without Riley noticing.

The shadowy figure started tailing them the day before. It stood still behind the darkened windowpanes and blended into the shaded corners of buildings. Never did it show itself completely, but it was obvious it wanted Connor to know it was there...watching. Why? What did it want, this bearer of gloom that went everywhere they did?

As he stretched his feet out before him on the sleeping bag, he stared hard into the darkness of night until the fire died down to only a glow. When he was a kid, he was never afraid of the dark. One night, after his father drank too much and hit his mum, he ran off and hid in a drainage ditch that connected their property to the neighbors. He spent the night inside the rugged tunnel, being careful to keep his backside out of the trickling water. The smell of wet grass and dank mildew imprinted itself on his childhood memories and he could still remember it...all these years later. Even after that night in the ditch, he wasn't afraid of the dark.

But now...now there were things that lingered, waiting for him to close his eyes and take over his thoughts. He'd wake at night after feeling someone next to him, but it wouldn't be Riley's touch on his face or her hands pulling at the sheet...it would be that of a person long dead. A person with a bloodied and sloughed off face or hands that were rotted to the bone. His mind had become a myriad of nightmares that firmly attached onto his psyche even during the light of day. And there was not a damn thing he could do about it.

He peered into the night around him, looking from one unlit structure to the next, playing a game with himself to see if he could name the items he spotted in the dark. A row of buildings here, the bed of a truck over there, A few spindly palm trees off in the distance. A sign that could be for the freeway or a gas station and...

What was that? He bolted upright, startling the horses that were tethered securely to a tree behind them. He was sure he saw movement. Yes, there it was - a figure walking down the road. Connor glanced at the fire, nothing but smolders left, and looked back to the road. This shadow was different. It had substance and...color. The person was wearing dark pants and a lighter shirt. The apparitions Connor had seen in the dead of night didn't have as much contrast to them. This figure was a real person. A living person walking down the streets of Escondido.

He was half-tempted to rouse Riley and point out the person, who apparently hadn't noticed them huddled under the grove of trees. But he was certain it was a man and he was quickly blending into the background, shrinking to just a dot in the distance. By the time she awoke enough to see clearly, the man would be gone.

More survivors, he thought. There are more of us.

That should have made him feel better but it didn't. He was traveling with two women in a world stripped of laws and protectors. Riley knew he'd lay his life down for her and even for Kris...but would he be enough to protect her if they came face to face with what she was searching for.

Mariah was dead. She had to be. Sacrificed by her selfish louse of a brother. The men that took her didn't want her for a trophy. The men that abducted Kris tried to break her and when that didn't work; they ripped her nearly to pieces. Too much time passed for Riley to get the answers she sought, he was sure of it. But now his fears were coming true - others were out there.

There would be no sleeping for him tonight. Connor rolled onto his side to watch Riley as she slept. Only the stars lit the sky, so he could just make out the shape of her face. He didn't need light to see the curve of her lips or how her dark lashes looked as they rested against her sun-kissed cheekbones. Many nights when he was afraid to fall asleep and dream about the young son he knew to be dead, he would trace her features with his eyes, memorizing every inch of her beauty. It was the only thing that allowed him to smile in the mornings - waking up next to Riley.

Kris sighed in her sleep before turning onto her back. He listened as her breathing regulated and only then, when he knew them both to be safely and soundly asleep did he roll over to watch the street again. More men could be out there. And if they were, Connor would be the first to see them.

CHAPTER thirteen

"Did you sleep at *all* last night?" I asked Connor as he scratched his fingers absentmindedly at the base of his neck beneath his wavy hair. In the morning sunshine, the russet coloring showed tints of red here and there, making his hair seem to glow at the right angle.

"I got enough. Do you remember your dreams from last night?"

"My dreams? No, why?"

"You tossed and turned a lot, like you were having bad dreams." He sipped on his small tin cup.

I didn't remember a nightmare. "Sorry, my mind is a blank,"

"Small favors." He winked and passed me his cup. "Drink up; we have a long day ahead of us."

With a salute, I blew the steam off the top of the cup before taking a sip. The black coffee was unpleasantly strong. But it would wake me up and get me going - something that was becoming harder and harder to do at six in the morning after sleeping on the ground fitfully for half the night.

Kris was already dressed for the day and eagerly rubbing the horses down with her hands. She scratched under their manes, around their ears and down their sides until they were jittery with excitement. She had a way with them and the horses had bonded with her most of all. All she had to do was click her tongue and they would follow her around like excited puppies. The most I got with *my* tongue clicks was a snort or two, or an impatient swish of the tail.

After turning away from Kris and the horses, I caught Connor staring up the street near where we had camped out. The wind whipped at my loose hair as I approached him, sliding my hand inside his.

"What are you looking at?" I leaned into Connor's hip.

"Just…it's nothing. Just staring off into space I guess."

"Really?" Pulling back, I peered up into his face. "You look far too serious for someone just spacing out."

"Guess I'm anxious to get a move on. You girls almost ready?" he asked without looking down at me.

"Almost, Kris is just fawning over the horses for a bit. Give us a few minutes, okay?"

"Sure."

I moved away from him, letting his hand slowly fall from mine. When my arm dropped back down to my side, Connor said over his shoulder, "Riley?"

"Yeah?"

His eyes twinkled in the dawn like wet slate. "You look beautiful this morning, baby."

৯৯৵

Sunny did not like the City. We stopped for lunch after only a few hours to give her a chance to decompress a bit. She was wound up and unable to relax, like something was bothering her. Foxy was her usual finicky self, however.

We were halfway to the coast and off the highway by the time the clouds rolled in. North of Escondido was packed bumper to bumper with civilian and military vehicles alike. There were more signs of fires and destruction along the way but it wasn't clear when the damage had been done. All we knew was that none of it was recent. It made sense to stay off the highway and the side roads weren't too bad, though it felt as if we were traveling through a town that had been deserted since the seventies. Grasses grew up through cracks in the concrete, turning into weeds many months before. Some reached straight up into the sky as tall as the horses and others spread out along the concrete into scraggly bushes. The horses would jump every time the wind would rattle through the dry weeds, causing the raspy foliage to drag across the ground. I personally found the sound comforting - it went together well with the clomping of the horse hooves.

Sometime before the end of that third day, Kris announced her iPod battery had died. I thought the silence might end up killing her but eventually she struck up a conversation with Connor. I listened to the two of them talk about his movies, his favorite characters and how much money he actually made. The figures he pulled in from his last blockbuster film astounded me. The other's found it funny that I didn't know who he was but it didn't surprise me. Sure, I had seen his face a time or two, but I wasn't a movie buff. Lifestyles of the rich and famous never interested me. But I was slightly embarrassed to know so little about his past when everyone else was so familiar with it.

"You were rich enough to buy yourself a small island," I laughed nervously. Money meant nothing to us anymore of course, yet it still felt awkward discussing his success. It made our relationship feel more like a fairytale and less like it really happened. That someone like Connor would ever end up with someone like me just wasn't meant to be.

"Maybe. But remember, I'm from an island, why buy one?" he laughed back. "Hey, look over there…see what I see?"

Kris and I followed his nod to our right and spotted the trees instantly. We were trained to look for food, especially *fresh* food. Small yellow fruits weighed down the branches of a tree, not much taller than the property fence it hid behind. The petite and round fruits were clustered around the branches in such large numbers it was hard to imagine it had ever been picked clean at one time.

"I've seen those before but I don't remember what they're called. Funny looking fruits, if you ask me," Connor said as I dismounted Foxy.

"I love these things, they're called Loquats. My grandparents used to have a tree in their backyard," I said while standing on my toes and pulled the closest branch down to my face. "It must have bloomed early…don't usually see the fruits till after the New Year."

"Loquats?" Connor mumbled.

"Kris, throw me your bag…I'll fill us up," I said with a grin.

I grabbed on a cluster and pulled, dropping the loose fruits into the front pocket of Kris's bag. By the time I had finished filling the pocket, my hands were covered in a downy powder-like residue. As I wiped them clean onto the thighs of my jeans, a fat drop of water splatted onto the brim of my hat, making a tapping sound on the thick, woven material. When I looked up into the darkening sky, another raindrop landed on the center my cheek.

"Looks like we're going to get wet. We need to find somewhere to put the horses," I sighed over my shoulder, swinging the bag up to Kris. We moved quickly, letting the horses trot until we came across an apartment complex with covered parking spots.

Connor dismounted first, pulling Sunny into the small lot behind him. It was too dark outside with the rain clouds to see into the nearby apartments, so we tied the horses to the frame of the driveway awning and peered into the windows that flanked the front door of the unit closest to the parking lot. The room we looked into was a modest kitchen - clean and empty. The only thing out of sorts was that half the cupboards hung ajar, as if they'd been riffled through quickly and emptied. I still had my face up against the window when Connor jiggled the doorknob, opening the unlocked door with ease.

"Huh. It's open...should we go in, dry off a bit?" he asked.

It was a silly question, really. Kris and I stood on the front stoop, shivering and looking like a pair of drowned rats in cowboy hats. I shoved him inside and closed the door after Kris passed over the threshold. The apartment smelled old, like dusty carpet but thankfully not like a dead person.

"No one died here," I said under my breath.

"How do you know?" Kris asked, glancing around the small kitchen and attached dinette nervously.

"We'd be able to smell them," I said with disgust. The decomposing flesh of a person was a sickening stench that all of us remembered well. It was a sweet, rotten smell that overwhelmed every sense of the body. One did not forget it easily.

"Right." She breathed out a long sigh of relief and collapsed onto the loveseat that sat below the wide front window. A small cloud of dust bloomed up around her before settling. "Ewww," she coughed, waving at her face.

"There are probably towels or sheets somewhere. I'll go look for them." I dropped our bedrolls onto the carpet and kicked them up against the wall. It felt good to be indoors, even if it was in a dusty apartment belonging to a stranger.

I found several sets of queen-sized sheets and four towels in a narrow hall closet. After draping one over the modest loveseat, stripping, and remaking the bed in the back of the apartment, I plopped down beside Kris, who was kneeling on the small couch nervously looking out the window. The horses were standing shoulder to shoulder, apparently sleeping.

"They'll be fine out there, don't worry," I said to her before dropping my head back onto the cushion. "Damn, I'm tired."

"And hungry, no doubt," Connor said from the kitchen. He went through the whole room and came up empty handed. Our food spread out on the round dining table didn't create any sort of appetite either. I looked with resignation at the granola, cereal bars, two apples, a few oatmeal cookies, three bruised tomatoes and more loquats then we knew what to do with.

"Kris, why don't you take the apples out to the horses?"

She jumped off the couch and snatched them from the table before Connor had a chance to object. "They need to eat something other than weeds, Connor…we'll find more tomorrow," I said.

"Tomorrow? So, are we staying here tonight?" He sat down beside me and dumped a handful of the fresh fruit onto my lap. I rubbed one against my shirt until it shined.

"Why not? We need a break and we need shelter from the rain. I'd rather not spend the next twelve hours sitting in wet clothes."

Connor popped a loquat into his mouth and just as I began to warn him, he spit the partly chewed fruit out into his hand. "Damn, why didn't you tell me there's seeds the size of rocks in here!"

I laughed loudly while nibbling the sides off one of the yellow orbs. "I was just about to but you beat me to it. You didn't break a tooth, did you?"

Kris walked back inside, shaking water droplets off her arms. The cold followed her in before she had a chance to close the door. "The apples weren't enough. I thought Sunny was going to eat my shirt," she sighed.

"We'll find something more for them tomorrow," I promised.

"Are we almost there?" Connor asked, shifting to make room for Kris on the sofa.

"Less than two days, unless the weather sticks around for more than a few hours," I answered.

"Good, the sooner we get there - the sooner we can head back home. I want my own bed."

Taking one of the throw pillows from beneath my arm, I swung it hard into his face until I was satisfied by his grunts of protest.

୨୦୧

We have this little piece of the park all to ourselves for the time being. Shannon lays on my right in her 'I love Music' t-shirt and cut off shorts with one hand above her head twirling a piece of my hair between her fingers. Dean squirms around on my left. His jeans are cuffed several times, exposing his pale feet and ankles. He wiggles a foot at me and I smile at the blade of grass that is lodged between his two smallest toes.

"Look at that one," Shannon sighs.

I turn my attention back to the task at hand, staring intently up at the cloudy sky. The shapes move slowly, merging and separating fluidly. The day is humid and overcast - the perfect kind of day for cloud watching.

"Hmm...I see...a snowman with a top hat on."

Shannon giggles and shifts on the picnic blanket. "A snowman? I see a giant mushroom," she laughs.

"Wearing a top hat?"

"Mushroom's don't wear hats, Mommy!" Dean exhales loudly and hooks a dirt-streaked foot over my knee.

"Well, what do you see?" I ask him.

"I see an ice cream cone!"

Shannon groans.

"One scoop or two?" I tickle his side with my finger.

"Two!"

"Dean! You always see ice cream!" Shannon laughs.

The clouds begin to roll above us, darkening until they look like iron balloons - titans of cold metal in the sky. I sit up quickly, scrambling to my feet to take in the vast show above us. When I reach down for the children - they aren't there.

"Shannon, Dean?" I spin in a circle, seeing nothing but rolling grass and trees.

A shrill scream echoes around the tree line and I squint into the dreary day shadows in an attempt to locate the source of the sound. "Where are you two?"

The sky answers by ripping itself into pieces, dumping torrents of icy water onto my head as it falls to the earth in colossal amounts. I'm drenched in a second, wet through my clothes and instantly *chilled to the bone. As I sprint to the nearest tree, wiping my dripping hair from my eyes, I search for the kids. Where are they, where have they gone?*

The jagged bark of the tree feels rough under my hand while I rest but I only slightly feel it beneath my frozen skin. In a panic, I scream their names into the storm. My voice barely a whisper over the sudden downpour. They're lost. My eyes flood with a mixture of tears and rain water as they dart from one still form to the next, seeing nothing but the disquieted forest around me. I have to find them.

A sound drifts between the heavy sprinkles, "Mommy…"

"Where are you?" I scream, lost in the darkness of the storm.

I push off the tree and take three steps before the sky above cracks like a whip. A jolt of electricity from behind throws me forward onto my hands and knees. The rain ceases as I look over my shoulder and I see that lightning has struck an oak, jaggedly slicing it down the middle. It stands open and gutted - the trunk aglow with bright red flames. While I scoot backwards in the mud a hand reaches out from the blaze, followed by a face I recognize.

"You set us free, Mommy…," she says in a sing-song voice.

"No…" I sob, "Shannon…no!"

Her hand stretches out toward me and hovers just inches from my face before her whole being bursts into orange embers - some floating up away on the breeze, others settling onto the wet earth at my feet. I blink at her ashy remains while the tree roars to life; the branches spewing flames into the air like fireworks.

I sat up so suddenly that I nearly rolled off the edge of the unfamiliar bed. Although it wouldn't help steady the rushed beating of my heart, I clutched at my chest with one hand and gripped the edge of the mattress with the other. The dream felt so real that I reached up to touch my hair - certain it would be dripping wet with rain water. When my trembling fingers came back dry, I released a choked breath of relief.

Beside me, Kris lay in the fetal position, wrapped up in her sleeping bag, obliviously lost in her own dream world. I blinked at her, for a moment forgetting why *she* was there and not Connor but then I remembered where we were.

I got up quietly, slipping my socked feet into my shoes before stepping out into the narrow hall. Connor's sleeping form lay draped across the loveseat. *Safe. He was safe.* With a sigh, I leaned over him to peer outside. The horses stood where we left them, underneath the covered car park.

Though it was dark outside, I could tell from the coloring of the sky that dawn was on its way. The dream was fresh and stacked up like a tower inside my brain - waiting to be climbed. But there was coffee to make and a day to plan. Nightmares weren't new, yet something kept nagging at me and by the time the coffee was percolating, I knew it was important not to forget. After fumbling around in the poorly lit kitchen, until I found a pen and a scrap of paper, I scribbled the words down before shoving it into my back pocket.

You set us free.

CHAPTER fourteen

As we rode away from the apartment complex just minutes after the first rays of day lit up the ground, I nibbled on a piece of fruit and lost myself in the smell of the clean earth. The rain scent that lingered in the air was refreshingly nostalgic. For a little while, I was lost in my twelfth year, hidden deep inside me, that used to dance and skip through the overflowing gutters after a storm. I wanted to hold onto that memory that was latched to the just-washed air instead of so many other sad and disturbing ones from the last year. However something startled Foxy, she halted in her tracks, tossing Kris, and I forward in the saddle. And just like that, my twelve-year-old self was lost in the past again.

"Shh, girl. What is it?" I patted her neck, scratching softly below her long mane. As I stroked her, dust lifted off her rusty-brown coat, leaving clean streaks where my hand had been. I didn't have to turn around to see that Connor was also having a problem with Sunny; her whinny was strained and she stomped her feet irritably onto the road. Her hooves made a clack-scrape-clack-scrape sound on the asphalt that made me wince.

There was another crater where our road met Interstate 5. Unlike the last blown out hole we came across, this one was shallower and had tossed debris hundreds of feet around it. We left the residential street and followed what was intact of the frontage road that ran along the highway until we found a blown out portion of the barrier to walk the horses through.

Cars lined both sides of the Interstate as far as I could see; they were packed in so tightly against each other that nearly every bumper touched another. Other than the missing section of road, there were too many vehicles to safely maneuver the horses through. So we opted to stay on the side streets for the remainder of the morning. Twice I thought I saw movement off in the distance but convinced myself that a ripped flag or a torn billboard was to blame. The city streets had an odd odor - sort of like upturned earth that had been fertilized with cow manure. *Sick. The city smelled sick.*

"See that, just over there?" Connor pointed ahead of us and to the east over a row of buildings. A slender plume of smoke coiled upward into the sky.

"Yeah, I see it."

"Should we check it out?" he asked, without looking away from the growing black smut.

"No, let's keep going. It's probably a gas station or something," I answered.

I didn't like the way this part of town felt. Only a few more hours and we'd be in San Clemente. We didn't have the energy for detours.

∞

Connor was the one that spotted the small stream below the Interstate. For five miles, we had followed the shoulder of the highway after losing access to frontage roads. Fortunately, most of it was dirt and weeds and the horses enjoyed the change from the hard concrete. Once we figured a way down to the stream, the horses drank freely while I sat nearby, scouring the map for alternate routes. The Interstate glittered with windshields all the way to the horizon and the closer we got to Orange County, the more cluttered the vehicles became - spreading out onto the shoulders.

"We can't rest here for too long," Connor said at my elbow.

"I know." I looked from one horse to the other as they greedily drank the stream water. Sunny was the first to stop and graze along the shallow bank, nibbling up all the grass she could find.

"Maybe we should stay on the trail from here and follow the 5 up north." I pointed at the map, tracing a line along the Interstate. The only thing that would hinder our path would be walls or fencing.

"You know this area best, you decide," Connor sighed.

"Yeah, cuz I go horseback riding through here all the time," I laughed.

"Shh! Listen," Kris dropped her pack to the ground and stood up, facing the hills to our east. Connor and I turned our head to follow her gaze, straining to hear whatever she had.

"What?" Connor asked quietly.

As soon as he spoke, a soft whooshing sound echoed off the landscape. A dull whoomp-whoomp sound bounced around the hills and down toward the highway several times - and then, just as suddenly as it came - it was gone.

The three of us stood still, watching and waiting. Minutes passed and all that could be heard was the sounds of the horses eating and the trickle of water down the stream again. And my erratic heartbeat. It thudded loudly inside my chest. If Kris hadn't broken the silence, I was sure I would have collapsed of a heart attack.

"I think it was a helicopter," she whispered.

"I think you're right."

Connor threw his hands up in the air and rested them tightly behind his head, like you would see criminals surrendering to the police. When he turned to look at us, his face was lit with excitement.

"Riley, there's someone up there, flying around. Do you know what this means?" His shirt was rolled up, exposing his forearms, and his jeans had permanent dirt creases from sitting hours on end in the saddle. With his wild hair falling around his face and a twinkle making his eyes glow, he looked like a different man. One who believed in something we had starting losing long ago.

Hope.

As Connor spun happily around in circles, I looked in all directions, remembering where we were standing.

"We're close to Camp Pendleton. The military is around here. But I don't see any signs of them," I murmured.

"So?" Connor asked.

I didn't want to do it, to burst the bubble he was suspended inside. But there were obvious questions to ask. "The base is so close that you'd think we would see signs of something if anyone was there. Tanks, military vehicles, choppers."

"Yeah, so?" He stood with his arms still clenched behind his head.

"Connor, anyone with training can fly. But this close to the base...you'd think if anyone was alive, there would be signs of them. Look around - all I see are civilian vehicles - where's the military?" I gestured up at the Interstate above us, hoping he would understand what I meant.

"Does it matter *who* is flying the damn thing, Riley?" He was pissed. His arms collapsed down to his sides and he glared at me. His bubble was sufficiently popped.

I sighed. No, he didn't get it. "Connor, if everyone died here - if the *Military* is dead - then anyone could be flying that helicopter, or whatever we heard. *Anyone*. It means that we need to be careful. We have no idea who is up there but if there was hope of any sort of order being left - of anyone with authority surviving this...don't you think we would see signs of that when we're standing on Government property?" My voice shook with emotion.

Connor released a sigh and stared up into the sky. "I saw someone the night before last," he said without looking at me.

"What?" We didn't talk about it freely, but we all knew we saw things in the shadows.

"A real person, walking down the road close to where we were camped. It was too dark for him to see us but I saw him."

"You know it was a man?" I stared at him, confused and upset that he didn't say anything sooner.

"It was late, but yes, I think it was a man."

We stared hard at each other, probably wondering what the other was hiding. Kris slowly moved beside me and said in a lighthearted tone, "Well, both of you prove the same point."

"And what's that?" Connor snapped. Irritation showing on his face and coating his voice.

She slowly bent down to pick up her canvas pack and swung it over one shoulder before answering the question Connor nearly spat out at her. "It's true. We aren't the only survivors out here."

∽✑

The horses hung their heads low to the ground, walking only because we still controlled their reins. The light had faded from the sky an hour before, setting over the ocean in a purple haze that left the fluffy clouds above us a pale pink color. The reflection of the light that moved further and further over the Pacific lit them as if a giant light bulb glowed from within.

"So this dirt road will take us east if we stay on it, but there's a campground just north of here. Mind going off the trail for a few minutes?" I peered up from the dark map and pointed my flashlight into the trees.

"In the dark?" Kris asked behind me, snaking her arm around my waist loosely.

"If we cut through the trees here it's a straight shot to the trail that leads into the campground. Connor?" I turned to look at him, and noticed he obviously was still brooding from our argument earlier in the day.

"Fine. Lead the way," he said with an indifferent shrug.

"Okay." I shined the light into his face. "Into the trees, we go."

We found a game trail right away, at least what used to be a game trail and most recently probably been where water had run off from the rain. But it worked. Only a few minutes of slowly maneuvering through the poorly lit ditch and we were out on the other side, in the open. The horses picked up their pace when we reached the campground trail, as if they could sense the end of the day's journey waiting for us up ahead.

It was too dark and we were too tired to spend much time checking out the camp area when we found it, so we set up at the first site we came upon. We let the horses graze while we laid out our sleeping bags. Connor was quiet while he set up the small camping stove to heat our dinner.

"Why are you so upset with me?" I asked him as Kris stepped out of earshot to take the saddles off the horses. He set a can of beans directly on top of the small burner and stuck one of the flat camping spoons inside the tin, stirring the gooey mess around in a clockwise direction.

"How long are you planning on ignoring me?" I didn't bother to hide the irritation in my voice.

"I'm *not* ignoring you," he sighed, "I'm thinking." He rocked back on his heels and ran his hand through his hair. Even in the glow of our small lantern, I could see the dirt beneath his nails.

"And…" I prodded.

"Riley, I want to turn around…and go back." He stared up at me until I blinked, then returned to stirring the refried beans.

"You want to go back..." I forced the words out through clenched teeth, "I don't understand...we're almost there Connor. Why now?"

He slammed the spoon down with a clatter and I felt Kris's eyes on my back. "Because, Riley, this is a colossal waste of time and only *you* don't see that!"

His form faded into the distance as he stormed off into the night. Kris shrugged at me and continued removing Sunny's saddle. Despite the fact that I wanted to smack Connor upside the head, I had to smile. A clump of grass protruded from the mare's mouth and with each sideways chew, clods of dirt fell to her feet. Whatever plant she had found was so good that she pulled the entire thing - roots and all - out of the ground for a snack. As she munched she looked at me, her eyes hooded yet knowing.

She didn't want to be there either.

୬∞୶

The tree branches whipped from side to side and bobbed up and down as the breeze rustled through the campsite. Connor hadn't said much to Riley when he came back from his walk. He upset her and Kris too, who wouldn't even meet his gaze. Brilliant. The hard-packed earth beneath where they lay hurt his pressure points, especially his hips.

It was cooler tonight. Probably just as cold as the night before had been with the rain. He could taste the sap from the pine tree they slept under. The sharp and woody smell left a tangy flavor on the back of his tongue. No matter how many times he swallowed, he couldn't seem to make it go away.

He looked over to his left, where the girls rested. Riley was asleep with her back to him. With her blonde hair out of her braid, she looked younger and wild. He wished he could see her face. Someone has to be the first to say sorry... right?

He leaned over and gently gripped her shoulder, pulling her toward him. Her body fell backwards with ease and he smiled as her head tilted to the side.

"Fucking Jesus!" he screamed, kicking the sleeping bag from his legs. "Fuck! Fuck!"

Her face was gone. Bloody sinew and muscle hung from her head in chunks, something had eaten down to the bone in places. He screamed for Kris to wake up but she didn't stir an inch. Connor stumbled to the foot of her sleeping bag and recoiled in fear from the blood pool collected underneath her body.

Smacking at his face he cursed the night, not noticing the warm and sticky blood that was splashed on his cheeks and chin, and looked down at Riley once more, hoping - praying it wasn't real. That she would reach over and wake him from this living nightmare before he stroked out. But she didn't. All he could focus on was the light color of her wavy hair the golden strands that fanned out from her damaged face. Her face. Her face…what did this to her? What in the bloody hell did this?! The metallic taste of her blood rushed into his nose and mouth and he gagged so hard it made him light-headed. The last thing he saw before he passed out was one of her hands resting awkwardly on her chest…curled up tightly around a tuft of his own dark curls.

He did this?

The pulpy blood dripping off his face was all the proof he needed.

Yes, he did this to them.

CHAPTER fifteen

"Connor! Connor, wake up!" I attempted to pin his flailing arms to his chest while yelling his name over his screams. His whole body thrashed beneath my hands so violently that I was afraid to let go. But after his elbow hit me squarely in the chest, I was flung ungraciously backwards into the dirt, landing on my ass.

He flew upright, punching at the empty air between us and even though his eyes were open, his expression was still tormented by sleep, by whatever happened to him in his dream. I raised a hand slowly after catching my breath and carefully touched his arm. He recoiled from my fingertips and blinked at me. A semblance of recognition slowly spread across his sweaty face and he flinched at my smile.

"It's okay," I said quietly as Kris softly wept behind me, "I'm here. It was just a dream, you're okay."

"Riley?" In one fluid movement, he was out of his tangled sleeping bag and in my arms, his face buried in the curve of my neck, his tears hot against my skin.

Kris's slender arms wrapped around me from behind. The three of us sat in the cold dirt, crying softly and holding onto each other until the only sign of our tears were the dried up salt trails that streaked down our faces. We slept huddled in a pile under the moonless night, arms and legs entangled - afraid to let go of one another for fear that sleep would snatch us away to somewhere awful, where nightmares really did come true.

∽∾

I woke with a cramp in my side. Kris's arms were coiled tightly around my left bicep and Connor's hand was draped over my waist - his hand clutching a fistful of my shirt. For a moment, I stayed perfectly still, half on and half off the sleeping bag below me, wondering what the three of us must look like from above. Two grown adults and a teenager afraid of their own dreams. Afraid to sleep alone under the stars. But the cramp in my side spread until the sharp pain became unbearable and a spasm tore through the muscles in my lower back. With a groan, I rolled; jostling both the other's awake with a start. As they rubbed the sleep from their faces, I stretched my legs out until my back relaxed.

"I'm getting too old to sleep on the ground."

Kris laughed but Connor groaned out a string of curse words in agreement. The sun had been up at least an hour, which meant we would be eating breakfast on the go. No time for coffee.

Twenty minutes later, we had the horses saddled and rubbed down with their daily morning scratch. Foxy playfully nipped at the ends of my ponytail until I gave her a small handful of loquats. She ate them happily - seeds and all.

"Ready to go, Foxy?" The mare snorted and tossed her head up and down in answer.

As Connor swung his legs up and mounted Sunny, I took a final glance at the campground. At the beginning of autumn, the place should have been packed with campers. Children running along the dirt roads on lizard hunts. Couples walking hand in hand up and down the trails. The campground host lecturing a group of men about their late night festivities and scolding them in the morning to pick up their beer cans. But no...nothing. The campground was empty and probably always would be. I wondered if the same time next year, the campground would be overrun by weeds. It would blend in with the surrounding landscape - the only sign that humans had ever marked the place would be the crumbled concrete picnic tables and sun-bleached bathrooms.

"You coming, sweets?" Connor said softly as he backed Sunny up.

"Yeah."

It was time to move on. By the end of the day, we would be only hours away from Los Angeles. Tonight would be our last night of traveling and then the next day would begin the search. Perhaps I knew it then on that sunny morning - that finding Mariah wasn't going to happen. And I was okay with it. The outcome was no longer the objective - finding *anyone* alive was. I put all my energy into rescuing Mariah that I forgot there were probably dozens like her out there, lost and just needing someone to look for them. Someone to care, someone to find them. For whatever reason, that someone had become me.

"Look how close we are," Kris said quietly as she held the map out while we led the horses back down the trail toward the highway.

"Almost there."

We didn't speak for hours. The three of us simply sat upon the horses as they took us out of San Clemente and up the Pacific Coast Highway to Dana Point. We took a break for water then climbed back on, continuing north until we stopped for a late lunch in Laguna Beach.

"Wow, what do you think happened here?" Connor asked.

As we neared the heart of town, more and more storefronts showed signs of damage or were blown out completely into the streets. It was like a warzone. Not one corner stood unscathed.

"I have no idea, but I'm glad we weren't around for it."

Every mile or so there was a pile of burned objects that sat in the middle of the side streets that ran into the PCH. It took me three miles to realize it wasn't just debris that had been burned.

"Jesus. There are bodies in there," I whispered.

We tried not to look, but all through the community of Laguna Beach, there were piles and piles of them, thrown together in the street like garbage. In some places, the heaps of 'trash' reached over ten feet high and twice as wide, as if every single body had been dragged out of the houses on that block and set to burn. Though it felt eerie, it was unusually quiet - unusually still. That feeling of being watched, of having sets of unseen eyes on my back had all but vanished. For the first time in a week, it felt like the dead were really gone.

We ate lunch on a grassy outlook near a gas station. Most of the structures in the area had long been burned to the ground, including what was left of the gas pumps. As the horses grazed along the landscape like living lawnmowers, we sat on the cool earth eating granola and ripe oranges we had picked along the way. The salty air of the ocean blew past us and into the hills, taking the wet scent of seaweed with it. As we listened to the crash of the waves along the shore, I closed my eyes and tilted my face upward to soak up the afternoon sun until my cheeks burned with warmth.

The horses had nibbled the grass down to the earth in places, moving from one spot to another to gobble up the white dandelion seed heads that starred the green landscaping. Sunny's muzzle was covered with remnants of the weed as if she had rubbed her face along the plants before eating them.

Kris laughed as she used the sleeve of her shirt to wipe the horse clean. In my mind, I took a picture of the two of them: the brown-haired girl with freckles and scars as she leaned against the gentle-eyed, honey-colored mare with tufts of dandelion seeds up her nose. It was a beautiful image of the two with the Pacific Ocean as a background. Sunny ran her mouth against Kris's neck as a thank you before the two parted and we all climbed back up into our saddles.

The outskirts of L.A. were just a few miles away. I glanced at Connor, wondering if his thoughts were on the next day, like mine were. He smiled only the way Connor could - dazzling and perfect. I clicked my tongue to get Foxy on the move and we started back up the coast, leaving the ruined remains of Laguna Beach behind us.

ৎৈৎ৶

By nightfall, we were in Newport Beach. The fading light cast an amethyst glow across the streets and just as we had seen in Laguna, many of the buildings had been burned or damaged from nearby military tanks. The wind picked up and whistled through the palm trees, rocking the narrow trunks softly from side to side. We continued down the weed-riddled sidewalks until we came upon West Newport Park.

"Seems like a good place to camp. Plenty of room for the horses to graze, plus we can secure them over there for the night." I pointed to the fenced in tennis courts.

We tied the horses to a tree next to the small playground and took turns breaking into the houses across the street on Seashore Drive until we had enough food items for a feast. Connor also found

126

a portable BBQ, so after an hour of settling in and warming a bag of coals, we had a dinner of boxed macaroni and cheese, canned peas and carrots and chocolate pudding. Kris opened up the remnants of the cheese sauce packet and licked it clean while Connor and I watched. It was the closest thing to a full meal we'd enjoyed since leaving the lodge.

The horses drank from a large plastic tub that Kris and I found in a nearby garage. After dumping the Christmas decorations from it, we had carried it back to camp and filled it with several gallons of water. Almost every home had at least two full gallons of water. Like the people that lived there had prepared for the worst. Only a handful of the lavish homes actually had people inside - dead in their beds. Most packed what they could fit into their Mercedes and Land Rovers and fled the City. I wondered as I picked through the items they left behind, how far did they manage to get before the traffic stopped them? Which cars had we passed on the nearby coastal highway came from that very street? It didn't matter anymore. The dead were gone and we became scavengers of what was left of their previous lives. *Like rats.*

"No, I can't eat any more," I said as I waved Connor's plate away.

He set the rest of the pasta down and picked up the bottle of wine, swigging from it until he needed to come up for air. With a satisfied grunt, he set the half-empty bottle of red down on the grass between us and looked up at me with a goofy smile.

"That was great," he mumbled.

"Dinner or the wine?"

He smirked at me, his eyes glossy. "Probably both," he laughed.

Kris jumped up and grabbed the paper sack off the ground. "I almost forgot!"

We watched her rush over to the tennis courts with her bag of treats for the horses. The sack was filled with guavas and ripe, red pears - a treat we found in the fenced off yard of one of the beach houses. It was the only one nearby with citrus trees. The salty moisture must have kept the trees alive and blooming; both had scraggy branches that grew up and over the wall that bordered the neighboring property.

"Riley," Connor pulled me up against his side while we watched Kris feed the horses, "I miss you."

"Miss me? I haven't left your sight in a week!" I laughed.

"I miss the feel of you," he whispered against my ear, his lips brushing along the curve of my skin.

"Oh," I sighed. Yes, I missed him too. I missed the feel of his strong hands between my thighs and the taste of his mouth. Judged on the wanting look he gave me, the desire was inside him, too.

"Soon," he whispered after kissing me softly.

"Yes…soon."

ഇം പ

The flames licked at the glass teasingly, dipping down below the windowsill before launching back up, high above my line of vision. There was nowhere to go, nowhere to run. The fire burned all around me, filling the open room with smoke. It roiled and curled beneath the wide door like it was alive.

"Help!" My raspy scream bounced off the columns of the empty warehouse.

Only the sound of popping wood and twisting metal answered as the fire ate its way through the curved galvanized metal sheeting above, dropping chunks of burned roofing at my feet. I jumped in fear as shadows twisted and writhed in the corners, a chorus of screams and shouts louder than the fire itself ringing out into the smoke and ash-filled air.

And then silence.

I was kneeling on all fours, struggling to breathe in what little oxygen was left in the room when the fire died down to embers and the shadows disintegrated. Daylight streamed in beneath the door in a thin strip and I crawled toward it, caring not what was on the other side as long as there was air - clean, fresh air.

Soot coated the inside of my nostrils and the rank odor of it burned down my throat, drying me out from the inside. My throat screamed for moisture, refusing to work as I attempted to swallow what little spit was left in my mouth. When I reached the door, I shoved my face against the slit at the bottom and greedily sucked in air, feeling the hotness of it fill my lungs. Too weak to stand and push the door open, my head fell down on the cold concrete with a soft thud.

This was it. This was how I was going to die. Stranded inside a burning building with no air. Abandoned even by the ghosts of the past. Completely and totally alone.

A girl's soft voice whispered inside my ear and I felt ash slide down my cheeks as my lashes fluttered open. I knew her voice, but when I parted my dried lips to speak, no sounds came out of my parched mouth.

Shannon's voice tickled the inside of my ear. "Mommy...they are free now. The fire, Mommy don't you see...it set them free."

৩৯৵

I sprung up from my sleeping bag with such force that I ripped the zipper open clean down to my knees. Kris stirred beside me, turning in my direction with a sleepy face. I scrambled onto my knees and practically sat on Connor, shaking his shoulders until his own eyes flew open and he sat upright to face me.

"What the hell, Riley? What's wrong?"

"I know what they want," I breathed heavily into his face.

"Who...what the hell are you talking about?" he asked, rubbing his eyes.

"The dead...I know what they want from me." He stared at me in the darkness, confusion on his face, exhaustion embedded into the wrinkles around his eyes, but I kept talking until a look of partial understanding registered in his gaze. "I know what they *need*. Connor, I know how to set them free."

CHAPTER sixteen

"We're not far. The 5 is just a few more miles ahead. Are we staying on the trail?" Kris asked. She folded the wrinkled map until it was small enough to fit into the front pocket of her shirt and stretched both feet out in front of her, flanking my thighs with her dusty boots. We were all restless, the sooner we found the gas station where Jacks discovered Kris, the better. From there, we would work our way back up the highway until she remembered the warehouse her captors had taken her. Once we found it, we planned on stashing the horses somewhere safe and staking it out for a few hours to see if they were still using it.

"Yeah, we'll stay along this till we hit the highway and then go north. Why, are you getting tired of the scenery?"

She laughed and rolled her ankles, flexing them from side to side before lowering her feet to secure them in the stirrups again. The last few hours were spent walking along the Santa Ana River Trail and even though we knew we were on a golf course, the only thing to assure us of that was the symbol on the map. The manicured lawns and neatly trimmed trees grew wild, encompassing the hills with weeds and tall grasses. Summer had been harsh however, killing off most of the green and replacing the softly rolling hills with a yellowish color. The horses tried to stop every few feet and snag a bunch of grass to munch on, which meant Connor and I were constantly pulling at the reins - something we weren't accustomed to. The extra effort at keeping the horses moving was wearing on us, but we continued along the trickle that time reduced the river to at a somewhat steady pace, stopping once for the horses to drink. I let

Kris take the reins for a bit and became the navigator behind her with the crinkled map opened up between my chest and her back.

With proper upkeep, the trail must have been a gorgeous one to hike on in the middle of the residential areas of Orange County. In some places, we were completely surrounded by growth. It blocked the fencing and rooftops from view, almost making it seem like we were riding through the mountains of Laguna again, except for the funky smell of rotting bones.

A pang of sorrow rippled through me as we neared a street underpass. I missed Zoey and the others. The dog must be confused after being left behind. With Kris and I both gone, I hoped the men were taking her on lots of walks and swims in the lake. It was this daydream world I was lost in when the first rifle shot rang out.

Clumps of dirt sprayed up into the air and showered down on us in dusty chunks. Foxy skittered to the side and nearly bucked me off her back before bolting. Instinctively I wrapped my arms around Kris and held on tight. There wasn't time to look for Connor behind us as we rushed into a small grove of trees. Within seconds, we came out the other side, exposed in the open landscape of the river bed. Shots rang out all around us, echoing around the golf course. It was impossible to pinpoint the shooter.

Foxy flew along the embankment as fast as her legs could take us. Something whizzed past my right ear and for the briefest of moments, I imagined it was a bird. A hummingbird racing us along the nearly dried-out river. But it wasn't. A bullet struck the top of my shoulder and just a fraction of a second later a small explosion erupted in my hip, sending me flying off the horse in a mid-air somersault. I landed hard in the dirt and rolled too many times to count before I came to a stop in a thick patch of flowers so purple that it hurt to look at them.

Struggling to inhale, I heard Kris scream, followed by a loud shout from Connor. What happened next became a blur. Sunny went down not far from me. Her front legs collapsed, sending her muzzle straight into the dirt. A cloud of dust bloomed out around her like a mushroom as her body flipped once and landed at an awkward angle. There was blood, a lot of it, coming from her crest and shoulder area. She didn't move again.

My voice wouldn't work. I couldn't call out to Connor - I couldn't return his cries of my name. The more he screamed for me, the more frantic he became. He couldn't see me. I was so close and he couldn't find me buried among the overgrown flowers. More rifle shots boomed from nearby and all went quiet. The only sound became the ragged catch of my breath in my throat and the subtle shift in the flower stalks as the slightest of breezes eased through them.

Alone. The word had a new meaning then. Connor wasn't coming. He wasn't going to save me this time. My right side was sloped at a downward angle. So that's the direction I rolled in, until I made it to my stomach. There wasn't any pain - not yet. I pushed through the flowers, following the slope of the embankment until it dropped out from beneath me and I tumbled down the sand, landing face first in a dried mud hole. It smelled of dead grass and old water.

I stayed still, breathing raggedly through my mouth, watching a dark pool of blood gather beneath my shoulder. The cracked mud soaked it up greedily, spreading my burgundy life force out along the shallow crevices in little streams. As I watched my blood flow away, I became aware of the heat on the back of my neck. The sun burned something fierce. An overwhelming urge to lather my neck with sunscreen came over me, but a bottle of SPF 50 didn't materialize in front of my face.

An unfamiliar pair of dusty-black combat boots did.

∽∞∾

Bubble baths and sateen sheets. Vegetable broth and crackers washed down with flat ginger ale. And sleep; days and days of it.

I walked around the lavish bedroom during the day twirling my full-length nightgown, giggling at the soft feel of the expensive silk as it danced around my freshly shaved legs. At night, I dined on salads full of every kind of vegetable, drenched in olive oil and vinegar. For dessert, I had wine - with a side of lemon gelato.

How glorious it was - this house. At least two stories, though I seemed only to wander around the same floor. In fact, I never left the bedroom or the attached bathroom with the whirlpool tub. But it didn't matter. I twirled the nightgown. I danced. I slept. I ate. And then I did it all over again until the rain came.

Like a child, I cowered under the blankets every time the thunder boomed in the sky. I yelped in fear when white light flashed outside the windows. I was alone in this room and the storm wanted in. The windowpanes shook as hail pelted the glass from outside, threatening to break through with every gust of the vicious and unrelenting wind. I knew it wanted me.

The storm was coming. And I was all alone.

⊱⊰

The pillow was the first thing I recognized as I drifted out of my watery dream and back into reality. It was soft and squishy and even though I knew what it was, it felt unlike any pillow I'd ever rested on before. For a moment, I rolled my head from side to side, enjoying the plush feel of it beneath my scalp. But it wasn't *my* pillow. The thought was enough to startle my eyes open.

I was lying on the right side of a massive four-poster bed with sheer curtains eloquently draped around each mahogany post. It was dusk, or dawn. At least according to the pale lighting that peeked through the slatted windows. Orange curtains with a paisley-like white pattern flanked each of the floor length windows to my left, just beyond the wide expanse of the mattress.

"So…she lives." A gravelly voice beside me purred into the quiet room, making me jump under the sheets.

A man lounged in a deep armchair next to the bed, with his bare feet propped up, heels resting just beside my covered legs. His face was all shadows but I was certain of one thing - he was not Connor.

His jeans rustled as he lifted his long legs off the bed and lowered his feet to the carpeted ground. When he leaned toward me, with his hands casually draped across his knees, I flinched and tried to push up onto my elbows but my left shoulder throbbed in painful protest from the movement.

"I wouldn't do that," the stranger said with a soft chuckle, "Unless you want to tear your stitches."

I let my head fall back into the pillow and tried not to lose myself in the luxurious feel of it. My side hurt too, just as bad as my shoulder. Worse, actually.

"Where am I?" Hearing my voice was startling. The sound came out strained and dry like my vocal chords hadn't been used in months.

"You're safe. For now," the man answered.

"And...who are you?"

"A friend."

"For now?" I asked, glancing nervously in his direction. He leaned back into the chair, obscuring his face once again in the shadows. After a pause, he laughed and I couldn't decipher if it was meant to calm or frighten me.

"Yeah, I guess you could say that."

"How long have I been here," I asked, lifting my hips as far off the mattress as they would go. This was only about half an inch.

"Three days," he said, standing from the chair fluidly. His form towered over me and I recoiled as a hand reached out to pull the sheet up to my collarbone.

"And my friends...are they here too?"

Instead of answering my question, he crossed the room, lifted something off a long dresser, and brought it to the foot of the bed, holding it up for me to see. *Kris's pack.* I tried to remember the last few moments of our ride. The golf course. The gunshots. The horses. Sunny down in the dirt - bloody and broken.

He tossed it into the center of the bed and turned to walk away, saying over his shoulder, "I found this but there wasn't time to stick around and hunt through the weeds for bodies."

I stared at the pack and the bright red stain along one strap, not noticing him walk from the room, leaving me alone in the bedroom with my thoughts and all that was left of them. *Kris and Connor.* They were right - all of them - I lost the two most important people left in my life before we even reached downtown Los Angeles.

"I'll find you," I whispered into the silence, *"I'll find you and make sure your souls rest. I promise."*

The surprising thing about losing Connor and Kris is that I accepted it immediately. I cried for one day and then the anger set in. It was the kind of anger that you can taste on your tongue and feel coursing through your body like an untapped electrical current. It was the kind of anger that kept me alive and fighting. For days, it was all I could think about, all I focused on. It festered inside me like a parasite until my need for revenge became stronger than my will to eat. Even despite the chip in my hipbone from a bullet graze and the one that was yanked out of the back of my shoulder after I passed out from the blood loss, the revenge was strong and alive inside me.

As soon as I could walk, I started doing crunches on the carpeted bedroom floor and push-up's against the wall. Using water glasses and then shampoo bottles, I did bicep curls, and lunges from one side of the wide bedroom to the other. And I disassembled and reassembled the handgun that was stuffed inside Kris's backpack until I could do it with my eyes closed.

I counted my bullets and touched them every day, making sure my DNA was left along the tip of each shiny point. I did this because one day soon I'd be firing each of those bullets into the heads of the people that took my family from me.

I was going to empty my clip into their thick skulls until their bodies stopped twitching.

∽◦↩

"You coming down for food, or staying up here again?" His gravelly voice vibrated through the heavy bedroom door.

"I'm not hungry, Drake," I said, ignoring the involuntary twitch of my stomach.

"Liar," he answered placidly.

I stared hard at the doorknob, expecting him to turn it and enter the room. He didn't, of course. Frozen in a sit-up, I waited for him to retreat down the hallway, but heard nothing but silence.

Cursing and groaning I rolled onto my side and stood up, ignoring the fuzzy feeling in my head as I stomped over to the door and flung it open. He leaned comfortably against the outer portion of the frame with a knowing smile on his face.

I didn't trust his hazel eyes just yet, regardless of the fact that he saved my life. There was a darkness hidden there, and his lack of free-flowing information didn't ease my doubt about his intentions. After spending two solid weeks holed up in the two-story house, I knew *nothing* about my rescuer other than his first name. Though he stood silently before me, the arrogant expression of triumph was spread smoothly across his face like a buttered slice of bread.

Pushing past him, I sauntered down the hallway and took the stairs slowly, as if I wasn't salivating at the idea of eating. By the time I was half-way down the stairs, I finally heard him descend behind me.

Canned vegetables. Canned fruit. Homemade bread with an olive oil and balsamic vinegar for dipping. Lunch never looked so good. My tongue curled and twisted in my mouth as I served myself a humble amount of food and poured a glass of what looked like fresh lemonade before carrying my loot into the next room to sit at the expensive wooden dining table. My meals had mostly consisted of oatmeal, over-ripe fruit and tons and tons of water. It wasn't until a few days before that my appetite came back. Drake could tell but I didn't want to eat around him, or serve myself food that he had scavenged or prepared. It was obvious, even to me that I had lost a considerable amount of weight since leaving San Diego. This reminded me of the conversation I needed to have with the man that sat quietly opposite of me, eating his lunch as if he was the only person in the room.

With a soft clank of metal against ceramic, I set my fork down and stared at the sheer curtains that obscured my view of the backyard. Having something to stare at while talking made it so much easier. It was hard to look at Drake. Something about his thick, arched eyebrows unnerved me. And his smile...it tweaked at the corner of his mouth, exposing his canine teeth, reminding me of a cougar.

"I need to know where the closest department store is," I said.

His silverware made a similar clanking sound on his plate before he spoke, "Why?"

I finally looked at him and shrugged nonchalantly. "I need stuff. Especially clothes that fit."

"Oh. Okay, before dinner we can go then," he said. I watched him shove a large mouthful of oily bread between his lips and chase it with canned pear.

"No, I can shop by myself. Just need to know where to go, is all."

With a sigh, he pushed away from the table, gathering up his dishes though he wasn't finished eating and said over his shoulder on the way into the kitchen. "I'll be ready at sunset. Maybe you should put a bra on or something."

❧ ❧

My hands stayed shoved into my pockets as we walked. The night was overcast, hiding the early autumn moon from us as we took the sidewalk through the ritzy neighborhoods that bordered the Riverview Golf Course. I quietly followed Drake, irritated as hell at the fact that he wouldn't just point me in the direction I needed to go.

With no map, I didn't know where we were or what was nearby. But I *did* know that it wasn't safe to travel through the area during the day, as I found out the hard way after being shot off Foxy a few weeks before. The little information Drake did share was that there were lookouts placed atop the tallest buildings flanking the 22 freeway in an effort to regulate who gained access to the 5. It was smart on behalf of the thugs - placing snipers along the Santa Ana River. The only reason why I hadn't snuck out of Drake's place already was because he knew where the assholes hid out. He had spent the last two months watching them and following them around parts of Orange County. Twice he saw them take down a random survivor. And that was all he told me. I knew he was hiding a lot more information and for some reason, he didn't feel comfortable sharing it yet. So I stayed, waiting for the day when I could pry the info I needed out of him to enact my bloody revenge.

But first, I needed clothes that stayed on my hips and didn't slide off my bony shoulders. It took less than half an hour to walk to the closest mall. After picking my way through a handful of stores, I changed right there in the aisles while Drake wandered off with a flashlight to find his own supplies. We both hit the sidewalk again with backpacks full of miscellaneous items. Plus a treat or two.

Halfway back to the house, the clouds parted above us and moon rays hit the sidewalk, lighting the concrete up with a pale blue glow. Most of the streets were empty but trash blew across the ground everywhere. Papers, plastic bags, cardboard and clothing filled the gutters. Most of the homes that faced the main streets had broken windows and busted doors on account of being pilfered over the last year. There weren't any signs of recent life on the streets, but obviously others had picked the area clean at some point.

"How long have you been here?" I asked, not looking at Drake.

A momentary pause went by before he spoke over his shoulder at me, "Long enough to know not to cross the river."

"What do you mean?"

"That's where they seem to pass through a lot. I don't get close enough to see what they're doing, just to see where they go." He shrugged and kicked at an empty milk jug that rested on its side in the center of the street.

"Then why do you stay if you don't care what they're doing?" I asked angrily. His lack of interest pissed me off. I wanted to chuck something at the back of his head. The visual image of my shoe bouncing off his buzzed and brown hair almost made me grin.

He whirled around to face me so quickly that I bumped into his chest. "I've seen them kill. I know what they can do, and I know they run all over this City like they own it. I'm adapting, just like you. Why is that any different than what *you've* done this year?" His eyes were dark and squinted as he glared at me.

With an uplifted tilt of my chin, I steadied my breath despite how close he stood to me. "It's not the same thing at all. You're hiding from them and from anyone else you could find out there," I threw my arm out beside me and gestured down the street. "If you aren't here to bring them down, then what's the point of staying and watching?"

Only an inch of space separated his nose from mine as he leaned forward and said in a low voice, "I *never* said there wasn't a point."

I gawked at his back as he spun away and continued down the street as if the conversation never happened. Fidgeting with the strap of my pack, I walked quietly behind him, lost in my thoughts.

What was he planning? And why wouldn't he tell me what it was?

CHAPTER seventeen

The wind howled like a dying wolf outside the windows and rattled the solar panels on the roof. It had a ferocity so intense I figured it was only a matter of time before they slid off the top of the terracotta tiles and landed with a crash on the driveway and back patio. They were what kept the house running, just as if the power had never been lost. Except for those few days where a storm ripped through California with one goal only - destroy anything and everything in its path.

I turned away from the moisture-clouded glass and readjusted my feet beneath me as I pushed deeper into the chair. Drake was lounged on the sectional, his feet propped on a pair of matching cushions with Swarovski crystals sewn delicately onto the silk fabric. I think he used the lavish throw pillows as foot props on purpose as a way to spite the previous owners who spent money on things that had no true worth. The house was full of valuable items from all around the world that meant absolutely nothing anymore. Value had a different meaning. Fresh water and food had become our gold and silver.

"How long are you going to stare at me?" he asked without looking up from his book.

I inwardly chastised myself for blushing but since he had yet to glance up at me, the embarrassment faded quickly. "I'm not staring. I was thinking," I said a bit too rough.

"Thinking…and *staring*." Again, he didn't look up but I thought I caught a hint of a smile playing at the corners of his mouth.

With an exasperated sigh, I glanced back outside at the cold wind that had the tropical plants in the backyard thrashing around wildly. Even after hearing the sound of paper rustle and the hardcover book snap shut, I didn't look at Drake. The feel of his eyes burned into the back of my neck and I wiped at the sensation on my skin nervously.

Eventually he spoke, "What's wrong? You're more pouty than usual."

"And you're just as rude, I see."

"You think I'm rude?" he laughed.

"Unpleasantly rude and not very thoughtful," I grumbled under my breath, finally looking at him.

His smile fell immediately. "If I was either of those things, I would have just left you bleeding out in the mud."

"Then why didn't you?" I snapped.

Drake's hands flew up in front of his face like he wanted to strangle something. "I'm not as much of an ass as you think. Have I proved otherwise?"

"Yes!" I nearly shouted the answer. "You seem to want to keep me here but won't tell me why! I know nothing about you, your story, or how you got here. You just expect me to sit here like some weak woman and eat the food that *you* provide and treat *you* like the master. That's not how I work!"

He kicked the crystal pillows to the ground and stood from the couch, crossing the sitting room in four strides, tugging at his shirt as he walked. I flinched away from him as he pulled the black top over his head and threw it into my face, standing before me bare-chested. The shirt smelled subtly of soap but it wasn't the clean smell that had me distracted, or by Drake's sudden and aggressive approach. It was the scars that streaked across his chest like an amateur landscape drawing.

With a yank, he snatched my hand and pulled me out of the chair so roughly I came up on my toes. Slowly, and almost as if he thought the touch might be painful, he placed my palm on one of the scars just between his pectoral muscles. His gaze settled on something over my head and he began to talk in a hushed voice, like he didn't want the walls of the house to hear his words.

"I came through this area with another survivor, hiking on the same trail you used. He went down after the first series of shots but I ran and I would have made it if my fucking boot laces didn't get tangled in a stray piece of wire fencing." As he talked, he moved my hand gently along the scars but didn't seem to feel it; his eyes were detached and hollow. "They were on me in seconds. Three men, all with guns," he paused and blinked slowly before looking down at me, "I think it's obvious one of them likes to use a knife."

When he let go of my hand, it lingered on his skin until he stepped back. I sucked my lower lip in before inhaling. The severe arch of his eyebrows relaxed slightly and for the first time, I saw him as a regular person just like me - a survivor.

"How did you live through that?" I tried not to stare at the series of scars that broke apart the fine spattering of his chest hair.

"Well, there wasn't anyone there to drag me out of the mud, if that's what you mean." He walked away, leaving me standing alone in the open sitting area, clutching his still warm shirt, stunned into a humble silence.

❦

For the rest of that evening Drake stayed upstairs, locked away in his room, just two doors down from mine. No movement came from the end of the hall. There was no sound. A few times I found myself stepping out onto the highly polished wood to check on him, but my bare feet never made it more than two steps from my door frame.

As the brutal wind picked up speed and the storm drenched the house from all possible angles, my time was spent propped on the bed in positions that didn't aggravate my wounds. Wood logs popped and sizzled in the fireplace that took up most of the lower part of the wall separating the sleeping room from the bathroom. The smell of the burning wood filled the entire upper level. Any other circumstances and I would have loved the home, especially after roughing it through town on horseback with Connor and Kris for almost a week. But a house with a glass and marble fireplace in the master suite didn't bring joy or happiness or even excitement - only sadness that I couldn't share it with them.

Every time the house creaked I would peek into the hall, expecting to see Drake passing by my room on his way to the stairs but he never appeared. It was clear he only told me how he ended up in that part of town because he was angry and not because he suddenly felt comfortable speaking with me openly. Guilt plagued me for doubting his intentions but a question nagged inside my head like a leech - refusing to let go until it was sated with an answer.

Where could I find this man with the knife?

❧

Drake hovered over his cereal bowl like he was afraid someone would snatch it out from under his mouth. After having skipped dinner the night before, he was working on his second serving of cinnamon oatmeal. He stirred a spoonful of raisins into the slop until I couldn't see them anymore.

"Hungry?" I asked, sipping orange juice.

Pulp settled at the bottom of the glass while I watched Drake eat. Our supply of fresh oranges was almost gone after making juice every morning that week. The great thing about Southern California was that every neighborhood had a fruit tree of some kind. The trick was finding the ripe ones.

He didn't answer, only continued to eat as if I wasn't there. It had rained off and on throughout the night and even with all four fireplaces in the house lit and roaring, it was still chilly inside. I thought I had heard Drake walk down the hall twice sometime before dawn, but I was too tired to slip out from under the blankets to see what he was doing.

"What time did you get up this morning?" I figured small talk would warm him up a bit.

He licked brown sugar off his spoon and set it aside before gulping down half a cup of juice. "When you did. I heard your door. Why?"

I set the glass down and looked at him curiously. "You didn't get up early this morning?"

"No, I was passed out." He looked at me clearly annoyed. "What?"

"Nothing. I thought I heard you walk down the hall a few hours ago. Must have been the house settling…or something." I stared at the orange pulp and picked a small seed out of my cup before glancing back up at Drake. He was watching me carefully.

"Or something," he repeated.

"Can I ask you a question?" I didn't pause to wait for his reply, "I'm just curious if this place was empty before you...you know...moved in." I met his eyes and stared at him.

"No."

Lifting an eyebrow, I waited for him to elaborate. When he didn't, I tilted my head and raised a hand in a gesture that meant I was eager for more information. My hand stayed suspended in the space between us, propped up by my elbow, until he finally gave in and exhaled an irritated sigh.

"No, the house wasn't empty. There was a rich couple in a car parked in the garage. My guess is they gassed themselves before the bug had a chance to take them out."

"Oh. Well, where are they now?"

"What do you mean? It's not like I left them there."

"I meant, how did you...dispose of the bodies?" My chest heaved as I attempted to regulate my breathing.

"What the hell kind of a question is *that*?" The kitchen stool scraped along the floor as he pushed away from the bar counter and snatched up his bowl and spoon before walking around me to the sink. It was rare to see him in a short-sleeved top and the t-shirt clung to his upper body like it was half a size too small. I knew how many push-up's he did a day, it was probably hard for him to fit his arms into *any* shirt that didn't hang around the waist.

"I'm just curious, is all," I said, picking up my own dishes and setting them beside his in the metal drop down sink.

He groaned before facing me with a look of displeasure seeded deep in his eyes. "I buried them - kind of. Happy?"

"No," I muttered.

Buried, not burned. This meant they could still be hanging around the property. Most likely, they were and that's who I heard walking down the hallway earlier. I sighed and cleaned my dishes, ignoring the questionable looks that Drake shot in my direction every few seconds. He was hiding things from me, so it seemed only natural to hold my own secrets close to my chest for the time being. It wouldn't be the first time I was guarded with Drake. No doubt, it wouldn't be the last either.

༂ೕೈ

A little alcohol was all it took to loosen Drake up and get him talking. And once he did, he wouldn't shut up. We sat on the sectional - me tucked under a throw blanket, half-buried beneath a mound of different shaped pillows and him in the opposite corner of the sofa. His feet propped up on the delicate coffee table, a large glass of wine in one hand. The rain had stopped but the wind made it seem even colder. There was only enough dry wood in the garage to last maybe two more fires. The next day we would have to bring home some more, or the week would end up with one or both of us freezing in the night.

"So you left your *dog* there? Why'd you do that?"

"Well, it didn't make sense to bring her when we would be on horseback. I don't know if she could walk that far." I sipped slowly from my own glass.

"Shit. If my dog lived, I wouldn't let her out of my sight."

"There are others at the lodge that need her."

I almost believed that to be true. The real reason I didn't bring Zoey with us was because in my heart, I was worried one or none of us would make it back. At least she was safe at the lodge with everyone else.

"Right. And this lodge, you think it's safe up there, tucked away in the mountains?"

He lifted one of his arms and propped it behind his head before leaning back into it. I was almost certain the gesture was done to show off his bicep. Impressive at it was, it wasn't enough for me to forget about Connor and the last time I saw him sitting in that same position.

"It's been safe there for the most part. No one else has found it. And we have solar power too, plus the lake."

"Huh."

"What?" I asked.

"It's just…what if there's a fire or some other natural disaster. You really want to be stuck on the top of a mountain for that?" He took a large swallow of wine.

"Where else should we go? Into the city, with all the-" I abruptly bit down on my lower lip, then tried to hide my slip by bringing the wine glass to my mouth, but Drake wasn't drunk enough to miss what I almost said.

"You mean, with all the *dead* people?"

I nodded. And sipped wine.

"In the city with the bodies...or the shadows?" He wasn't teasing me, he was waiting for me to confirm that he wasn't the only one that had seen or heard something paranormal.

I shrugged, trying to play off my reaction like neither option bothered me, "Both, I guess."

"Right," he huffed, "Something tells me it would take more than a dead body to spook you."

"I guess that's true now. It wasn't nine months ago."

The day I found my mother dead in her apartment flashed through my memory. And the baby still strapped into the stroller inside the bus depot. That day brought me face to face with enough death to last one hundred life times.

"It wasn't for any of us." Drake's eyes glazed over as he stared at the wall.

"Who was the person you were traveling with?" It was a personal question. One that I intended to lead into the conversation about what he saw over the last few months.

"Someone I met on the road. He was a nice guy. A good guy. Had a family before the bug hit. Was a couple years older than me."

"What was his name?" I asked.

"Lewis. Lewis something." He finally blinked and looked from the wall to me again. "More?" He leaned forward, snatching the bottle of wine - it was our second - and poured some in my glass before waiting for my answer.

It was as good a time as any to bring up my questions. "Drake, do you know where the asshole that nearly killed you is?"

His hand tightened around his glass, but instead of getting defensive or shutting down completely, he surprised me by nodding. "Yup. I've known where that fucker's been hiding out for a while now."

"Really? Mind sharing?" I sipped my wine and tried to stay calm. But I felt like my intentions were written all over my face. I didn't want to tell Drake that the moment I knew that information would be my last moment with him.

"There's not much to share. They mostly hang out at one of those food warehouses. It's smart, really. There's enough packaged grub in that place to last the lot of them for years. They stay the night there in shifts and took over a housing complex near the building."

I looked away from him, lost in thought. *A warehouse. A housing complex.* It was a lot of ground to cover by myself.

"How many of them are there, exactly?" I chewed on the inside of my cheek. This would take more thought than I first imagined.

"There were thirteen men. Now I think there's eleven or so," he said with a crooked grin.

"Were?"

"Let's just say an opportunity presented itself," he laughed. His wine glass was empty again. I watched him refill it and take another gulp.

"What did you do?" I was genuinely curious and leaned toward him while he spoke.

"About a month before you came along I followed a pair of them across town while they were on one of their patrols. Pathetic really, the two of them were. They spent an hour talking about naked women and golf. Golf. I mean fucking really? It wasn't hard. I waited for them to split. When the younger guy went to take a leak, I snuck up behind him with my hunting knife. The other one got it in the back. Right between the shoulder blades." With one hand over the other, he made a swift, downward motion in the air between us.

"Really? It was that easy?"

"Taking a life, or taking out those two idiots?"

"I don't know, both?"

He shifted around in the seat and for a moment, I thought he was going to get up and leave me there alone with the wine. "I'm not sorry. Fuckers deserved it. I know they've taken down more like us, who were just passing through here. And I think they have a girl or two tucked away in that building. Haven't stuck around long enough to find out what for, but I can imagine."

I sat upright so suddenly that wine sloshed out of my glass and Drake flinched. "What do you mean, like they have them there as prisoners?"

"Why the hell is that exciting?" he asked, looking at me sideways with an arched brow pointing toward the beamed ceiling.

"Oh, you have no idea," I jumped off the couch and nearly broke the stem of my glass as I slammed it down on the table. After pulling the magnetic notepad and pen off the refrigerator, I hurried back into the sitting room to find Drake just where I had left him, with the same surprised expression on his un-groomed face.

"Here, show me," I said, handing the notepad and small pen to him.

He waved them at me. "Show you *what*?"

"Where this warehouse is."

The wine had gotten to him, I could see it in his foggy eyes but he wasn't at all fooled. After setting his own glass down on the table with a clink, he stood to face me and tapped his finger into my chest almost hard enough to make me sway.

"What are *you* doing here, Riley?" he asked, emphasizing each word with another sturdy poke of his finger.

"Stop that!" I said, slapping his hand away.

"Are you looking for someone?"

"Maybe. It doesn't matter. Just…just please tell me where this warehouse is. And I promise you won't have to worry about me anymore."

He rocked back on his heels like I had struck him in the face. "I'm not forcing you to stay here, you can leave whenever you want," he said through gritted teeth.

"That's not what I meant," I sighed. "Don't you think that I'm just as mad at them as you are? They took Connor and Kris from me. And, yes, if you really want to know, we were looking for someone. A woman."

"I think I'm entirely too drunk to have this conversation right now." He turned to walk away and I grabbed at his arm, getting a fistful of shirt instead.

"No. Let's talk about it now. Why *won't* you tell me? What does it matter to you?"

With a shrug, he loosened my grip on his shirt and snapped at me, "Because you'll fuck up my plans! Damn, you're nosy!"

"You *are* planning something. I knew it! Why else would you stay here after what happened? Oh, this all makes perfect sense now. What is it, what are you going to do? And don't think you can just walk away and not tell me, I'll beat it out of you if I need to." Drake was half-way up the stairs with me hot on his heels, reluctant to allow him to end the conversation by escaping into his room. Which is exactly what he was trying to do.

"I'm sure as hell not telling you! You'll go out there and get yourself killed. Stop, let go!" He growled at me as I yanked at the back of his shirt, efficiently stopping him in the hallway before he could get to his room.

"No way, tell me. It's not your right to keep this to yourself," I hissed back.

In a blur, I was slammed up against the wall and nearly lifted off my feet before I realized Drake's mouth was on mine. My first instinct was to kiss him back but, seconds later, it was Connor's face that I saw. In a panic, I squirmed out from beneath him, pushing firmly on his chest but getting no leeway. When we parted, he brought the back of his hand to his mouth and I noticed it was shaking - just like my knees were.

"Shit," he mumbled, "I didn't mean to do that. Sorry." He turned away and left me standing in the hall. His door closing behind him so softly that I barely heard it click.

"I'm sorry too," I whispered. Unsure if I meant it for Drake or for Connor.

CHAPTER eighteen

I wasn't surprised when I heard him stomp down the stairs at dawn. It sounded like he left through the front door and I didn't dare go downstairs till I knew he was gone. The spacious house seemed too quiet with just me inside it. Full of nervous energy, I cleaned the kitchen, the sitting room and took several bags of trash out into the garage. Drake didn't return until I was finally sitting on the couch, peeling back the wrapper to a stale granola bar.

When he opened the front door, he seemed surprised to see me. "Hey," he said awkwardly.

I nodded, covering my mouth as I chewed. He propped the door open and stepped back outside, pulling a wagon full of chopped wood bundles into the house. A gust of cold wind followed him inside and I shivered, pulling my sleeves down to my wrists.

As if he felt an explanation was needed, he grumbled under his breath without looking at me, "We're almost out of fire wood."

"Okay," I managed to say, with a mouthful of food tucked into my cheek.

After a few minutes, there was a wooden bundle at the foot of every fireplace and then he promptly disappeared into the kitchen. I waited for him to come back out but after nearly twenty minutes, I figured he wasn't in a hurry to speak with me. I found him leaning against the counter, flipping through a luxury boat magazine with an open jar of dill pickles within reach.

"You don't have to avoid me, you know," I said, startling him.

"You don't have to sneak up on people like that," he said, not taking his eyes off the open magazine. "Plus, I'm not avoiding anything."

"Can I have a taste?" I asked.

"What?" He looked almost panicked as I moved toward him with my hand out.

"A pickle. You're not going to eat the whole jar, are you?"

"Oh. Sure. Here," he said, handing the open jar to me.

"What did you think I meant?"

He shook his head, returning back to the magazine. I tried not to laugh at how intently he was staring at an advertisement page for some sort of medication.

"Look…about last night," I started.

"It was stupid, I know. Won't happen again," he said quickly.

"It's not a big deal. It's just, I can't."

"Really, I didn't mean it," he said, glancing over his shoulder. "Think I was just drunk and being stupid."

"You were mad at me," I pointed out.

"Maybe a little," he laughed. Finally he closed the magazine and dipped his fingers into the jar I was still holding. After biting a pickle in half, he gestured at the front of me. "You wouldn't get far."

"What do you mean?" I tried not to sound insulted.

"You're all balls-out. These shits have been running this town for months. They've got a system down. There might not be a lot of them, but you won't get five feet if you just try and storm the place."

"Oh."

He lifted his eyebrow at me. A gesture I was beginning to become familiar with. "I'm sure I could manage. Especially with a little help," I said.

Both his eyebrows shot up that. "You aren't serious."

"But, I really am," I winked.

Shaking his head, he took the pickle jar from me and walked into the sitting room, kicking his shoes off before propping them up on the glass table.

"So, tell me about this plan you seem to be hatching," he said with a grin.

After a considerable amount of arguing from Drake and pathetic begging on my part, he finally agreed to take me to one of his lookout spots. The safest way to go unnoticed was to sneak in at night, he told me.

"We're only going to watch, unless something unplanned happens, understand?" Drake asked as we quietly walked down the sidewalks until the darkness of the nearby golf course came into view.

"I got it," I whispered back, adjusting the straps of my pack on my shoulders, making sure they were tight enough to stay on if I had to run.

Both of us were armed but our guns were tucked inside our packs, buried under the modest rations we would need for our overnight stakeout. Strapped securely to my right thigh was a six-inch hunting knife with a wicked serrated edge. It was an exact match to the blade that Drake wore on his left thigh. He spent several hours showing me how to properly thrust and maintain a strong hold on the blade. After a day of practicing with it, I was confidant I could use it if I had to.

It was a moonless night, perfect for creeping through shadows and around buildings. But still, I was nervous about being seen or worse - caught. I followed Drake closely. I stepped only where he stepped, touching only what he touched. Within a half hour, we were crouched at the fence that bordered the backyard of a residence and the course. Except at that particular spot, there were trees obscuring my view of the wide area between our side of the Santa Ana River Trail and to the side we needed to get. It was the perfect place to wait for a safe time to cross.

"Got your scope ready?" he whispered.

It was already out of the pack and in my hand, so I held it up for him to see. I nodded at Drake as he signaled at the tree and watched him scale the trunk in silence. The night was dark enough that all I could see around me were the shapes of structures. It was hard to tell in the distance if they were houses, apartments or office buildings. If it was hard for us to see, hopefully it was equally as hard for anyone else looking out along the golf course to spot us.

A hiss sound came from the tree above me, so I flattened myself onto the damp grass and pressed the pocket scope against my eye, scanning the buildings across the way with the night vision tool. The rooftops were clear but it was impossible to see inside each window. I stayed on the ground, sweeping back and forth across the buildings until a soft thump landed beside me.

Drake crouched at my elbow with his own pocket scope held to his face. "It looks clear, but we have to hurry just in case." He tucked the scope into the front pocket of his camouflage jacket and waited for me to do the same before standing. "We'll run straight that way, through those trees," he pointed northeast. "Don't stop until you get to the last one and then we'll check with the scopes before crossing the water."

"Okay."

"Are you really ready? Once we get out there, we'll be exposed and if they see us…well, you know the plan."

I did know the plan. We would separate - one of us fleeing east, while the other went west until we were certain we weren't being followed. Not until then, would we work our way back to the house.

I nodded but Drake squeezed my arm until I said the words out loud, *"Yes. I'm ready - let's go."*

Without another word, he rushed into the trees, following the curve of them across the south side of the course. I pumped my legs hard to keep up with him. Within seconds, we were huddled behind our last bit of cover. After doing another sweep of the nearby buildings, Drake sprinted out across a weed-filled sand trap and I bolted in line behind him. When our feet hit the riverbed, we ran through less than an inch of water but it still sprayed noisily up around us. The sound seemed to echo through the entire area but I didn't stop until my feet hit the north side of the course and I almost collided into Drake as we both came to a stop under the same tree. He was barely out of breath but my lungs were on fire. My nostrils flared as I kept my hand clamped to my mouth in an attempt to stay quiet, but what I really wanted to do was double over and breathe like a woman in labor.

"This way," he whispered, heading off through the few bent and scraggly trees nearby before the course trail came into view. We waited there, listening for sounds in the buttoned up night. Something chirped in the grass a few meters away, but it was otherwise silent.

We jogged along the concrete trail, following the curve of it around a small berm. The walking trail opened up before us with a residential neighborhood just on the other side. Drake nearly collided into the fencing that was obscured under a severely overgrown bush. After launching ourselves into the heavily weeded backyard, we crept our way along the side of the stucco house until we reached the street. From there we walked quietly and quickly, stopping only to crane our necks and listen to the inhibited night.

Only a few minutes through the neighborhood I noticed a burnt smell that drifted in the breeze overwhelming my senses. My nose became raw from rubbing it, and the further east we walked, the stronger the smell was.

"What is that?" I whispered.

"I don't want to know," Drake answered. *"There, see that building?"* He pointed between two houses at the next block where several buildings stood tall and dark in the distance.

We pulled our scopes out and scanned the area, seeing no activity. "Is that the one?" I asked.

After jogging between the houses and scaling more fences and brick barriers, we crossed a major road before ending up in a parking lot. I stayed close to Drake as he led me toward one of the large, brick office buildings, dodging debris and blown out remnants of windows from the lowest levels. Once inside, we took the stairs up to the roof. After eight stories of taking two steps at a time, I was exhausted and ready for a nap, but once we stepped onto the roof and cool air slapped me across the face, my adrenaline kicked in.

"See that shiny building over there," he said just above a whisper.

I crouched down below the ledge to look at the building across the street, half the height of the one we were hiding on top of. "Yeah."

"That's where they usually camp out and keep an eye on the trail. There's another one just up there," he pointed east and I followed his hand further up the street where a similar building stood. It was hard to make it out in the darkness, but it was there.

"Is that where they were when they shot me?"

"Probably. They have the advantage there. It's not the highest viewpoint, but anyone passing by will be seen. If they're looking. Plus, if the first sentry doesn't have a good shot, the second one will. Now they only come here in pairs."

I grimaced at the buildings, as if it was their fault that this group of post-pandemic terrorists had staked their claim on the river passage. With our height advantage, I could see the entire roof area and with the scope, I could also make out a pair of camping chairs and a small chest set near the low ledge right in the center of the building. Facing the golf course.

"Why aren't they there now?"

"It's still early," Drake said, sliding down against the ledge. We had enough room to stand without necessarily being seen, but I slid below sight too, tugging my pack off my shoulders before leaning against the cool cement wall.

"What do we do now?" I asked, rifling through my pack, pretending to look for something.

"We wait," he answered with a shrug.

❦

The first lookout didn't show up until midnight. I had gone through half a bottle of water and a granola bar waiting. Even though we popped out from our hiding spot every five minutes or so to look down at the building or the streets, it was the screech of a walkie-talkie we heard that let us know we weren't alone anymore.

The mechanical sound echoed down the street below and we both peered through our night vision scopes to see a dark shape walk into the closest glass building. Drake looked between the two structures, finally spotting the other lookout crossing the adjoining parking lot.

"Where'd they come from?" I asked quietly.

"Not sure," he paused, scanning the area around and below us. "I guess they're staying somewhere closer now. We might have walked right by their house."

A chill spread up my spine at his words. "Perfect."

He laughed softly and put the scope back up to his face. "Well, there's our boy."

It was definitely a man that paced the perimeter of the roof before settling into one of the chairs. He sat there for a good ten minutes before the other lookout appeared on the much larger roof of the next building. They sent a series of signals to each other with flashlights and then both appeared to settle into their chairs, riffles draped across their legs.

"So, we know they are still coming here," I said softly, "But the question is where will they go when they're done?"

Drake's arm brushed mine as he leaned against the wall, moving his scope from one building to the next. "That's what we're here to find out, right?"

৯৩৵৻

"Where'd you do it?"

"Do what?"

"The two men you killed…where did it happen?" I asked.

"Oh. You really want to talk about this *now*?" He looked at me sideways, his brown eyebrow arched upward. I couldn't tell if he was interested or annoyed with me.

"What else are we going to talk about?"

He grunted before settling back against the ledge. It was almost dawn, with no sign of movement from the two lookouts or the relief pair that Drake said would show up soon. I had to pee, but for some reason was embarrassed to do so on the roof of a building.

"About a mile from here. South of the house," he said.

"In the neighborhood?"

"Yeah, why?" He handed me a baggy full of orange slices and I took it from him.

"What were they doing out there?" I sucked some juice from a slice of fruit while Drake fidgeted uncomfortably.

"I don't know. Scoping out the area, probably."

"What happened after? Did the others come looking for them?"

"I don't know, Riley. I just dragged their bodies into a nearby house and split. Like I said before, it was sort of unplanned, you know?"

He bit into his orange slice just as the sky paled in the east. The sun was coming. When I couldn't hold it any longer, I mentioned I had to use the restroom and Drake gave me directions to the closest bathroom on the level below us. Most of the floor was pitch black, since the windows of the office building didn't reach the inner rooms. Thankfully, the bathroom was unlocked. After shining my light around the small space, I used the first stall and rushed back up the stairs to the roof just in time to see that part of the sky and a handful of clouds were dyed with a lavender coloring.

"Oh wow, that's beautiful," I said.

"Quiet!" Drake hissed, and I immediately dropped to the ground, afraid I had blown our cover in some way.

After crawling through the loose gravel to where he was flattened against the ledge, I reached into my pack and pulled out my pocket scope. I didn't hear anything - no voices or walkie-talkies or birds or insects. Just air as it flew over my head, nearly one hundred feet above the ground.

"Look," he said, pointing to the second lookout's rooftop, "I saw another guy over there, but not sure where he went."

"So there's three of them?"

"Hold on a second…do you see that?"

I shoved the scope against my eye and followed his line of sight in between the two glass buildings until I saw movement on the trail. There was definitely someone walking alongside the golf course. Neither of the lookouts seemed alarmed, but both stood with their rifles, glancing up and down the riverbed.

"They're looking for something," I said quietly.

"Yeah, but what?"

"Or *who*."

We watched until the man was out of our view, following the curve of the land below to the west. He was also armed, but it was hard to tell what he looked like beneath a bundled up coat and thickly lined bomber hat.

Nearly an hour passed and the sun was fully awake by the time the same man returned, but this time he came up the streets, walking an almost identical path as the one we had taken. He entered the first glass building and Drake snatched his bag off the ground and crawled toward the door.

"Come on, we have to get off the roof," he said over his shoulder.

"Is something wrong?" I crawled behind him, my pack slung over only one shoulder so it dragged along the gravel.

"The windows downstairs are tinted, now that it's daytime, the roof is too exposed."

Once we were inside the stairwell, Drake ran down the steps to the same floor with the bathroom I had just used, practically running down the narrow hallway to the south facing offices with windows. He found one that seemed to be just below where we were on the roof and pulled a desk up against the window. After some rearranging, he had two chairs in front of the desk, both raised to their highest points.

"There," he said. With a thump, he tossed his pack onto the table and sat in the chair, resting his boots on the desk and hooking his fingers behind his head.

"Okay, now what?" I sat stiffly in the empty chair beside him, too uneasy to get comfortable.

"Now we wait again to see who goes and who stays."

"For how long?" I wiggled in the chair, my behind glad for the cushioning.

"For as long as it takes or until one of them is on his own."

I turned to look at his profile. His rugged face was almost perfectly shaped. He had a straight nose, with a slightly rounded end, a square jaw that evoked a kind of strength, thick eyebrows, and lips that seemed to have been stenciled on his mouth. He was the kind of handsome most women would swoon over only to have their hearts broken, but when I looked at him, I wanted to see Connor's blue eyes staring back at me, not Drake's hazel-green ones.

With a gulp, I swallowed the lump in my throat before speaking. "And if one of them heads off on his own…then what?"

He finally turned to look at me, his eyes cold and hard with determination. My body betrayed my mind and I had to force myself not to look away from him even as my cheeks flushed at the way he stared me down.

"Then we strike."

CHAPTER nineteen

We got lucky.

The year I turned twenty my cat jumped out of our second story apartment after the kitchen window was left open. She pushed the screen off and dropped to the ground like a stone, landing on all fours as a cat should, but the momentum smashed her face into the concrete, chipping three teeth and scraping her chin. She was otherwise unscathed. A week later, I was still picking gravel out of her skin. I swore that she cashed in at least one of her nine lives that day. Luck had been on her side. Sometimes luck is funny that way.

When the night watchmen left their glass towers an hour after daylight arrived, they headed off in the same direction, going north toward where Drake said the warehouse was, instead of east or west where the houses fanned out toward the horizon. This left only one lookout. It was the opportunity we hoped for.

It took nearly a minute to sprint across the parking lot of our building, cross the street and rush into the lobby of the glass structure. We ran straight up the stairs, stopping at the top only to catch our breath. The door to the roof was propped open with a medical book of some kind, thicker than any book really needed to be, letting in a spray of sunshine against the staircase. The air from outside was warm and dry and if our adrenaline wasn't coursing through our veins like a drug, we might have noticed it was too quiet on the roof.

Armed with our knives in hand, we eased outside and stepped onto the roof. Quickly sliding around the wall to the right in an attempt to dart behind the small roof access door, but instead we came face to face with the man we were trying to sneak up on. Drake was immediately knocked backwards into me, the force slamming us both against the wall.

With a grunt, Drake brought his fist up into the shorter man's jaw, forcing him back a step. The glint of metal reflected off the bright white flooring of the roof as the man lifted his sniper rifle up with one hand and grabbed at his bleeding mouth with the other. We both rushed him at the same time, Drake from the front, me from the side. The collision nearly toppled all three of us to the ground. The man fought back but Drake was larger, stronger and angrier, and slammed the rifle into the stunned lookout's face, simultaneously breaking his nose with a sickening crunch and splitting an eyebrow open. At the same time, I thrust my knife into the man's side, twisting it under his ribs before jerking upwards.

The man's face paled instantly and his last exhale of air was full of bloodied bubbles before he fell to his knees. With an almost comically slow lean, he went down on his left side, arms and head limp. *Seconds.* It only took seconds to kill an armed man and took even less time for him to die. My first thought was how lucky we were. Mentally I ticked off how many lives I would have left if I were a cat. No doubt I had used up half of them just in the last year.

"Jesus," I rasped. I was terrified, but unable to look away from the dead man's face. My pulse throbbed in my ears, making a *whoosh-whoosh-whoosh* sound that reminded me of a helicopter that you know is nearby but can't quite find in the sky before the sound is gone.

"See, nothing to it," Drake said. Large beads of sweat stood out on his forehead as he blew out a loud breath, kicking the man's leg. "He's a goner."

"Obviously," I said, trying my hardest not to sway. *I will not faint, I will not faint, I will NOT faint.* I had to say it in my head over and over until I was certain I would stay conscious. It was not the first time I took a life but it *was* the first time I took a life in cold blood. It wasn't really cold blood though, not really, because I knew it was that man's job to shoot down anyone he saw. He could have very well been the one that put two bullets in me just a few weeks before.

Even though I tried to convince the darkest part of my being that he deserved it, all I saw when I looked down at him was a man. A Hispanic man with short brown hair and pale eyes. He was dressed in jeans a size too big, his thin frame practically swallowed up in layered shirts. Nothing about his face seemed menacing or dangerous. Plus, he couldn't have been over twenty-five.

And then my eyes settled on the rifle near his hand, the same one he pointed at Drake just moments before. The one he would have used on me, given the chance. That dark corner inside my heart grew a teeny bit bigger and I forced myself to look away with dry eyes. It was done. It was over. This was what I wanted, wasn't it? *To make them pay.*

"We should move him, dump him in a room downstairs or something," Drake said, picking up the rifle and slinging it over his shoulder. He'd obviously handled one before.

"Why bother? The next guy to come up here is going to see the blood right away," I said with a sigh.

"No body will mean questions. Right now we don't want the rest of them out looking for us, not if you want to follow the next pair back to their *lair*," he said sarcastically, bending down to hoist the dead man's shoulders off the ground. "Grab his feet, it won't take long."

The man's ankles were still warm when I wrapped my fingers around his legs, lifting when Drake did. Dead weight was heavy and though the guy wasn't much taller than I was, it was still a struggle to get him down the first flight of stairs without dropping his corpse every foot or so. His coat held most of the blood from his side, but a few drops still decorated the steps and hall. Drake shoved the body into a closet on the fourth floor and used a rag to wipe off the stairs leading to the roof.

He shrugged at my confused look. "This buys us a little time. The others won't know what happened, at least not right away."

As we hurried down the rest of the stairs with our packs bumping against our tailbones, I got a whiff of something antiseptic in the staircase. Just short of the first floor, I stopped on the steps and inhaled deeply.

"Drake, wait," I warned, "Do you smell that?"

Two steps from the bottom, he stopped and turned to look up at me, "What?"

"It smells like medicine in here."

"It's a damn medical office building. Why does that surprise you?"

"Because this smell…it wasn't here before." Even after waving the air around my face, the odor didn't fade.

"Riley, let's go," he said impatiently. He slapped his palm against the wall in irritation, lowering his foot down one more step. From where he stood, he was able to see out the door into the lobby.

"Drake, wait-"

The glass from the lobby door blew inward and showered down around him. With a startled cry, I fell backwards on the step, landing hard on my ass as Drake dove to the ground and flattened himself onto the tile. Another series of short bursts ripped through the door and it took me a second to register the fact that we were being shot at from at least one person in the lobby.

"Stay there!" I shouted down to Drake, who had nowhere to go but into a narrow corner. He filled the small space at the bottom of the steps with his frame, his boots skidding and squeaking along the tile as he pushed his body as far into the wall as it would go. He sat on the ground, legs drawn up, grabbing for his knife.

I scrambled up the top steps and around the turn point of the railing, fumbling with my pack zipper the whole time. Once open, I thrust a hand in, pushing aside granola bar wrappers and water bottles until my fingers settled on the cool grip of my loaded pistol.

With my finger pressed to my lips, I signaled for Drake to stay quiet. Eventually whoever was in the lobby was going to get close enough to the door to open it and when he did, I'd have a straight shot down the stair case to his head. All I had to do was wait.

Seconds ticked by. Minutes passed. Hours could have come and gone before we heard the crunch of a shoe on broken glass. I held my breath with one shaky hand pointed at the door. Drake nodded from below, still pinned in the corner at the bottom of the stairs, unable to see into the lobby area. I stretched out on my stomach, exposing only my head and arms and saw the first peek of a tennis shoe come into view before quickly vanishing with a squeak.

"Romero, come in," a high-pitched male voice boomed below us. The sound of static from a walkie-talkie answered him.

"Romero! Pick up the fucking radio, bro!" Another click...More gravelly silence. *"Shit! Shit!"*

Something large and metallic made a bouncing sound before coming to a stop against a wall. *A trashcan maybe?* Another squeak of a tennis shoe echoed in the lobby, followed by mumbled cursing.

"Are you dead in there, mother fucker?" the man screamed into the stairwell.

I held my breath, waiting for him to walk into my line of sight again. I only needed one good shot. *Just one.* Shoes squeaked and the large metal object bounced along the lobby floor again.

"I saw you assholes! I saw you run across the street, stupid *shits*!" he wailed.

Damn. There wasn't anyone on the other rooftop, but that didn't mean there wasn't someone *inside* the building. I suddenly felt like an idiot. Drake was still squatted in his corner, the gun held less than an inch from his nose but his eyes closed momentarily while he pressed the barrel against his slick forehead. Obviously, he was feeling just as much the moron as I was at the moment.

"You fucks dead in there, or what?" the man screamed again.

I wanted to laugh. As if, we'd actually answer him either way.

The clean white shoe came back, followed by another. A pair of loose jeans came into view then a shiny metal buckle followed by a yellow sweatshirt that poked out beneath a puffy coat the color of coal. My breath froze in my throat when I saw his elbow. A few more inches to the right and I'd have a clear shot of his chest. But he stopped and fired several more rounds at the stairs. One of the bullets ricocheted off the metal railing and whizzed by my head close enough to move my hair.

One more fucking inch.

Finally, he leaned toward the door to peer into the rectangular space where the window had been, and there it was - the front left pocket of his coat. My finger squeezed the trigger twice, the bullets lodging square into his chest. Like in an action movie, his arms and legs flew up into the air as he was catapulted backwards, as if a giant had punched him in the gut.

Drake jumped up from his corner and kicked the door open, firing freely into the lobby. Something shattered, but the only person inside the open space was bleeding out on the shiny lobby floor, staining the expensive white marble a rich cabernet shade. Drake kicked the gun out of his hands and it spiraled across the tiled floor, coming to a stop with a loud clunk sound after hitting the base of the check-in counter.

As I stepped out of the stairwell and into the much brighter room, the boy, barely out of his teen years, stuttered one blood-bubbly word before his head lolled to the side and the light went out of his chocolate brown eyes, *"F-fuckers."*

৽৽৽

Two men. I had killed two men in the span of ten minutes. Who...what had I become?

"Did you hear me...Riley?!" Drake shouted in my ear, pulling hard on my right arm, "I said we gotta get the hell out of here!"

With a yank, he pulled me away from the impressive blood pool already forming beneath the body, and pushed me out of the glass lobby door that Drake had managed to completely shatter with his wild shooting from the stairwell. Our feet were still crunching on the glass a good twenty feet from the entryway.

"Huh?" I finally asked when we were half a block away, running down the deserted and cold street. I looked over my shoulder at the glass building and it stared back at me, sad and damaged from our brief shootout.

"Jesus-FUCK!" Drake hissed, still pulling me by my arm. "Damn, that was close! We gotta move fast - they'll hear those shots for sure."

Words finally found their way from my blank mind to my numb mouth, "Wh-where are we going?" I fought the urge to upchuck all over Drake's side at the juvenile and vulnerable tone of my voice.

I will not cry, I will not cry, I WILL NOT CRY!

"Damn, woman. You weren't kidding, were you?" He glanced over his shoulder, his hand still attached to me. I was surprised when I looked down to see that he was actually holding my hand.

"What?"

"That you know how to take care of yourself," he said with a manic grin. I didn't like it. I imagined his face held together from the inside by scotch-tape and that if he grinned like that hard enough, the tape would tear away and he would become nothing but cracks and bloody gashes. He was gripping my hand too hard for me to pull it free, even though I jerked my arm several times.

"They're dead?" It came out a question, though I knew it was a fact. Two men, their bodies leaking out the blood they spent the last year trying to keep inside their bodies.

Drake stopped in the middle of the sidewalk in front of a building that had boarded over windows and unreadable graffiti splayed across the entire façade. I blinked at it, curious what monsters lingered inside the darkness.

"Are you okay?" he asked.

I flinched when he reached a hand up to my face and attempted to fight back as he tilted my chin up. "I'm fine," I said through my clenched teeth.

"No, you're not. Drink some water." He reached into his pack and tossed a bottle at me, then turned away, continuing up the sidewalk at a brisk pace.

As I walked-jogged behind him, I drained the bottle of water and tossed it into the street, instantly appalled at my lack of concern for the environment as the plastic cylinder bounced twice before it rolled to a stop in the gutter. The environment - what a joke that had become. The millions of dead bodies polluting the ground and air outranked one empty plastic bottle.

But I still felt a pang of guilt. Because that's who I was. My guilty conscious would never leave me be. It nagged at me - picking at my brain like a small child does at a splinter in their toe that they won't let their mother touch. Every thought was followed by guilt. Every smile, every laugh I had over the last year made me feel like shit because of it, but some of it was warranted, I knew that. I was a *shit* for smiling when my kids were dead. A *shit* for laughing after Fin was blown away in front of me. A *shit* for bringing Connor and Kris into the urban wilderness of California, when we had all been perfectly safe at home in the mountains. A *shit* for thinking I could storm a warehouse full of armed men and shoot them down without a care in the world.

I was a complete and total shit.

The first chance I got, after this mess in Orange County was over, I was going to walk to the coast and throw myself off the first cliff I found, letting the Pacific ocean claim me like it tried to do earlier that year.

CHAPTER twenty

Drake was right, the others did hear the shots and they scrambled down the street in our direction like two-legged cockroaches. I loathed roaches. They multiplied faster than rabbits and came out into the open only when it was dark. Except it wasn't dark when two fully armed men in black coats came running toward us. The tall one held a radio to the side of his head and as they neared, I could hear static growling from it angrily. Pointless, really - we had the walkie-talkies in our packs. Turned down low, of course. It's how we knew what street they would be taking.

From across the residential lane, squished under a pickup truck, Drake sent me a thumb's up sign. This meant we were a go. I flattened myself beneath the massive bush I had crawled into and with a heavy exhale leveled my gun at the shorter man's head. He was closest to me. Drake had the sniper rifle he pinched off the first dead lookout pointing at the duo and when they were almost five feet from the bumper of the truck, Drake gave me a firm nod. *Do it.*

My eyes involuntarily closed when my finger squeezed the trigger and my guy went down hard, landing on the ground a second before the radio guy. I didn't even hear the rifle shot. From under the bush, my knees began shaking so violently that they banged into the coarse dirt hard enough to leave bruises. Spittle flew from my mouth as I struggled to hold the cry in.

Drake scrambled out of his hiding spot, only needing to crawl a few feet before he reached the first dead man's jean clad legs. I looked at his still boots as if the heels would magically click together and we would all wake up in a black and white world again - the color of blood no longer visible. Unlike Dorothy's ruby-red slippers, these boots were the kind that had a steel toe and laces that tied up the calf. *Military boots.* One of them twitched slightly when Drake nudged the man's side. After Drake shot him a second time in the face I turned my head to the side and did what my body so badly wanted to do for the last hour - I heaved up my meager food intake for the day into a wet, sloppy and grainy mess, missing my arm by a mere inch.

ৎৡৢঔ

There's something macabre about hunting the hunters. After I threw up in the bushes, I yacked all over the street while helping Drake pull the two dead men behind a house. A hole the size of a quarter replaced the taller man's right eye. The first shot had torn through his throat. As I stared down at what was left of the still warm body, I wondered if Drake was aiming for his freshly shaven neck on purpose. I wondered if Drake wanted the man to drown on his own blood, like he almost had that summer. There wasn't time to ask. The radio in the street screeched as another man's voice cut in and out. There were more of them - close by.

"How many do you think are left?" I asked breathlessly, wiping the rotten drool from my chin. I would worry about my embarrassingly weak stomach later.

"Let me think…maybe half a dozen or so. You know I haven't been out here for weeks, there could be more of them now," he said, briskly rubbing the top of his head with one blood-streaked hand.

"Or less," I said softly.

"What?"

"You said there could be more of them…but there could be less."

He stared at me like I was speaking a foreign language. "Don't *count* on that. I doubt we'll be that lucky," he said with a grunt. There was that word again - *luck.*

As we walked north, following the curve of the road to the west, I said confidently more so for myself then for Drake, "Oh, I don't know about that. Seems like we've been pretty lucky so far."

It was the hottest day of the week and we were in two layers of clothing, not counting our warm jackets. The thick canvas-like

170

material had a green camouflage print that was meant to retain heat. And it worked well - I was hot. Sweat soaked the collar of my shirt, pooling in unpleasant places around my armpits and crotch. I walked with my legs slightly further apart than my normal gait because I wanted - no, I *needed* airflow between my legs. In California, the weather in the fall was always a gamble. It could be hot and dry or cold and wet. We didn't have dependable seasons in this part of the world.

With my lower lip pinned between my teeth to keep from complaining out loud, we rounded a bend and found ourselves at a major intersection. The street sloped uphill over the freeway. The overpass fencing shimmered in the distance like a mirage.

"That's the way," Drake began walking down the center of the street, the rifle slung over his shoulder like an urban gunslinger.

"You sure you want to do this. Today?" I bit the inside of my cheek. I was the one that pushed him. I was the one that demanded this from him, yet *I* was willing to back out. To retreat to the safety of the solar paneled mini-mansion just a short walk away from anything and everything we could need.

"Why not? We've already taken almost half of them out." He looked me up and down and then grimaced. "You're right. It's too much, isn't it? Doing all of this in one day?" With his hands outstretched before me, he looked like he was waiting for rain to come. It wouldn't.

"It's afternoon. Let's find a place, wait for the others to come back. They have to regroup. *We* have to regroup." I nodded across the street at a school.

"No way. That place gives me the creeps," he pointed behind me, into the neighborhood we just exited. "I think we should find a place around here, but keep it dark tonight."

I nodded. "Lights out. Sounds good." And it did. I wanted a pillow to bury my head under. I wanted the darkness of sleep to take me over, consume me until there was no option but to allow my body to relax.

The first house we approached smelled. We didn't bother to see if the doors were unlocked. The dead lived there. The next house had a unique design to the outside from the rest on the block. A more modern build, a sleeker yard with a waist-high wooden fence, that Drake grumbled was completely useless, and several bushes growing up around the front windows. We hopped over the painted fence and a piece of the rusty-red coloring flaked off against my palm. I felt like an animal, standing on the front stoop sniffing the air, hoping it didn't linger with the smell of rot.

"It's locked," Drake said. He jiggled the handle in his hand before leaning over the porch railing to peek inside a window. "Looks clean. I'll go around back…you keep a lookout, yeah?"

I nodded and watched him jump off the porch, his shoes making a scraping sound on the gravel that bordered the steps. A minute or so later, a crack of glass echoed through the house and I jumped back up the steps to look through the front window. The sheer curtains made it hard to see, but a shadowy figure moved slowly across the room, approaching the front door almost hesitantly.

Already half-way to the fence with my pack thumping against my back and my heart crashing against my ribs like a feral cat stuck in a cage, Drake opened the front door and stuck his head out.

"Hey, where you going?" he smiled, "Man, you've *gotta* see the master bedroom."

∽∽∽

Nightmarish. There wasn't a better word to describe what we saw. "I am not sleeping in here," I said finally, thumbing the room over my shoulder as I squirmed around Drake in the doorway.

"Ha! And I am?" he scoffed, staying close behind me, no doubt just as wigged out by the master suite as I was.

We set our packs on the kitchen table and took turns combing through the cabinets. Two cans of green beans, a pack of peach cups in heavy syrup, a can of cooked beets and a bag of peanuts later we displayed our loot on the table with mocked pleasure.

"We'll be feasting tonight!" Drake cheered.

"I'm allergic to peanuts," I lied. Drake dropped the few shells he had cracked open in his hand like they were radioactive and flung the bag off the table with a frantic swipe.

It had to happen. That manic laugh one has when your psyche is just one warped event away from splitting into pieces, fracturing your mind beyond repair. The laugh was so violent that the convulsions brought me to my knees. I rocked back on my feet, not caring about the tears and snot flowing freely from my face as Drake stood next to the table, a look of shock plastered on his face.

"You're losing it," he said.

I nodded in agreement and his hazel eyes widened, which made me laugh harder of course. Even with a hand clamped over my mouth, I sounded like a rabid hyena. Ignoring the warning stitch in my side, I shrieked, giggled, guffawed and bellowed until my bladder threatened to empty itself - with or without a toilet nearby.

Drake stood with his feet widened, his arms crossed at his chest and a curious look in his eyes as I fought to regain my composure and control of my cramping bladder. He furrowed his brow, the expression saying something like, *'What the actual fuck?'* and that brought on another bout of giggles. With my knees pressed into each other, I struggled to right myself and swayed a bit before taking a deep breath.

I was going to piss my pants if I didn't find the bathroom. Leaving Drake standing in the kitchen efficiently concerned with my mental well-being, I said over my shoulder on my way down the hallway, "I was just fucking with you, I'm not allergic."

A peanut shell promptly flew into the back of my head, getting caught in my braid. "You little shit!" he laughed as I rounded a corner.

Laughing. We killed four men and we were laughing.

Yep, I was a shit alright.

৩~৶

The sofa had a lump in it that pressed uncomfortably into my ribcage and sagged in a way that made my hip dip into the cushion awkwardly. Every half hour or so I turned like a piece of grilling meat on a rotisserie spit. My mind wandered through the past, present, and ignored the future completely. I didn't once think about the next day and what our plans were. I didn't think about the warehouse. What I thought about were walks on the beach. Hikes through the mountains. Holiday dinners and birthday cakes - all with the kids. Their smiling faces floated around my mind like helium balloons, a constant reminder of the person I used to be.

How foolish it was to think I could start over with a new love - a new *family*. As if it was really that easy. Somewhere in the tangled web of synapses, firing inside my skull was a memory. A reason why I got out of bed and decided to leave my house in the first place. But it was just out of reach, like searching for dropped keys on a moonless night. I knew it was there - the reason - but what it *was* escaped me.

With a sigh, I rolled over again, this time facing the rest of the room, the other side of my hip sinking into the sofa. Drake was asleep on the recliner, his head turned away from me, one socked foot poking beneath the blanket he was loosely wrapped in. It occurred to me that we had lived together nearly a month and yet that was the first time I had seen the man sleeping. Memories of the angry kiss in the hallway came back to me and I groaned, rolling over again onto my back. It's not that Drake wasn't an attractive man - we just weren't attracted *to* each other. He treated me like he would a rebellious little sister and I treated him like…well, I didn't treat him the way I should. He saved my life, offered me shelter, food, and the opportunity to seek revenge. The kiss was just weird. Though he didn't speak of his past, I wondered who he lost, who he had to leave behind.

The rest of the night was like that - lost in thoughts, memories, and rotisserie squirming on the couch. When the temperature dropped, I knew dawn was soon approaching. I flung my blanket off, not trying to be quiet as I padded across the living room and down the hall to the bathroom.

We closed the master suite door the night before on account of the hundreds of dolls that lined the walls, decorated the bed, and filled the floors two feet deep. They weren't cute, girly dolls. They were the kind with realistic glass eyes that followed you around the room and creepy grins that seemed to smirk at your back the moment you turned away. Old dolls with cracks in their ceramic skin and paper thin clothing. The lot would have been a collectors dream, but for two relatively normal people, it was like a scene from a slasher movie. The kind where evil dolls come to life and won't die no matter what you do to their little plastic bodies.

The only other room in the house was an office/hoarding room full of decades' worth of papers, unopened mail, recyclables, bags of clothing, and miscellaneous junk. Since neither of us wanted to spend any time in the dolled-out master bedroom, we opted for a fitful night of tossing and turning in the living room instead.

The cobwebby curtains did little to block out the impending light of day. By the time I returned to the living room, the darkness outside was unfurling around the edges, streaking the sky a violescent color. Rubbing the chill off my arms, I stood behind the curtain, looking through the gauzy fabric at the changing sky, marveling at how quickly the streets and buildings came into shape. Almost like someone above us was turning a dimmer switch, lighting the world up below with the flick of a massive wrist.

Of course, I knew there wasn't really a universal dimmer switch but I liked to imagine things like that, especially when nothing made sense in the new world. The sound of Drake stretching turned me away from the window in time to see him untangle from his blanket and sit up with a groan.

"Morning," I said quietly. He only nodded.

After his bathroom break and tossing me a bottle of water, we ate a modest breakfast of peanuts and fruit cups before saying goodbye to our overnight haven. The air outside felt fresh on my face and smelled of dry earth, with a lingering scent of dead things that I was sadly growing accustomed to. Dead trees, dead flowers, dead grass, dead bodies - all emanating the same dried-out and overripe odor that filled the sour streets with a fetid tang. Before I threw myself off a cliff and landed in the ocean to drown in an endless supply of sea-foam, I intended on burning the cities of California to the ground. It wouldn't take much; one spark here, another there and the decomposing buildings would burn like fireplace timber. The fire would spread where the wind took it, which in the southern parts of the state meant the fire would eat up everything it touched from all four points of the compass.

Just as it should be. Burned to the ground, wiped out so life can start again. A rebirth from the ashes. Maybe then, the dead would finally leave and give the living a chance to survive.

Retracing our steps from the day before, we left the residential street and turned to follow one of the main roads toward the freeway and the large shopping area that was across the street from the warehouse. It was dark enough that we hoped to slip through the landscape unseen, choosing to think that anyone on the other side of the freeway was still clueless about the events of the previous day. I was relying on luck again.

Not in the mood for small talk, we walked side by side with at least five feet of space between us. Before making it even a block up the street, we both stopped in our tracks as an image formed, still shrouded in the shadowy remnants of night. I peered hard ahead of me, at the small figure that stood in the center of the inclined road. As my eyes adjusted to the changing surroundings, a peek of sunlight lit up the road and we were able to clearly see that it was a boy standing in the distance. He was young, maybe five years old, wearing loose pants and nothing else. Unable to control it, my chest began to heave up and down as I fought to keep the panic and fear at bay. Spinning around, I saw no one behind us, but that didn't mean *they* weren't coming.

"Oh God, not again," I said to myself.

"Jesus - that's a kid!" Drake made a move to run after the boy but I yanked on his arm, pulling him close to my side.

"Don't," I warned.

"What? It's a *kid*," he repeated.

"No. It's not."

He turned to look at me, his face slack with shock and pulled free from my clingy grasp. "What the hell's wrong with you, Riley? We can't just leave him there!"

I shook my head at him and begged him to stay. Not to walk up the street toward the small child that stood motionless and eerily quiet in the car-cluttered road, but it didn't stop him. At first, he walked, then he jogged, and when he was almost there it finally happened. It must have been what it felt like for Connor - to see no one and then dozens of bodies come out of the shadows and surround me. I finally understood how terrifying it must have been to see that from the outside.

Drake was leaning down toward the child, but something must have spooked him, since he jumped backwards and cursed, gripping at his backpack straps as if he was ready to bolt. He didn't realize there was nowhere to run. Small misty shapes began moving toward him, merging into little people as they got closer. Children. Only ten at first but then twenty, thirty, fifty. All in their bed clothes, all the color of death - pale grey skin with bloody faces. Scraggly blooms of burst veins shimmered beneath the skin like fireworks - the signature calling card of the virus.

He didn't know what to do; the circle closed on Drake so quickly. Some of the children holding hands, others reaching up to touch him, pulling at his clothes, tugging at his shirt, as small children like to do and all he could do was panic. With his hands fused over his eyes, he saw little of this but I could hear his distress. It was my name he yelled over and over.

I ran for him. Even before I knew what to do, I ran. I plowed right into the group, barreling into the shoulders, heads and backs that barely came up to my hips. So young; they were all so young. Hands reached out for me, and I felt their cold and slimy fingers through my clothes. I kept my momentum going, even after something snagged my sweatshirt, tearing the seam open. Gagging to avoid choking on the smell, my eyes watered with the memory of my dead children's faces before I burned their bodies. Not bothering to slow down, I collided into Drake and we clutched at each other, our eyes sealed shut to block out the horror. We crumpled to the ground in a muddled mess of limbs, bringing our bodies as close together as they would fit. My head was beside his, jammed into his chest, leaving my neck exposed. Small hands continued to touch and grab at us, but it was different than my first experience with the dead - the sensations felt less angry and more eager. Almost impatient, exploring rather than trying to cause harm and fear.

It's not real, it's not real, it's not real, I chanted in my head over and over until I almost believed it. I might have been saying it out loud, Drake might have been saying it too, but my knowledge that the tiny dead bodies would eventually vanish into thin air did little to stifle my screams. Especially, when something warm and sticky dropped onto my neck, sliding off my skin and landing at my side with a wet plop. *It's not real, it's not real.*

We shivered, cursed, screamed and shivered some more, until the air went still and sunlight warmed the place on my neck where some sort of flesh had fallen off one of the children. Fighting to calm my stomach, I kept my eyes closed while running my trembling hand along my skin, feeling nothing but my own sweat. Funny, even after no physical trace of the dead was left on our bodies, the lower hem of my sweatshirt hung at an awkward angle, torn clean along the seam.

"It's over." My voice wavered and creaked like an old board.

Drake's soft brown hair brushed against my cheek with each shake of his head. Such a strong man, an arrogant, independent man, and he was kneeling on the asphalt, refusing to let go of a woman half his size. After muttering something I hoped sounded soothing into his ear and pulling away from him, I looked quickly around us. We were alone again. The street seemed massive then, as if the lanes spanned one hundred miles wide and we would never be able to reach either shoulder before the road cracked in half and swallowed us whole.

I imagined the waves of the ocean as they lapped around me. What the salt water would taste like as it filled my mouth and drained into my body. I was not going to die on that dirty street; that wasn't how I was supposed to go.

∾∾

We didn't talk for the next hour. It took a considerable amount of urging on my part to get Drake up and on his feet. We sat on the sidewalk next to the bumper of a dusty Audi with bird crap dotting the hood. I glanced inside just once; it was long enough to see the dead family of six partially huddled under an array of different colored blankets. Like so many other people, they died in their cars trying to drive away from the virus. But you can't run from the air you breathe. I doubted they got far before the driver lost control of his bodily functions and the passengers, too sick to notice, died beside him soon after. The first words spoken after the early morning event that nearly made me pee my pants came from Drake.

"Holyfuckingshit." It came out in one breath, strung together like a solitary word. He said it over and over until I placed my hand on his knee and gave him a friendly squeeze.

"It's over," I told him again. Knowing full well my words didn't matter, I tried to smile anyway.

"*Holyfuckingshit,*" he said again, staring at one of the Audi's flat tires. His short hair just barely grazed the top of his tanned ear. It blended effortlessly into his centimeter long beard that he hadn't once shaved off completely the entire time I knew him.

"Yeah," I agreed. After draining the water I handed to him, he stood up too quickly and swayed a bit.

"Don't you dare pass out on me - you're too heavy to carry. I'll just leave your ass here on the sidewalk," I joked half-heartedly. But I felt creases digging deeply between my brows as I watched him with concern.

With a curt nod, he let go of my shoulder and bounced his empty water bottle off the roof of the dirty Audi. It slide down the windshield and topple off the other side of the car. It rolled to a stop somewhere in the street - just another piece of litter for me to feel guilty about.

ço∂ç

"Do you want to talk about it?" I finally asked. It had been twenty minutes of silence - me following Drake along sidewalks, in between houses and over freeway walls.

We were slowly moving our way east through the bumper-to-bumper cars. The sun was already warming the day, and though I wasn't sweating yet beneath my layers, I knew that by noon I would be. If I was still alive at noon.

"Do I look like I want to talk?" he grumbled without turning around.

"Hasn't that happened to you before?"

I accidentally stepped on his foot as he abruptly stopped walking and whirled around to glare at me. "What did I say? *Don't.*"

Blinking up at him, I tried not to feel offended and nodded. We crossed the rest of the highway in silence, reaching the other side with our hands and knees dirty from crawling over the hoods of cars and trunks. With a final glance back at the vehicles before following Drake down the shoulder of an exit, I wondered how long it would take the cars to break down and rust. A lot longer than it would take their occupants to turn into skeletons. I shivered. The image wasn't a pleasant one.

When the highway wall dipped down low enough to hoist ourselves over it, we landed feet first into the backyard of a private residence. The yard was an open and weed-filled lot with brown grass. In one of the corners, there was a large doghouse. Lying on its side, still attached to a thick and heavy looking chain was a dead dog. Something had eaten most of the soft organs out of the body, exposing the dried out ribcage and spine. The animal was so badly decomposed and disturbed that it was impossible to tell what color, sex or breed of dog it had been. I yanked a starched and sun-bleached towel, rigid as a board, off a nearby clothesline and rested it on top of the corpse. After crying over the body, I joined Drake at the side gate, where he patiently waited with his hands in his pockets.

"Is there something wrong with me, that I feel worse for that damn dog than I do the men that we killed yesterday?" I nearly sobbed.

Drake reached out and swiftly pulled me into a rough hug, releasing me almost as quickly as he grabbed me and planted a dry kiss onto the top of the head. It was a brotherly act and I sighed in thanks for the gesture.

"No. There's nothing wrong with you," he said.

We walked through the quiet neighborhood. Me avoiding looking too closely at the yards that looked as if a pet had lived there, and Drake scanning every corner, peering into every window with caution. The warehouse was only two neighborhoods away, according to him.

Whispering so I could barely hear him, Drake pointed to the houses on the south side of the street, "Behind there is a newer apartment complex. It's the one I told you about, the one they sort of took over. At least, that's where they were. The warehouse is just on the other side, close to the shopping center. It's new too. Or it was."

"Are we circling it?"

"Yeah. We'll go all the way around, come up on the warehouse from the north side where the delivery docks are. I don't think they'd expect that." He scratched at the side of his scruffy face, lost in thought.

It was a gamble. A risk - but then again there was no right or wrong anymore. Just survival of the fittest. Everything I had been was gone, not much of me would be left in the end. The way it should have been from the beginning. Why not risk what little was left?

Drake stopped just before a major intersection, stepping off the cracked sidewalk to lean against the wall of a three-story office building. I stood next to him in semi-baggy clothes that didn't quite fit right, my hair pulled back in a tight ponytail. We stared across the street where dozens of medical tents stood, cordoned off from the street by a slew of haphazardly placed military vehicles. Even from hundreds of feet away I could hear the flap of plastic as the breeze moved through the tents with a lazy kind of lull. A separate area inside the barrier was partially obstructed from my view, but a single story tent with a white dome top had a rip down one of its long sides, exposing the contents to the elements.

Stacked on top of each other in tight rows were thousands of white body bags. Just iridescent enough that even from beyond the street and across the parking lot, I could make out the brunette, blonde and occasional redheaded bodies through their milky-colored plastic wraps. It wasn't the first time I saw a medical quarantine zone but the sheer volume of people sickened me. The way each body, no matter the size, was piled neatly on top of the next, meant there was a system in place on how properly to store infected human remains. Someone with a title wrote up a plan, pointed at a pile and said, *'That one goes over there'*. It was depressing and sad and made me want to puke.

"Sure is something, isn't it?" Drake said in a hushed tone. His eyes were glazed over, like he was looking through the death across the street, rather than at it.

I glanced between him with his stoic and faraway gaze and the parking lot turned military base with a numb feeling. It should hurt to see such a thing - thousands of dead people - hundreds of dead *families*. It should hurt every time, like a knife straight into the heart, seeing a body bag with a person half my size rotting inside. But it was only a detached and numb feeling. A feeling of 'been there and seen that'. *A crappy feeling.*

Drake cleared his throat to bring my attention back to him. "Warehouse is just over there," he nodded down the street, beyond the vacant office building.

I stared at the side of his head, wondering what the story was behind the closed hole in his earlobe. A random thought for a fractured mind, made sense.

"So, when do you want to do this?" I asked, still staring at the tiny hole in his ear where a piercing used to be.

"No time like the present." He grinned the wide Joker smile that creeped me out.

Sighing, I knelt to the ground in a small patch of brown grass, letting the moisture from the night before soak into the knee of my jeans. Mudding up my pants wasn't a concern. Being dirty was a normal part of my new life. Besides, the jeans would be easy to replace when needed. Stain your clothes and break a shoelace? Pilfer new ones from the closest mall. Lose your brush and run out of shampoo? Pilfer more from the closest mall. Of course, that philosophy wouldn't last forever. Eventually even the malls would dry out just like the bones from the bodies under the dome tent.

My pack was full of weapons, handguns, clips and knives of different shapes and sizes. Most of them pulled off the dead men from the day before. My own knife was strapped securely to my leg, just like Drake's was. A gun was tucked into the back of my jeans, loaded and ready for action. The day before, I didn't even bother to take one of the long-range rifles. My shoulder wouldn't tolerate the kickback. Drake was the only one with a rifle draped across his torso like a pageantry ribbon.

All we needed was a little bit of greasy paint to streak our faces and those cool lace-up combat boots and we would fit right in with the thugs we were conspiring to kill. Well, maybe the camouflage paint was a bit much, but the idea struck me as a funny one and I imagined Drake's face covered in hunter green, mine in black. The image of our thirty-something year old faces in paint was so appealing at that moment that I almost dragged my fingers through the mud and rubbed them under my eyes.

Instead I sighed, doing it over and over, filling my lungs with air as rapidly as possible. Sort of like a swimmer would, right before launching their body into the water for a race. When my head felt efficiently light-headed and cleared of all the gunk that lingered around in there like the day old smell of skunk, I tightened my pack straps and nodded at Drake that I was ready. Of course, all he had to do to prepare was hitch his jeans up half an inch or so. Men were easy that way.

"Ready?" he asked, gun in hand, muscles taut and eager.

"Ready enough," I said with a smile. If we were going to die in five minutes, I wanted a smile to be the last expression we shared between us.

CHAPTER twenty-one

Only one doubt went through my mind before we edged around the corner of the office complex and ran down the buckling sidewalk from tree to tree for cover: If I *did* die, will Zoey ever forgive me? I could have turned around right then, leaving my morbid and stupid curiosity right there on the street corner and fled out of the city, back south into San Diego. But I didn't. The crazy inside me had been unleashed.

There was no sign of life outside the warehouse - not even the wind wanted to touch the squatty bushes lined around the building. The little things stood as still as rocks, rigid and dried out like an old skeleton. They seemed like shrubby versions of suspicious garden gnomes to me. I almost expected them to shudder and move out of the corner of my eye and end up five feet away from where I swore I last saw them. They didn't of course.

We were only a few yards away when the first bullet took off a chunk of the tree I hid behind. Instantly a startled scream flew out of my mouth, taking a good deal of spit with it. I cursed so hard between my clenched jaws that it actually hurt my front teeth. They vibrated in their sockets like hummingbirds strung out on sugar water. My first coherent thought not related to the pain in my mouth was if the shooter had noticed Drake creeping up the street. Since no bullets were ricocheting off the dead cars or shattering the cloudy windshields, I assumed he was still out of sight.

"Stay the fuck back!" Someone yelled from the warehouse. The angry and guttural cry sounded like it came from above me, from somewhere up high. I risked a brief glance at the roof and snapped

my head back behind the tree trunk after catching the glint of sunlight reflecting off of something shiny.

Another crack and more splinters flew by me. The tree was barely an inch wider than I was and wouldn't serve to keep me covered for much longer. Something wet trickled down the side of my face, dripping slowly from my jaw. But I couldn't reach up to feel what it was, or my arm would have been exposed, so I waited, trying to ignore the steady *dripdripdripdripdrip* sound of what had to be blood landing on the canvas shoulder strap of my pack.

The sun bounced off of a crumpled soda can, causing me to squint against the glare. If it was only a foot closer, I could have kicked it away, toward the gutter. The more I tried to ignore it, the brighter the glare seemed to become and though only seconds had passed with it in my peripheral vision, I was sure I would end up blind. With my cheek pressed firmly against the cool, rough bark, there was nothing to do but ignore it.

Struggling to fight the compulsion to step out from behind my tree and launch the can as far from me as my spindly leg could propel it, I heard a hiss from the street and turned my head in time to catch Drake's hand signal. With my gun out, I nodded and angled it around the tree, firing toward the warehouse, hoping it was distracting enough to keep the guy on the roof from looking down at us. One, two, three, four, five shots rang through the air - cracking through the silence with a deafening thunder that echoed down the street and bounced back around me like a hug. It was just enough time for Drake to disappear from my view, hopefully making it to the next set of cars before more rifle shots pocked the tree. He didn't hold back. So many rounds had been fired that I was sure half of the tree was blown away. I could feel each bullet as it struck into the trunk, like a knock on the other side. A deceivingly subtle *let me in* sort of knock.

"Not by the hair of my chiny-chin-chin," I laughed. The sound was foreign. I immediately swallowed what I could of it, chastising my rapid loss of sanity before firing again, stopping only to reload with a full clip.

"Come out, come out, wherever you are," I yelled in the most annoying singsong voice I could.

The answer came in the form of more cursing from the rooftop and another round of bullets into the tree. I started to giggle, that last bit of reason slipping away from my mind. I was in a John Wayne movie, dusty, dirty, and shooting at the bad-guys. John Wayne would have a horse though. I had a horse, but I lost it.

The image of Sunny's remains came to me. Drake had taken me back to see her when I was able to walk without assistance but not much of Connor's horse was left. The birds and something with canine teeth sharper than mine had made a mess out of the beautiful and sweet palomino. Tearing her flesh away and scattering her ribcage in a twenty-foot radius around her downed body. My eyes filled with hot tears that stung and prickled at my eyeballs like thousands of tiny needles. That was it - the image of Sunny dead on the overgrown golf course that shoved me over the edge of what was left of my reality.

Brazenly, but still mindful enough to use what little speed I had, I bolted from behind the tree, firing wilding at the rooftop through my blurry vision. I ran up the sidewalk toward the waist high utility box that was nearly twenty-five feet away, pausing only slightly to kick the damn soda can as hard as I could into the street.

I never *did* hear it fall.

 споэ́соу

Kneeling behind the utility box, I was finally able to touch my face. Just as I expected, my hand came back sticky with bright red blood. It pissed me off even more, and I popped up to fire the gun, catching just a glimpse of Drake closing in on the side of the building. He was crouched down, running full speed and slammed into the wall with enough force that his feet slid out beneath him and he landed on his ass.

It was the last time I saw him outside. Ten painfully long minutes of cursing, yelling and name-calling, that reminded me of playground bullies, and random rounds of back and forth gunfire went by until my legs began to cramp from the squatting and kneeling. Plus, by then I was bleeding from more than my head.

After a long moment of silence, I screamed myself hoarse, letting the wind take my voice up and away from me. *"Did you give up already, assholes?!"* No one answered. No shots, no attempts to debase my sex or slurs of frustration carried down to the sidewalk.

With a quick look above me, the roof seemed momentarily still - vacant. And then the sound of muffled gunshots sang again.

Drake was inside.

I believe there are only a handful of reasons to run so fast that your knees come higher than your hips: when you are running from something bigger and meaner than yourself, or when a gold medal is at stake, of course. But there's another reason - when you need to get somewhere so fast that you know your heels can't afford the split second of time it takes for them to roll off the ground. So you sprint with only your toes gripping and moving you forward. That's how I ran the rest of the way down the sidewalk. Not even slowing down, before my shoulder slammed into the door Drake went through.

The door opened with a bang and inside I flew, but I wasn't expecting my feet to instantly lose traction. After sliding across a puddle of something slippery, I crashed face first into a chain-link wall. Bouncing into it with such force that I was flung backwards like a deployed rubber band into the sticky mess again, my feet failing me, slipping out and to the side. My ass will never forgive me for how hard it hit the ground.

"Unf," I exhaled, coming to a stop after spinning clockwise on my backside. The pistol was gone, catapulted somewhere away from me during my ungraceful entrance.

The chain inside the room rattled loudly, taking nearly a full minute before the links stopped jiggling. By then I had mostly caught my breath, the labored sound being the only thing that whispered through the dark room. It was some sort of utility space or a side office - I wasn't sure. But the blood was fresh; it was still warm and uncongealed. An enormous amount. A fatal amount. Enough blood that no one could've walked away and lived more than a mere handful of seconds.

The *rat-a-tat-tat* of gunfire snapped my head up and to the right, through an open doorway that led into a much larger - and darker room. Crawling in an awkward slipping motion on my hands and knees, I slid to a stop just before the doorframe, my knife in my right hand. Craning my head cautiously into the next room, there was only a shadowy aisle upon aisle of bulky boxes and pallets. And a shoe. My wet, left hand stuck to the linoleum floor as I crawled, using the knuckles of my other hand to balance myself. The shoe was connected to a foot, a leg, a body. It wasn't Drake.

Not realizing I was holding my breath, a gust of air whistled out between my lips. There was a slash across the man's throat and several bloody holes dotted across his torso. Drake was using his knife, stealthily making his way through the building. Just as planned. The image of him with a bloody bandana tied around his forehead, his face streaked with mud and paint, came back into my mind and before I knew what I was doing, I dragged four of my bloody fingers across both cheeks - one finger down my chin and neck and wiped my hand dry on the thigh of my jeans.

It was war, damn it. Why not look like a fucking warrior?

∽∾

Two more bodies - both slashed with a blade. Several more bursts of rifle fire, handguns, screams, shouts, lots and lots of cursing. I followed the trail, sneaking glances up and down the aisles, looking for a sign of life. Looking for the women. Drake said they were kept there.

My daughter hated to wear shoes. Everywhere she went she had naked, dirty feet. The sound of her walking across our house would *slapslapslapslap* against the hard floors. It was an organic sounding step I always recognized as purely hers. So, when a similar slapping of bare feet reverberated in the darkness, I knew whoever was running toward me was barefoot, which was odd.

I quickly ducked down the nearest aisle with my blade held out in front of me like a flashlight and waited. The slapping sound slowed then stopped completely. Whoever it was, they knew I was close. The blade glinted from the pale reflection of something and I tilted it, struggling to find the source. Peering at the knife with my head down, I almost didn't notice the air change as something long and metallic whooshed over the top of my head and slammed into the metal frame of the aisle. The shelves beside me throbbed loudly from the impact and I scuttled backwards, tripping over a large box and landed on my backside for the second time in five minutes.

The barefoot slapping resumed, this time running away from me - toward the side door. After scrambling to my feet, I darted around the aisle corner just in time to see the shadow of a young girl with flowing hair dart into the entry room, disappearing into the light. *Freedom.*

The warehouse - a behemoth of a structure creaked and groaned as if preparing to swallow me in its gut as I pushed deeper and deeper into the shadows. It never occurred to me to pull out my flashlight. An animal instinct in me took over, bending my spine forward so I crouched, curling my hands so they looked and felt like claws instead of fingers. The smallest refractions of light gave my eyes all they needed to see into the dingy space around me.

Like a bloodthirsty animal, I hunted. Following the sounds of grunts and moans and discovering nothing but a handful of freshly killed men. Until I found it. In the corner of the warehouse was a walled off room - most likely used once upon a time as a break room. A lamp from within glowed softly but the space seemed quiet - almost too quiet.

The door was ajar just enough to slip my body silently inside without disturbing it. The narrow room was long - stretching a good hundred feet from the doorway. Lining the furthest corner was a row of twin mattresses. Some with ruffled sheets, some naked so that they exposed the dark stains that spread out along the diamond pattern of the beds. The sharp odor of urine and feces made me gag. And the hot, iron smell of blood. Thin sprays of blood decorated the walls, still dripping downward in places. I gaped in shock at the bottom of the furthest wall where a woman with matted hair, that might or might not have once been blonde, lay in a crumpled heap of chopped up limbs - intestines and brain matter spilling out around her like a gutted fish.

My stomach lurched but didn't have time to do more than that before gangly arms jumped out from behind the door and slimy fingers coiled around my neck. Creative curses words flew out of my mouth as the knife clattered to the ground and spun across the room. We struggled against one another, falling to the scuffed linoleum and rolling around until we were fused together - a tangled mess of scratched, bleeding and trembling limbs.

Stringy hair caught in my mouth and I spat out the sour strands in a panic before they became stuck in my throat. One of us kicked at the table that held the battery operated camping lantern. When it crashed to the ground, it rolled away from me, stretching the light in waves over the walls, letting in the shadows. When a pale face came close to mine, I jerked my forehead into it, feeling something crack and my attacker screamed - a high-pitched cry that only a woman can make. Wiggling a knee between us, the greasy hands left my neck. I kicked at the girl's soft midsection, sending her flying into the blood-streaked wall, landing just inches away from a severed hand.

Scrambling from her, I pushed myself back until my shoulder blades hit a metal filing cabinet. My left shoe had come off and my backpack was lying on its side by the door, one of the straps ripped.

"Jesus," I muttered, sucking in air, pressing my back as far into the cabinet as my skin would allow.

She moaned - the crazy lady. When she stirred I flinched as if struck, denting the metal drawer behind me with my head. Instead of getting up for another attack, she curled into a ball and began to sob. It was an eerie sound in a space as large as the warehouse. The cries drifted in and out of the aisles with a strange kind of ebb and flow, like the building itself was breathing her sorrow.

The smell hit me again. It was the scent of dirty *living* bodies, shit and urine mingling with fresh and rotten blood. This was where they were kept - the women. In a dungeon, in squalor - left to rot, die, and be used however the men saw fit.

Raising a shaky and bleeding hand in front of me, and speaking as soothingly as my damaged throat would allow, I said to her, "I'm not here to hurt you." The simple statement was absurd even to me, especially after punching, slapping, scratching and kicking the small yet surprisingly wily woman clear across the room.

A holler boomed outside, sounding faraway but dangerously close at the same time, and the woman's sobs cut off abruptly. We both stayed frozen like that. The girl curled in a tight ball, hands clamped around her mouth, me with my arm projected in front of my body, fingers splayed open to reveal an empty palm. We waited. Listening to each other's hushed and erratic breathing.

"Riley!" Drake's voice boomed again.

"Drake!" I squeaked, causing the woman to jerk. "In here," my voice wavered. "Drake!"

Every muscle in my body protested as I dragged myself toward the door, flinging it all the way open to look out into the darkness. Something rustled behind me and I braced for the woman's hands on my body again but instead she had retreated deeper into the room, hiding in the shadows.

"Where are you?" Drake hollered, his voice closer but still not close enough.

"Here, the far corner...over here!"

He found me resting on my forearms, my hand freely bleeding from a bite wound, my face bloody and my arm leaking a dark amber color. My clothes were soaked with the blood of the first man Drake had killed.

"Holy fuck!" he breathed, dropping down to his knees to pull me into his arms. His face was splattered with red droplets, his dark clothes soaked in the same wet sprinkles.

"Fine," I mumbled, "I'm okay."

"Like hell," he lifted me to my feet and snaked an arm around my waist to hold me up.

"My shoe," I said.

"Huh?"

"I lost...my shoe."

He blinked, his eyes watering. And then his chest heaved into mine as he began to laugh. "You lost a fucking shoe? That's it. That's all you have to say?"

My body swayed in his grasp as I looked down. That's when my mind finally broke, when I took in the pathetic sight of that white, socked foot. Not many people remember that moment - the very *second* when their reality finally leaves them and the hysteria walks in - loud and proud to be there.

I laughed so hard it hurt. So hard in fact, that tears flowed down my face, leaving clear tracks through my sticky finger painting. I laughed until the only pain I felt was a sharp stitch in my side that threatened to separate my muscles from my ribs. Drake held onto me as if he feared I would run away and we laughed and bled against each other until a scared voice interrupted from just behind us.

"Riley...is it really you?"

CHAPTER twenty-two

It wasn't supposed to happen. I mean, not *really*. Finding Mariah was a dream; a fantasy I clutched to in order to stomp some of the survival guilt back down my throat. Yet, there she was standing before me. Battered, used up and broken - but alive.

We stared at each other in the poor light, recognizing only our voices. Drake's arm was still wrapped tightly around my waist but even with the support, my knees threatened to buckle beneath the weight of my body. *It was actually her.*

"Mariah?" I squeaked.

She looked awful. Her brown and curly hair was longer, the matted clumps showing several small bald spots on her greasy scalp. Part of her left earlobe was missing and she stood before us practically naked. Only a torn pair of boy shorts and a men's ribbed tank top covered her pallid skin. At one point, her meager clothing might have been white in color, but in the dark employee room, the stretched out material was dirt-grey and bloodied.

In an attempt to defy gravity by sliding out of Drake's grasp, I stepped toward her with my bleeding hand out in a non-threatening way again. Without another word, she ran into my arms, knocking me into Drake. Hot tears flowed from my eyes as we pressed against each other, the chill of her flesh absorbing what was left of my body heat. I gave it freely, since it was the only thing I had left to give. Her frail and frozen limbs sucked my heated life-force dry, draining me until I was empty.

֍

At first, the cool ground was inviting. As I slumped against the concrete wall where Drake leaned me just before passing out, I fingered a crack between the bricks gingerly, as if a story was tucked deep inside the mortar waiting to be discovered by the right set of hands. The only story they told though was one of death - one of immorality and injustice. It was written out in bloodstains along the half-dozen dirty twin mattresses. It was a nightmarish story about lust and desire and pain. *It was Mariah's story.*

Her feet stood a few steps away, ash-black heels tucked close together, stubby toes curled down into the linoleum with her arms entwined out before her in a braid. As I blinked in the sight of her, I marveled at how slender her figure had become - almost starved to oblivion. She was all skin and bones, so thin her breasts were barely nubs. Over the last year, my own soul had been gutted again and again, yet life had continued anyway. But Mariah had lost all signs of life. Except for the basics - sleep, eat, breathe and repeat again in the morning. Perhaps we weren't as different as we looked. What was left of either of us?

"We should go. Can you walk?" Drake asked tenderly, sending a cautious sideways glance at Mariah.

After a quick nod, he hoisted me back to my feet and helped me locate my fallen shoe. There was nothing, no items of clothing to cover Mariah with, so Drake zipped her into his thick canvas coat and pushed us out of the rank room with an urgency I didn't need to question. Her feet padded in unison with the scuffing of my shoes as we rushed from one aisle to the next, Drake searching in the darkness for someone or something.

"Are they all…dead?" I asked just above a whisper.

"No, shush…keep moving," he snapped.

We escaped the way we had entered, through the side door that was still propped open from my embarrassing entrance not even ten minutes before. Drake clasped my hand and tugged me behind him, and I pulled tightly on Mariah's hand - the same one that dug into the flesh of my neck moments before. I shivered at the thought of my skin embedded beneath her nails, but of course, she didn't know it was me. That's what I told myself - *she didn't know.*

The sunlight felt alien; an orb of light so bright after being in the dark warehouse that it didn't seem real. My pack swayed violently from one shoulder as we ran to the sidewalk, taking cover behind the expertly planted rows of shade trees that had grown up and over the power lines. It was hard to tell which of us was bleeding the most. Drake had oozing wounds on both arms and though he tried to hide it, I saw him clutch at his waist more than once.

"What is it?" I asked, trying to lift his shirt off his abdomen, "What's wrong? Are you hurt?" What a stupid question. Of course he was; we all were. In response, he impatiently swatted my hand away and looked up and down the street as if it simply wasn't the right time to bleed to death.

"I don't know where he went," he said, using his hand to block the sunlight from his eyes.

"Who?"

"A guy took off but I couldn't follow him," he paused to glance down at me before scanning the street again, "I heard you screaming."

"Oh."

I didn't remember screaming as Mariah tried to tear my head off, but it didn't surprise me. She scared the shit out of me. Silently and with no objection or complaint, she ran down the streets with us, Drake in the lead with me pulling her behind like a toddler. We ran most of the way back to the house after making unnecessary turns every other block, stopping only to gasp in breath and for Drake to scan our path for any followers.

By the time our feet stumbled over the front stoop of the house, it wasn't even noon yet. Drake was the only one of us that stayed alert, watching from the front windows for nearly half an hour to make sure we hadn't been followed. Mariah and I were collapsed on the living room floor on our backs, uncaring about what kind of grimy stains we left on the expensive beige carpet.

When he finally stood over us, one leg in between mine with a Glock still clutched in his maroon-streaked hand, I started to giggle. It was the only emotion I had left: insanity.

Drake shook his head, allowing just the hint of a smile to tug at his mouth. "You are one crazy woman, you know that?" I giggled harder, letting the shakes take over my entire body in waves. "You did it. You actually found what you came for," he said breathlessly.

Still giggling, I turned my head to the side to face Mariah, but as she stared up at the ceiling I knew I hadn't found her soon enough. How did one come back from the hell she had endured over the last year? Was it even possible? *Could* Mariah come back?

But Drake was right. I did find what I came for. My giggling fit stopped - cut short in my throat. Yes, yes, Mariah was saved but at what cost? I lost Connor and Kris. Darkness bubbled up inside me. I sat up and stared between Drake and Mariah as my stomach acid churned and toiled. It was right there, clear as day. And the expression on Drake's face as he stepped around me to collapse into one of the heavily cushioned armchairs said it all.

Would Mariah be worth it? Was finding her worth losing the others?

That sick feeling in my stomach rushed up my throat and I clamped my mouth shut in an effort to keep the water inside me down. The realization hit me then - what was left of me would never recover from the guilt of screwing up. *Never.* The difference this time around was that there were others waiting for me - depending on me. I only hoped they wouldn't miss me too much.

୨ৎ

For hours we showered and took turns tending to each other's wounds. Drake had several bullet grazes on his arms, and a shallow stab wound just to the right of his belly button that I had no clue how to treat other than to stitch it up. For the first time since leaving the lodge, I missed Win so much I wanted to cry. After being patched up the lot of us looked like Frankenstein experiments. Mariah seemed to be in the best shape with just one scrape along the side of her head and the two deep, purple bruises below each eye from my head-butt to her face. She was damn lucky her nose was still on straight.

"Is it okay...I mean, can I clean myself?" Mariah was fingering the edge of her filthy worn out boy shorts while Drake knotted a stitch in the two-inch gash on my shoulder.

"Of course, you don't have to ask. There's an extra bedroom upstairs, the bathroom is across the hall and the shower works...last door on the left." I winced as Drake poked the needle through my skin again. "I'll leave out something clean for you to wear, okay?"

She nodded at me and quietly retreated up the stairs. When her dirty feet were out of sight, and the bathroom door closed above us with a soft click, I said over my shoulder, "Poor girl. Think she'll be okay?"

With a soft brush of his thumb against my cheek, Drake looked up the stairs with a sigh, "Riley, only time will tell that."

"And that's all we have left, right? Time?" I asked bitterly.

"It is what it is, I guess. Are you taking her back to San Diego? To be with the others?"

"Where else can she go?" I avoided looking at him, not ready to divulge the part about me shooting Mariah's brother to death. I hoped she never mentioned Matt.

Another tug of the needle made me jerk slightly as he threaded it through my skin. "Sorry, this is the last one."

"How many?"

"I hope you don't mean total?" he laughed.

"Never mind. No point in counting, I guess." His fingers moved gracefully along the thread, pulling it tight into a knot before he clipped the ends off and patted my arm. "All done. For now," he smiled.

"I promise not to tear open any more parts of my body, at least not tonight."

"Good. Because my fingers are tired of tying all those little knots."

Leaning forward, I lifted his shirt up to look at the one-inch line on his stomach, running my fingers gently across the stitches. "Are you sure you're okay here?"

He made no effort to remove my hand. "Yeah, I'll be fine. Might take tomorrow off from fighting bad guys though…if you don't mind?"

"You've earned the break," I laughed. After removing my hand, his shirt fell back into place, hiding the spot where a small pocketknife had sliced into him. "Thank you."

"No need to thank me," he smiled, staring at the carpet, "I told you I had my reasons."

The room felt hot and humid and the fact that I was covered in blood and things I never, ever wanted to identify, I pushed up from the carpet and stood up with a groan. "I'm going to get cleaned up," I told him.

"Save me some hot water, will ya?"

"I'll do my best." I started up the stairs, holding onto the railing to keep from falling backwards. "I make no promises, though. Oh, and Drake?"

"Yeah?"

I waited until he looked up at me, the skin around his hazel eyes crinkled just slightly from age. "Thanks again...you know, for everything."

With a smile big enough to melt my heart, if only mine wasn't broken beyond repair, he said with a nod, "Anytime, kiddo."

The only sound in the room was the whooshwumpwhoosh sound of the fan as the blades rotated slowly above my head. I was tired, more tired than I had ever been in my life and even more so uncomfortable. No matter which side I rested on, my body protested. Vehemently. I was stitched up in several places, making it nearly impossible to lay in a way that didn't irritate one of my numerous, fresh wounds. Maybe I could do what the Conehead family did, throw the mattress against the wall and sleep standing up. But, that wouldn't work because even my feet hurt.

Whooshwumpwhoosh. Whooshwumpwhoosh. The sound might soon drive me crazy if I didn't pass out. Was I going mad? Was the whooshing and wumping actually coming from my head? I tried so hard not to focus on the day before but the madness was swallowing me, a giant black hole inside just gobbling me up - feet first. It found its way to my throat, sucking the life out of me, making it hard to breathe. With my eyes closed, I struggled with my body's instinct to fight and stayed as rigid - as still as possible.

Let it take me. Let the nothingness consume me and end the suffering, the pain, the guilt. Please, please take me away from this place.

There were hands on my throat again. My eyes flew open, heavy from sleep and dreams about spinning fans and dark places. Fingers tightened, greedily digging into my already sore and bruised skin. I sure as hell wasn't dreaming anymore.

There was a flash of a colorless male face. The feel of scratchy flannel rubbed against my chest. Pressure from two knees dug into my hips and abdomen. The smell of nicotine and sweet liquor filled the room. The taste of blood on my tongue after biting down on it made me gag. A ringing in my ears threatened to blow my eardrums. And I couldn't breathe.

The man sitting on top of me with his icy hands around my throat was not Drake. I kicked; a pathetic sort of movement that did nothing to dislodge my attacker and an even more pathetic sort of whine came out of my mouth.

This was it? This was really how I was going to die? After everything I'd been through, everything I'd seen? I was going to be killed in my bed, in the middle of the night with the fan spinning noisily above singing 'whooshwumpwhoosh' over and over?

Dark spots began to explode around me and I panicked, feeling consciousness fade away as my vision clouded over. Another glance of the man's face and I saw a strong jaw with a mouth pulled back in a sinister grin. He was enjoying it - taking my life. Releasing my frantic grip on his hands, I jabbed a thumb into his left eyeball and then pinched the inside of his right arm as hard as I could. With a painful grunt quickly followed by a startled cry, the man's hands were gone and my lungs inflated, sucking air in with ravenous need.

I was *so* wrong. In that moment, as I lay gasping for air, I knew I was wrong - maybe my life was worth fighting for. And fight I did.

For just a second I was worried I had swallowed my tongue - I couldn't feel it, my mouth was swollen and doing a bang up job of sucking oxygen in as fast as I needed it, so I snorted air in and out of my nose instead, sounding not too different from an excited pig. The pressure on my hips eased slightly and I launched my torso forward, slapping my hands at anything and everything I could find. That's how it went for a minute or two - like children play fighting we slapped at each other. Eventually my brain remembered how to form a fist and I balled up a hand and nearly pulled my shoulder out of socket with a right hook to his jaw. It knocked the man off of me and I rolled away, slithering over the side of the bed onto the floor like a snake, taking a pillow and the bedside lamp with me.

Hoping Drake would hear the commotion, I pulled the small table down as well, and grabbed for the glass I used before bed. Nearly slicing the tip of my finger off, I found the broken base of the drinking cup and hurled it at the dark figure still hunched over on the bed. With a satisfying *thunk,* it struck the side of his head and for a second I saw nothing from my bedroom floor view. And then he was up and off the bed, rushing out of the room and into the hallway in a drunken stagger.

The fan was still making its whooshing-wumping droll as I sat stunned and gasping on the carpet, unable to scream, unsure of what to do. And then Drake's words came back to me, *"There was a guy that took off..."* and I knew what was going on. He was there. In the house. The man Drake saw run away from the warehouse. Seemed we were followed after all.

"Mariah," I wheezed.

୨◦ঔ

My limbs shook as I crawled around the foot of the bed, seeing no sign of any movement in the hall. Like a dog, I moved on all fours toward the door, noting the dark smear along the wooden frame left by someone's hand. Good. I had drawn blood.

The hallway was empty. And quiet. It was the kind of quiet where you know something bad is lurking nearby just waiting for the right moment to strike, just as quiet as Mariah's prison was. My ankles popped as I used the wall to stand, my slight frame suddenly feeling like the weight of a car.

"Drake...Mariah?" The words were scratchy in my throat, like broken glass lined my larynx. There was no answer, just the same no-sound response from the empty shell house.

Drake's room was closer, so I slid against the wall, upsetting picture frames from a family long dead until I reached his room. The door was wide open but there was no sign of him in the messy bed. The night allowed the slightest amount of light in through one of the windows, and along the ban of white that reached out like a finger toward me was a small pool of blood. Not enough to be fatal, but possibly enough to be missed.

Like an idiot, I had left my room without my gun. I had nothing to fight with but my two hands. Peering down the hall, I was able to see that Mariah's door was still closed so I pushed off the wall with a soft grunt and swayed back to my own room, being careful to step around the broken glass that sat pointy side up on the carpet.

The gun wasn't in the nightstand. Resisting the urge to rip my hair out in giant fistfuls, I snatched the broken glass up and padded back out into the hall, the air hot and dry in my throat. The fabric of my white shirt tightened around my chest as I heaved in and out, still struggling to get a full breath into my lungs. My cheeks flamed with heat as anger coursed through me; I was damn tired of people trying to choke me to death.

Something thumped from Mariah's room and I inched closer to her door, stepping carefully, the glass gripped so tight in my bleeding hand that I couldn't feel the cut on my finger any longer. My pulse raced, my heart thudded wildly and my stomach cramped nervously. With my hand on the brass doorknob, I put my ear to the wood, listening to the sounds within the room.

It was as if someone was repeatedly pounding on something soft. With a sharp inhale, I realized what it was. A beating. Turn the knob slowly, I kicked open the door and raised my hand above my head, ready to throw the glass at the first person who rushed me.

Drake was kneeling next to Mariah's bed, his face bleeding profusely, his arms secured behind his back. The man from my room stood over him, his arm frozen in the air while Mariah rocked herself on the bed.

"Well, look who decided to join the party," he said before bringing his fist down on Drake's face again. Blood sprayed the side of the bedspread.

"Stop!" I pleaded. My voice was shrill and damaged.

Mariah's rocking motion slowed when I spoke, but she stayed in the fetal position with her head tucked down tight. She wouldn't look up. Inside the room, the man stood up tall, turning to face me with an unwelcoming smile. His hair was shaved down almost to the scalp, making the sharp angles of his thin face stand out. He showed off a defined brow, high cheekbones and a jutting chin. His sculpted jaw line was bloodied on one side where the busted glass hit his temple. If it wasn't for the injuries and wicked glint in his eye, he could have passed for handsome.

"Come on in, have a seat," he gestured to the bed and I continued to only stare at him with my hand still ready to throw the glass. With a theatric sigh, he stepped around Drake and sat down on the edge of the bed, patting the place beside him. Still I only looked at him. "Now, now. Didn't your parents tell you in was rude to stare at people?"

With an exhale, I cleared my throat before speaking, "Who the hell are you? What do you want?"

The man laughed. It was an almost genuine laugh for someone. My eyes squinted into the darkness as the twenty-something year old shifted on the blankets, crossing his legs and patting at the mattress again.

"Come sit down and I'll fill you in," he said with a grin. White teeth glinted back at me as he tilted his head to the side, catching the starlight from beyond the open window.

"I have a better idea," I said, tightening my grip on the broken glass, "I think you should get the fuck out of my house before I split your face open."

He laughed hollowly. "*Your* house? I don't recall seeing your face smiling back at me from all those expensive picture frames on the wall."

"It's my place now. And you need to get out," I hissed. My arm was getting tired.

"You know," he stood up and turned his back to me, "I think we got off on the wrong foot. Let's start over, shall we? My name's Hunter and it seems I'm in need of a new crew thanks to you guys."

"Get out!" I screamed. At least, I tried to. My voice sounded strangled.

When he turned around with a gun in his hand, I threw the glass with all my might, which wasn't much. It struck his mouth before landing on the floor, splitting his upper lip. Stumbling into the room, I flailed at the wall until my hand found the light switch. When the room lit up, we were all temporary dazed from the glow but he was faster on his feet. With a grunt, he had his arms around my waist and lifted me off the ground effortlessly. My body bounced onto the bed and his fist pounded into the side of my head three times before all went black.

CHAPTER twenty-three

The faintest trace of carpet deodorizer was the first conscious thing I noticed. That and the throbbing ache that came from the side of my head. It was hard to straighten my legs for some reason and moving my hands sent pain up my arms. Something scratchy tightened around my wrists every time I moved a centimeter.

"Riley."

"Mmm."

"Riley. Open your eyes."

"Connor...?"

I followed the gentle sound of his voice with my head, opening my eyes as prompted, even though the sunlight amplified the painful humming in my brain. Drake's battered face stared back at me. He wasn't my Connor. It was impossible to see what his expression was buried beneath the bloody cuts and bruises but his eyes said enough. There was sadness and pain there.

"Drake?" I struggled to right myself but my body wouldn't cooperate.

"You okay?"

"I can't move." With my eyes closed the pain was almost worse.

"Riley, we don't have much time," he said, waiting for me to look at him once more. When my eyes were open again, he nodded at the bed. We were still in Mariah's room but she wasn't there.

"Where is she?"

"He took her. Riley, this is *bad.*"

We looked at each other. Both of us having so much to say but not knowing where to start. The realization that I wanted to know more about Drake before we died overwhelmed me and question after question cramped my already swollen brain. *Where are you from? Did you have a family? Were you a dad? A good lover? What's your favorite song? Your favorite food? Are you a cake or pie person? Beach or mountains? What do you like to read? Do you read? Who are you? Who are you really?*

He spit onto the carpet - a globby mix of blood and saliva. The shirt he slept in was soaked in a scarlet color along the bottom. "Your stitches," I said.

"Least of my problems, don't you think?" He tried to smile but his puffy lips barely moved.

It was rope that was tied around my wrist and ankles, that's why I couldn't move. I had a burning rash on my skin where the rough cord rubbed me raw. *Hog-tied.* The bastard had tied me up like an animal. The only thing I could do was roll on my stomach from one side to the other.

"You need to get that glass, cut the ropes," he said, nodding his head toward the bed.

"I can't move, Drake," I said through gritted teeth.

"I'm tied to the fucking bed frame, Riley, I can't get it," he hissed.

And so began my roll across the room. It might have been funny under other circumstances, but my hips hurt from digging into the floor and my limbs objected every time I attempted to flip myself over like a fish on the shore. After a series of ungraceful revolutions, I opted to squirm along the floor on my side, using my toes to dig into the carpet fibers for leverage.

The glass lay on its side, just under the foot of the bed, waiting patiently for me. My bad shoulder creaked like an old tree branch as I scooted myself closer to what was left of the cup, dragging my body almost the length of the bed before feeling the cool glass touch my finger-tips. I imagined myself in a horror flick as I fumbled with the jagged base, rotating it to fit into my hand securely. In a scary movie, I would be able to slice through the rope with ease just in time to get away from the attacker. But it wasn't a movie and using the bottom of a busted drinking glass slippery with my own blood to cut through one inch of rope was a lot harder than I thought it would be. Several minutes passed, and the rope had barely begun to fray when I noticed movement in the far corner of the room. The surprise caused me to jerk backwards, knocking the glass out of my hand. I wiggled around on my side to get a better view of whatever it was that shared the room with us.

Hovering in the empty corner was a dark, pulsating mass. It shimmered slightly before taking the oily shape of a man. Its gloomy color stood out against the pale yellow of the painted walls like a dark water stain.

With my eyes shut tightly, my head collapsed to the floor as I moaned, *"No, no, no...no...not now, please not now."*

"What?" Drake snapped, "Did you drop it? Pick it up!" And then seconds later, "Oh shit!"

There's only so fast one can move with their hands and feet bound behind them along carpeting, but I gave it my best, getting maybe four feet before the shadow was standing just beside me. A feeling of cool foreboding covered me like a wool blanket, pushing me down into the floor, pinning me in place.

"Go away!" I cried into the ground. Like a child, I hope that if I couldn't see it, it wouldn't be real. If I didn't look at it, maybe it would leave.

Voices, small and rushed, echoed around the room in a chaotic chorus. The vibrations of sound tickled my ear canals. It was the sounds of the lost - wanting to be heard. I yelped as the bed moved beside me and still I refused to open my eyes. I knew the shadow man was still there, standing somewhere next to me, I could feel his sorrow, his anger and pain radiating out into the room like a toxic gas.

It could have been an earthquake but the bed was the only thing that bounced around the room. So violent was the shaking that the feet of the metal frame actually lifted off the floor more than once, causing my forehead to bounce against the thick carpet with soft little thumps. And still I did not open my eyes.

When a banging shook the closed bedroom door from the outside accompanied by shouting and cursing, I finally looked to see if our intruder was letting himself into the room or not. The doors had no locks on them but the handle rattled in place as if stuck. Our attacker continued to scream while the bed shimmied one final time, settling against my back a good foot away from the wall. The erratic bouncing of the bed was all the leverage needed for Drake to slip his ropes out from under the frame.

The voices stopped. The shadow man drifted over my trembling feet, hovering only a moment before it faded back into the yellow corner as if passing through the wall and then Drake's hands were on me, fumbling clumsily along my wrists. At first, I thought he was trying to free me, but realized it was the glass he was searching for.

When the bedroom door finally flew open, Drake launched himself forward with the busted glass held tightly in both hands, the cords of his muscles bulging from both arms and brought it down into the startled younger man's chest before the two catapulted into the hallway out of my view. Too afraid to move, I listened to the muffled cries and grunts of fighting as the struggle moved further away. A piece of wooden furniture fell over - most likely the small decorative table at the top of the stairs and picture frames flew off the wall. After an eerie silence, the crunch of breaking glass being stepped on made me flinch.

"Do it!" a male voice bellowed.

After a slight pause there was a loud, wet crack, like something was split open and then - nothing. Someone was still alive though - I could hear their raspy breathing.

"Drake?"

No answer. Then someone from the hall rustled around a bit and thumped against a wall. Arching my back to loosen the rope behind me, I shifted my legs, rolling to my side and then upright. With my shoulders pulled back, I crawled forward on my knees until the hall came into view.

Mariah stood over a body with an antique brass bookend in one hand. When our eyes met, she dropped it to the floor where it made a solid thud before falling over. Blood splatter had sprayed the lower half of her naked legs in the shape of a rainbow. But there wasn't a pot of gold at the end of this one. Just a broken skull leaking its contents.

"What'd you do?" I whispered.

"What I told her to." A breathy answer came from the slumped figure by the wall.

She grinned at me and nodded, her gums bleeding where a tooth had been knocked out. Though she had showered the day before, her hair was still a ratty mess and standing naked in the hall she looked every bit the definition of crazy.

"He's dead," she laughed, "I killed him. He's dead...*dead-dead-dead-dead-dead,*" she cooed and giggled. The hairs on the back of my neck stood up at the sound.

"Mariah. Mariah, can you help me?" I asked, trying to keep my voice calm.

She froze, her face stuck in a manic grin, her bloody slobber drooling from the corner of her mouth. "Help? Yes, *yes-yes-yes*, Mariah can help you," she said quietly with a series of brisk nods.

No. That was the answer to my question from the day before. Mariah wasn't going to come back from the Hell she'd been thrown into.

She was lost forever.

⊱◈⊰

I dressed in jeans and a long sleeve top, pulling a thin denim jacket over my shirt so my cuffs stuck out at the wrists. In the last few days, I had lost another five pounds or so, as was evident by the way my pants hung from my hips again. Even with swollen and injured joints, my body swam in my clothing. After tugging on socks and shoes and pulling my hair back for a braid, I walked through the room taking a mental image of the supplies I managed to stock up on. There wasn't much, but now that I was leaving, I realized I didn't want to take any of it with me.

After fidgeting with the strap around my thigh where a new knife was tied in place, I used the restroom and splashed my face with cold water before smoothing back the loose strands of my hair. *Water.* All I wanted to pack was water.

When I stepped out into the hall, the body of the boy who was once ruggedly handsome was still sprawled out on his back on the floor. He was probably a football star at one time, voted best smile or most likely to succeed by his high school class and there he was, dead on the top landing of someone else's house, head crushed in by a sculpted *Rodin* book end. Amazing how the choices you make can determine not only your fate, but also the fate of those around you. As I stepped over the towel I draped over his face a few hours before, I caught sight of his closely cropped brown hair and had the sudden urge to feel it.

Squatting above him, I ran my hand along the top of what was left of his head, feeling the downy hair prickle my skin. His scalp was almost room temperature. Not that long before he had been just a kid and in only a year, he morphed into a local thug - the worst kind of urban monster there was. Taking what he could from those who lost everything. I wouldn't miss him.

"He's not coming back, you know."

Startled by the sound of Drake's voice, I looked up to find him leaning against his open doorway, a full backpack draped over one shoulder and a clean shirt dangling from his hand.

"I don't *want* him to come back. It's just," I looked back down at the boy; Hunter Mariah said his name was. "I can imagine him being a nice kid before all this. And look what he became."

"Yeah, well, tragedy brings out the worst in some people."

"What has it brought out in us?" I stood up as he pushed out of the doorway and walked toward me.

Moving a loose section of hair off my face, he let his hand linger for a second too long on my cheek before dropping it back to his side. "Well, in your case, nothing bad."

I shook my head in disagreement. There was nothing good left in me.

"Riley. *Riley*, look at me," he shoved his hands in his pockets and I wondered if it was to keep from touching me again. "You know that dark survivor cloud that's hovering above us, just drowning us in shadows? Well, you can see my cloud and we can both see Mariah's. But *you*," he leaned closer and lowered his voice, "I can't see your cloud, though I know it's gotta be up there somewhere." After he smiled, he walked away. I listened to him take the stairs down two at a time and not till he got to the bottom did I let my eyes water up.

⚬⚬

Mariah shaved her head. While changing and washing my face, she took the clippers Drake used to trim his hair and removed the guard, shaving her hair clean off. The torn patches of skin from her time as a captive stood out more but without hair, her head had a smoother, universal look to it. She stood in the kitchen all smiles, dumping miscellaneous food items and bottled water into a backpack she found in the guest bedroom closet. She smelled of fresh sunscreen and lavender body wash.

"I'm so excited, I can't wait!" she gushed to Drake. He stood on the other side of the counter, picking the chocolate chips out of a bowl of mixed nuts. "Is there snow up there? In the mountains? I love the snow. I *really* want to see some snow. It's been cold enough. Might as well have snow if it's going to be cold, you know?"

"Hi," I said as I entered the room.

"Oh, Riley, are you ready, can we *go* now?"

"I'm ready," I said to Mariah.

Drake lifted his eyebrows at her as she struggled with the pack zipper. "Here, let me help. Why don't you go get some shoes on, okay?" I asked.

"Shoes, oh, I don't have any." Her smile was plastered to her face like it was stenciled on.

"There's some shoes by the door for you, but if they don't fit well, we can stop somewhere along the way and pick up a new pair. Okay?"

She bounded out of the room with a nod, the cuffs of my jeans skimming the ground even though they were folded up her legs. From behind, she looked like a malnourished thirteen-year-old boy.

"Better keep an eye on that one," Drake said over my shoulder before following her into the living room.

With a sigh, I joined them, my hand fingering the small metal object that rested in my pocket. Mariah pulled her socks on and then pushed both feet into a pair of canvas shoes I grabbed while at the mall with Drake. She wiggled her toes inside them and held a foot up for me to see.

"They're a little big. I'll definitely need another pair, because these are just a tad too big…*see?*" She wiggled her foot again and I smiled. Mariah was teetering closer to the brink of insanity than I had *ever* been. It put things in perspective.

For instance, I knew looking at Mariah that I had someone to take care of again and I couldn't fail her, not a second time. Which meant I had to take her back to the group. Even though they weren't *her* family, they were the closest thing to a family that *I* had. She would fit in. *Eventually.*

"Are you sure you aren't coming back here?" I asked Drake as we walked out the front door and stopped on the front steps.

"Nothing will bring me this way again," he turned around to look at me, "I told you I'd see you back, but remember what I said, I'm not staying."

In a mock salute, I brought my bandaged hand up and watched the two of them follow the walkway to the sidewalk. When they got there, Drake turned around to see me still standing on the top step.

"What's wrong? Did you forget something?" he asked.

"Yeah. Give me just a second."

But I hadn't forgotten anything. I stepped back inside and walked up the stairs to the rooms at the back of the house. Inside the one I spent the last month in, I took a good look around, my eyes settling on the gauzy and expensive curtains. My fingers found the small metal tin in my pocket and removed it, flipping the top off. After dragging my thumb down the side twice, I smiled at the small fire that was born.

Touching it to the base of the curtain, I quickly stood back as the flame shot up to the ceiling, eating away at the fabric hungrily. After repeating the same process on the other window treatments and the foot of the bed, I closed the door and did the same thing in each room. Downstairs I set the kitchen curtains and the living room curtains on fire, then hunted around the couch until I produced the Swarovski crystal adorned throw pillow. I set that ablaze too and threw it onto the couch where it swiftly spread to one of the blankets. Pulling the door shut behind me, I joined the others on the sidewalk and not until we were several houses down the street did the windows start popping, exploding from the heat.

Drake knew what I did, but he didn't ask why. I thanked him silently for that. But the house had to burn. For miles, every block we walked, I stopped and went inside a home or office building and set it on fire. By the time we reached the coast, the others had joined me and it became a game of sorts. We walked, jogged, stopped to set fires and then walked and jogged some more. We even raced each other down Pacific Coast Highway during that first day, the loser getting the heaviest backpack for the next mile. We set over fifty structures on fire before nightfall.

Part of me knew that the others thought I'd lost my mind and decided to become a pyromaniac overnight. But it wasn't that. In fact, a huge chunk of me felt guilt for committing arson, but it had to be done. It was the only way to help those left behind.

Everything in the city had to burn.

CHAPTER twenty-four

Behind us, Orange County lit up the sky. An eerie terracotta glow pulsated from distant neighborhoods where flames leapt from rooftop to rooftop in a frenzied hunger. The wall of curling smoke hovering over the horizon just below the fading light of the blue sky should have been a terrifying sight but it made me feel giddy, almost delirious with joy. I was sure this was what they needed - all of them. The dead told me so. The feeling was so right that it tingled through my skin all the way into my bones leaving behind a dull ache.

Mentally buzzed but exhausted physically, we walked south on Pacific Coast Highway until the day came to a close. Mariah spent the hours mostly talking to herself and I spent the time looking for shadows. When I thought I saw something move that wasn't our reflections off the shop windows or expensive coastal homes, I would start a fire. That's how the day went as we neared the hills of Laguna Beach. But when night encroached, I stopped setting things ablaze so we would be safe overnight wherever we chose to sleep. The wind was in our favor - blowing northeast of us, but I knew that could change at any moment and send the fire nipping at our heels, which was why we stayed close to the coast.

"How about over there?"

Drake pointed to an open grass area that wasn't quite big enough to be considered an actual park. The border was overrun with bushes and palm trees but the furthest side opened up to a sandy slope. We crossed the ankle-deep grass and stood where it met the hard-packed sand, just feet away from a steep drop off. Below us, the ocean churned and bubbled, the high tide slamming repeatedly into the rocky bluff, tossing sea-spray into the air in an aquatic ballet.

"We can lay some blankets out. It's warm tonight, we don't need a fire," he said, as we stared down at the midnight-blue water.

"You don't want to sleep inside?" I pointed behind us to the row of million dollar homes with three stories. "Each of us could have our own floor for the night," I laughed.

"But it's a perfect night. Look, you can even see the stars already." Drake nodded at the sky.

Mariah bobbed her shaved head at me while tugging at her mangled ear. "Uh-huh, perfect night. It's a perfect night, I think."

"Okay. Well, let's grab something to eat then." I turned away from the edge, leaving Mariah standing there in her baggy clothes with her bruised face looking out at the water.

"Yes. Yes, a *perfect* night," she mumbled.

"What, honey?"

"A perfect night. A perfect night to go," she said to the ocean with a small laugh. As I looked back over my shoulder to ask what she meant, she took a step closer to the drop off. I froze.

"Mariah, step back honey, you're too close to the edge." She wasn't just close, she was teetering over it with several inches of her left foot dangling above at least thirty feet of open space.

She tilted her head to the side and gave me a lip-splitting grin and then her face fell, taking on a more somber expression. Her brown eyes were large and round with concern, "Riley, did I thank you?"

With the booming sound of my blood rushing through my head competing with the crash of the ocean waves, I almost couldn't hear her. Turning, I took a step toward her, ignoring Drake's quiet warning behind me.

"Thank me for what, Mariah? You have nothing to thank me for," I said with a cautious smile.

She shook her head before nodding so vigorously it made me dizzy. "I do, I do. You found me you came to find me. You saved me, you know. Thanks, Riley. Thanks for *saving* me," she said. The delicate frame of her body shook as she let out an empty laugh.

For a brief moment, the muscles of my shoulders that had hardened into tight knots relaxed. She wasn't going to jump, she was grateful to be alive still. I could see it on her face. There was joy there - a little crazed and psychotic, sure, but it was still elation for life. The salty moisture of the water drifted with the wind and whipped at my hair and I pushed my loose bangs out of my eyes in irritation.

With an outstretched hand, I said calmly, "Come on, Mariah, let's go."

Her smile was warm enough to melt a hole into my heart. *"Yes. It's time to go,"* she whispered.

And then she leapt.

With her arms out like a bird, she jumped into the air and almost floated on the cool breeze before falling like a stone. The only sound was my scream as the wind pushed it back into my face and made me choke on it. Drake's arms firmly wrapped around my waist and I struggled to get free, to get to the edge of the bluff, to see if she was okay. After dropping to the ground and crawling across the sand, I dug my nails into the hard earth as tears poured from my eyes, screaming her name against the assaulting air current that pushed against me with invisible hands.

Mariah's body was face down, caught in the jagged rocks at the base of the bluff. Her hands floated at her sides in the white water that was quickly turning pink around her. As I watched through my tears, with Drake's fingers hooked into the waistband of my jeans, the waves quickly lifted her limp form and gobbled her up into the surf. She was gone in seconds. The only sign she had ever been there was a solitary shoe that floated on the water for a few minutes before it became too waterlogged, sinking in submission to the ocean floor.

Shaking with pain and anger, I screamed at the waves that devoured Mariah up as if there was nothing to it, like she was just another piece of debris to be pulled out to sea by the unyielding currents. My hands pawed furiously at the side of the drop off like the crumbling ridge was a giant remote and all I had to do was find the rewind button.

"No! Why?!" I screamed at the fading day, *"Why'd you do this?"*

"Riley," Drake dragged me away from the edge by my kicking legs and pulled me hard against his chest while speaking soothingly into my ear, *"Sssh. She's gone.* She's been gone, Riley, you have to let her go."

"No! *No!* Why would she do this? *Why?* Connor and Kris. Sunny and Foxy. All those men," I blubbered, "Drake, Jesus - all those men, they're all gone because of her. *Because of her!* Why would she do this?"

"Don't do that to yourself," he said softly against my ear. But I didn't hear him. It was all for nothing, just like I had feared. She cost me everything. *Everything.*

"Why?!" I sobbed, the scream catching in my throat.

"You saw her, Riley. She's been gone a long time. Some people-," his voice hitched and he cleared his throat before continuing, "I think some people can't be saved. But you gave her freedom. You *did* save her, Riley."

I shook my head against him, hitting his cheek with mine and still he didn't pull away. My mouth was full of the sandy and salty air and I spit it out with disgust. Sitting in Drake's lap, I stared at the spot just above my left foot, where the sun was dipping below the Pacific horizon. It dropped lower every time I blinked, like a shimmering gold diamond in the sky. Even after it was gone, the sunset stretched out above our heads like a quilt; warm bubble gum pinks bled into deep ambers that reminded me of the fire burning in the north. Breathing heavily, I looked up the coast where we came from, seeing nothing but a black outline of angry smoke above the land. *How ironic.* Not that long ago I imagined throwing *myself* off a cliff like this - my last kiss being with the crashing waves of the ocean and yet here I was still fighting to live. *How fucking ironic.* Drake lifted me off the ground, turned my body away from the sea, and led me through the deep grass and across the street into a glass-walled house. After settling down on the couch, I stared at all the windows. Floor to ceiling, the glass was cloudy from salt and calcium buildup and my last thought of the day was imagining the popping and cracking sound all that glass would make in the morning as the house exploded in a giant fireball.

I'll burn it. I'll burn it all to the ground and let the ashes float like snowflakes into the Ocean where Mariah rested. She said she loved the snow. I'll burn it all...for her.

We stood too close, but even though my eyes stung, my cheeks burned, and my lips were drying out from the heat, we didn't move. The windows cracked before imploding and then the glass rained down in front of us in jagged shards from the force of the roiling fireball inside the home that spit and shrieked in anger. As it leapt outside an upstairs window, the embers caught on the neighboring roof. In ten minutes seven houses were burning. Only then did we leave, but not on foot.

As Drake stood with his gloved hands resting on his thighs, straddling the shiny silver and black Ducati we hauled out of a nearby private garage, I shook my head. If Connor could only see me, what would he say? Surely, it would be something along the lines of 'I told you so'. Drake knocked on the top of my black helmet and I gave him the thumbs-up sign before climbing on behind him. It was such an intimate way to travel; one person molded into the back of another. With my inner thighs pinned against his legs and my arms secured around his fit midsection, taking care not to rub against his sutures, I held on tight as the tires squealed against the asphalt as we took off.

Drake eased us through the cramped streets with ease, slowing when necessary but for the most part keeping the speed over twenty miles an hour. When we hit clear patches of road, he would open the throttle and propel us forward like a bullet. Every hour we stopped to look for water, fuel and to set a fire, of course. The smell of smoke followed us, but I ignored the shift in the wind and enjoyed the ride.

A few times, I imagined that Drake was Connor and squeezed his chest, or rested my chin on his shoulder. But everything about him was different. I didn't want Drake as a lover - just as a friend. And his words echoed in my head - the declaration that he wasn't going to stay with us in the mountains. Sure, we had bled together, we had killed together and slept next to each other, but it was unclear how much of a friend Drake considered me.

Nearly five hours on the road and we reached Oceanside. Not long after, Drake followed my directions and went east on the 78. It was the way I came with Connor and Kris, it was the way I wanted to return. What took us days to travel on horseback was covered in mere hours on the bike. Except the air was cooler and the scenery was backwards as we steadily worked our way out east. We didn't dare start a fire in the countryside, but the lighter in my pocket itched to be used every mile the bike ate up. After stopping at a corner gas station and chugging down warm bottles of soda, we refueled with the help of a hose and I rifled through the dusty office, shoving a piece of paper and a large marker into Drake's backpack.

Our lunch consisted of stale cheese crackers and bruised apples we found that had fallen off the tree and rolled down the long sloped yard of a nearby residence. When Drake put his helmet on a peek of his brown hair showed at the base of his neck and the only way I could tell he was smiling was that the skin around his eyes crinkled softly.

"What?" I asked, before shoving my helmet on. It was still warm from the long morning ride. I secured my braid into the back of my jacket, shoving it as far beneath the collar as my hair would allow.

He shook his head, causing a glint of sunlight to reflect off his visor and temporarily blind me. "Nothin', I was just thinking," he said with a muffled voice.

"About what?"

"Just. I don't know. This has been a fun ride."

I cocked my head to side and studied him. He was still smiling, his eyes proved that, but I couldn't figure out what he meant. "You're actually having *fun*?"

"Aren't you?"

Was I? Everything around me was still; no breeze rustled the trees or the weeds that sprouted out of the split sidewalks, no creatures chirped or chittered, it was as if nature itself wanted to know if I was indeed having a good time. The windows of the building stared at me with large, open eyes, waiting for my answer. All the circumstances of the previous days, weeks and months should have made me miserable but it was true - the ride *was* fun. The fresh air pelting my neck as the bike charged up the hills was invigorating. Sort of like a cleanse.

"I shouldn't be," I said guiltily.

Drake's smile must have vanished because the lines around his eyes smoothed out instantly. With a curt nod, he gestured to the bike and we both straddled the monster. "Let's get on with it," he yelled over the roar of the engine.

With a tap of his shoulder and a hand signal to stop, Drake pulled off the highway onto the shoulder just before Horizon View

Drive. He tugged his helmet off his head and swiped his sleeve over his sweaty brow. One difference between men and women is that men could make sweat look sexy. With my hair plastered to my face, I felt grimy and not in the least appealing, not that it mattered. The sun had passed over us hours before and long shadows from the manzanita and oak trees stretched out across the highway.

"Hold this? I'll be right back," I said after tossing my helmet into his lap. He called after me as I ran up the hillside but the words were drowned out by the vibrating sound of the idling bike.

There it stood, tall and sun-bleached. The barn that we slept next to on our first night out with the horses stood tall above the highway. It was hard to miss as you drove by. This was where Connor said he could live one day, even though there was nothing spectacular about the scenery. The dead grass crunched beneath my shoes as I approached it, unfolding the paper from the gas station. Inside the barn, just next to the sliding door was a bulletin board. After prying some of the rusted thumbtacks out of the cork, I rounded the barn to the side that faced the road below and tacked the paper to the rough wood.

In thick, black strokes, I wrote my first letter since finding the lodge the year before. After finishing, I stepped back to look at the bright white sheet against the maroon color of the barn. The smoothness of the paper looked out of place against the cracked paint and I squinted in the light to read the words one final time.

Connor and Kris,

You won't read this but I had to tell you how sorry I am that I lost you. Wherever you ended up after leaving this place, please look for Mariah there so she isn't alone anymore. I hope I find you in my dreams.

I love you…so much. - Riley

CHAPTER twenty-five

Once we left Ramona, an anxiety built up inside me that was impossible to ignore. *What was I going to say to the others? How would I explain what happened to Connor and Kris when I didn't know that answer myself?* They weren't in the warehouse from what I saw, and there was no sign of the other horse either. But Connor would *never* have just left me there. He would have searched until he found me. Which meant only one thing - they were dead.

The bike roared up the mountains with ease and soon we were surrounded by the pine trees of Julian. The tall and bushy conifers felt like home. The smell was so different there than anywhere else. Fresh air, heavy with the scent of pine, sap and earth saturated my senses. The town of Julian looked the same as it did the last time I passed through, except for a few deep and wide puddles in the gutters. Too nervous to stop and prolong the inevitable, we continued on the 79 until it met with Sunrise Highway.

It was as if I had been gone for years instead of months - that's how much I craved the peaceful solitude of Mt. Laguna. The din of the motorcycle echoed loudly around the summits creating a dull reverberation through the trees that sounded less like the purr of the expensive bike and more like a dying tractor. A few times since we passed through Ramona the engine hum morphed over the valleys, coming back slower and more propeller-like, but there were houses and rocks and water for the sound to bounce off of, distorting the sound. Plus, we had our helmets on and the drone of the bike beneath me was the loudest noise of all. With one arm comfortably hooked around Drake's chest, I held onto the side of my seat with my free hand and looked out at the passing trees. As the sun ran away toward the coast, it stole the light of day from us and replaced it with a cool, steel sky. The stars multiplied by the hundreds every time I glanced up and just before the last rays of light disappeared beyond the forest the lodge sign came into view.

Drake pulled off the asphalt after I squeezed his shoulder and pointed to the right. He took the drive slow, easing the tires around potholes loosened up from a recent rainstorm, being careful not to run over the disturbed rocks or small branches that had fallen out of the encroaching trees. When the remnants of the main house came into view, he came to a stop and he eased the bike toward a cluster of burnt roof beams. Without waiting for him, I dismounted and yanked the helmet off, letting it fall to the ground as I jogged toward the lawn. Summer had finally gotten the better of the grass, replacing it with an ugly brown color, leaving funky green bunches every ten feet or so. It still looked beautiful to me though.

"Riley, wait up!" Drake called from behind me.

I stopped in the middle of the lawn, almost underneath the branches of the great oak that was centered there. An image of Connor sleeping beneath the tree and Fin taking me down the trail where the greenhouse used to be came back. With a slow blink, the memory faded. It was just a tree again. Cold air pricked at the exposed parts of my skin with curiosity, as if the mountain air was feeling me out and saying; *I know you, welcome back.*

Pieces of hay still lay scattered about the base of the fence post by the Recreation building, as they were waiting around for a wind strong enough to relocate them to somewhere else. It looked like a horse hadn't been there since we left several weeks before. Even though I knew it was too good to be true, part of me still ached when I realized Foxy hadn't made her way back with Connor and Kris.

Drake caught up with me just before I reached the trail, still peeling the gloves off his hands. "Were you planning on leaving me with the bike, or something?"

"No, sorry. I just need to know. I need to know if they're here." I breathed heavily, picking up the pace as the narrow dirt trail began to slope downwards toward the lake.

"*Where* are we going?" he asked from behind me.

Halfway down the trail, I stopped to whistle loudly and Drake bumped into me, knocking me off balance and into the trunk of a tree. "Damn," I said, brushing loose pieces of bark off my shirtsleeve. A glint twinkled in the distance between two pines and my heart leapt at the sight of it. *The lake.*

"Sorry, what'd you stop for?" Drake flicked a sappy cluster of pine needles off my shoulder with a smile.

"Shush, listen," I answered. When my call wasn't returned with a familiar bark, I whistled again. "That's...odd."

"Huh?"

"My dog. She's not answering me." I rushed back down the trail, Drake mumbling something behind me and when we reached the bend that took us toward the lake, we could see the cabin tops.

Not sure what to expect, I simply stood before them, looking at each for signs of life behind the windows and finding none. The fireplaces were unlit, the doors all closed, the curtains drawn. I saw the cabins like that once before - when Connor and I first arrived to find only Fin living there. *The cabins were empty.*

"No," I gasped. Drake put a hand on my shoulder and I shrugged it off so hard the muscle in my neck cramped. "They wouldn't. They *wouldn't* leave me."

"Maybe something happened. Um, maybe they found a safer place?"

I sent a disgusted look at Drake, "Ana's pregnant, they wouldn't just *move*, Drake."

"Okay, well, go knock. Maybe they are just... I don't know, hiding out in there or something. The bike is not exactly quiet you know. They could've heard us coming."

Right. But Zoey would be barking. She knew my whistle. Even though I'd been gone awhile, she wouldn't have forgotten my call. Plus, the more I thought about it, the more I realized some of the vehicles might have been missing.

"Stay here in case someone's inside, okay?"

He nodded and kicked at the dirt, looking bored with a snarky expression on his face. Of course, this was all a monumental waste of his time and he couldn't wait to be rid of me so he could move on to bigger and better things. Like eating beans out of a can in some rest stop off the freeway.

All of the cabin doors were locked - even mine. After peering inside the front door through a gap in the curtain, I saw nothing out of the ordinary. It didn't look any different from the way we left it, but I hadn't exactly taken a mental picture of the place on my way out the door.

"Where would they have gone?" I asked my reflection in the glass.

Nothing was broken, damaged or missing. The water spigot on the side of the porch came on, releasing cool, clean water when I turned the valve. The small makeshift greenhouse behind the cabin was teeming with greens and ripe tomatoes. There was shelter, water and food, but no *people*.

"Where the *hell* did they go?" I demanded an answer from the empty air but only got my bangs blown into my eyes in response.

"Riley? What do you want to do?" Drake followed me to the back of the cabin and kicked a loose rock out in front of him. It bounced down the dirt slope that led to the edge of the lake but didn't quite reach the water.

Reflections of the sunset danced along the ripples, drawing my eyes out to the center of the lake where the pinks and purples merged in and out of each other. I wanted to float there, just forget about everything and everyone and float for a while. When I opened my mouth to tell Drake I didn't know - I didn't know what to do, something in the tree line on the far side of the lake moved. At first, I closed my eyes. If it was Fin, I didn't want to see him.

"Well, look at that!"

Tentatively, and with my teeth biting down on my lower lip I opened my eyes. Standing tall and proud in a slick brown coat was our deer. I hadn't seen her in months, so long in fact that earlier in the summer we thought she might have left the mountains or been taken down by a starving cougar. Yet there she was. And not alone. She had a mate, a strong looking buck that couldn't have been much older. She flicked her ears at me, her way of saying hello and I returned the gesture with a slow raise of one arm. That was our greeting. A subtle flick and a gentle wave. She grazed nonchalantly, as if that was her purpose for being at the edge of the lake but I knew it wasn't. Curiosity had brought her there. Maybe it was her way of telling us that she had found a love of her own, and that she was going to be okay.

When they trotted off, I turned to find Drake eying me. "So, what…are you the deer whisperer now?"

"No. We're family."

꧁ঐ꧂

"You sure it's okay, crashing on the couch?" Drake murmured from behind an empty tumbler. His breath smelled of whiskey vapor and chocolate chips. Only three drinks in and he was sleepy. After taking the glass from his limp hand and setting it down on the coffee table, I dropped a folded blanket on his lap.

"It's been a long day, Drake. Just crash here. We'll figure out what to do tomorrow."

"I already told you, I can't stay...'member?"

"Yeah, you've said that twice tonight already. Just get some sleep, we'll figure things out later."

Before shutting off all the lights and locking the front door, I picked his shoes up, set them under the coffee table, and put his glass into the sink. The place felt so familiar but also foreign. Connor wasn't there. Kris wasn't there. Zoey wasn't there. My body ached and as I used the wooden banister to pull myself upstairs, I was already unbuttoning my jeans in anticipation of the longest bath possible. With one foot on the top landing and the other in mid-step, I froze.

"I think I'm out of bubble bath."

꧁ঐ꧂

The shampoo bubbles didn't last nearly long enough and after adding warm water twice, I got tired of listening to the gurgling noise of the overflow every time the water sloshed above the drain lever. Pissed off and exhausted, I kicked my way out of the tub leaving the bathmat soaked, and toweled off roughly over the parts of my body that weren't stitched, gently patting the areas that were, leaving my hair stringy and dripping onto the floor as I padded over to the dresser. If Win was there he would have chastised me for bathing with fresh stitches, but there was no way I was going to bed without soaking my sore muscles.

Ignoring the blip-blip-blip sound of water falling onto the carpet I pulled out a clean pair of everything and sifted around in the lowest drawer that Connor used for his sleep shirts. Rubbing the towel against my head once more, I untangled most of the knots from my hair with my fingers and twisted the whole mess back into a high bun. The reflection in the mirror said I looked to be thirty-something but the aches in my body, the swelling in my joints and every torn muscle laughed. I *felt* more like ninety.

The bed was large and familiar but unwelcoming. Not ready to climb beneath the cool covers alone, there was nothing else to do than go back downstairs and pour white wine into the largest drinking container available. Halfway down the steps there was a commotion in the living room. A heavy item slammed against a wall, there was a squeal then a shout, something fragile shattered onto the ground, someone cursed but a dog bark boomed loudest of all.

"Zoey!" I screamed from the stairs, leaping over the last step and sliding a good twelve inches in my socked feet along the slick wood at the base of the stairs.

Though the lower level of the cabin was still dark, I could see her small form shoot across the living room. Her excited whimpers matched my cries as she jumped and wriggled and licked while I pet and hugged and kissed.

"Riley!" There was that squeal again. But by then I recognized it.

Someone tripped over a table and Drake's baritone voice cracked as he shouted, *"Get the hell off me, man!"*

"It's okay, he's with me!"

A light flickered on from the corner where the floor lamp rested on its side. Two end tables and the ceramic lamp near the front door had been knocked over. Shiny orange shards lay scattered out toward the sofa where several sets of shoulders protruded. Kris stood in the center of the room, her hands held up to her face in shock. A baby-like cry came from her before she ran into my arms, knocking the breath out of me.

"I-I can't believe it, you're *okay*." My hand shook against the back of her head, mimicking the waver in my voice. She smelled of sweet pea and pears - her favorite body wash.

Kris cried into my shoulder. It was an ugly, gut-wrenching cry that hurt my heart. "We thought you were dead, you *looked* dead," she sobbed.

So. They *did* leave me behind. Suddenly my mouth was parched, sucked entirely dry of moisture. It took two attempts to unstick my tongue from the roof of my mouth. "I'm fine. Look," I gently tilted her chin up with one finger, "I'm fine. Are you guys okay?"

Kris nodded, refusing to let go. For a moment, it was just the two of us in the room. And then Drake's voice bellowed out from the floor beneath a pile of struggling bodies.

"Guys! Guys, *stop*, he's with me!" Kris kept her arms wrapped around my waist even while I crossed the room and leaned over the side of the couch where Jacks, Skip and Winchester fought to keep Drake pinned to the ground.

"Jesus!" he yelled as the three men slowly clamored off the couch where he had fallen asleep.

"Sorry, are you okay? Drake?"

"Fucking peachy," he rubbed at his shoulder before standing up, "Your friends here really know how to introduce themselves. Could have given me a heart attack, jumping on me in my sleep like that. *Damn.*"

Jacks glowered at him with his feet spread wide apart, his hands held stiffly at his sides. He looked like he wanted to rip Drake limb from limb.

Skip broke the awkward silence first, "It's damn good to see you kiddo." We hugged tightly before Winchester squirmed between us and lifted me off my feet.

"Riley, I'm so happy you're home!" he said before setting me down and kissing my cheek. It was so out of character for him that I almost wiped the kiss away like I had seen him do so many times before.

"Jacks," I said softly, rounding the corner of the couch to put myself between him and the equaling unimpressed Drake. The two stood close to the same height and though Jacks had wider shoulders, which made him appear larger, I knew he couldn't compete with the sheer power of Drake's muscular build. "Jacks, this is Drake. Be nice to him, he saved my life."

He flinched but only nodded before licking his lips and kissing the top of my head. I spun around and waved at the room, "This is my family, Drake. Kris, Skip and Win. Even Jacks over there."

The spot was empty where he'd been standing and as I panned the room Kris made her strangled cry again. Except the sound wasn't coming from *her*. She stood next to me with her hand hooked into the pocket of my sweats and the cry I heard was coming from the doorway where Jacks had moved. He bent down toward the ground and lifted something with care before settling it into the crook of his arm. At first, it looked like a blanket balled up and ready for the laundry hamper but then a tiny foot poked out of the bottom.

With a gasp, my hands flew up to my mouth. "Oh my God! Jacks!"

His angry demeanor dissolved as he held the squirming bundle out to me. "Riley, meet baby Lily."

Gently, and with careful attention spent on making sure I was properly supporting the baby's head, Jacks transferred her into my arms. At first, she was just a colorful blurry blob through my tears but eventually my eyes dried. There in my arms, was a beautiful newborn baby girl with a full head of dark hair and even darker brown doe eyes that stared sleepily up at me. I counted her fingers; long and slender with carefully trimmed nails, and counted her toes, just as dainty and expertly groomed. She had that baby smell that I remembered from my own two children, sweet, fresh and brand-new. For months I had loathed the day she was born, as if it would remind me of my own lost babies and wreck my heart, destroying me in the process. But the opposite happened.

"Jacks," I whispered, *"Lily's beautiful. She's perfect."* I looked up at him to see his own eyes swimming in tears but he swallowed and blinked and they never had a chance to spill onto his cheeks.

"She is. She's amazing."

"I love her name. I can't believe you and Ana finally agreed on one," I laughed.

It was something they argued about every time it came up - what to name the baby. She had a notebook with dozens of names, none of which Jacks liked, of course. I didn't remember Lily being on the list.

"Um," Winchester cleared his throat but Jacks waved a hand at him and he stopped talking.

"You two did a good job, she's just beautiful. Where's Ana? I need to compare faces to see whose nose she has," I paused to coo at the baby, "Because she doesn't have yours, thank God."

"She's not here, Riley."

"Right. Where did everyone go? The entire lodge was abandoned, you know anyone could have come in and claimed it," I said everything in a happy voice as I smiled down at Lily while using my knee to gently push Zoey off my leg. She sniffed at the blanket like a treat was hidden inside.

"No, Riley. That's *not* what he means," Winchester sighed. One of Kris's arms curled around my waist again and she buried her face into my shoulder like a small child.

"Did she...leave?" I stared between Winchester and Jacks in shock. Surely Ana wouldn't abandon a newborn child. The woman was no saint, but she had a heart in there somewhere. For the first time since riding Foxy, I looked down at my wrist where she tied the bracelet onto my arm. It was gone, most likely torn off when I rolled through the bushes and dirt after being shot off the horse.

"She's dead, Riley. She...she died just after delivering Lily," Winchester dropped his gaze and lowered his voice to a whisper, *"Ana only got to hold the baby for a couple seconds."*

Jacks stepped forward as if to take Lily back but I held her to my chest and cried silently against one of her round, pink cheeks. *"Oh sweet baby, don't you worry, you will be loved more than you could ever dream."* As I rocked her in my arms, Jacks leaned into us with his arms around my shoulders. We stood like that for a moment until Kris's arms circled us, then Winchester's and finally Skip's. Huddled around the baby, we cried for what she lost and for what we found.

A new life to love. Another chance at happiness. A new beginning.

ে৯৵ঌ

"Win delivered her, can you believe that?" Jacks rocked the baby carrier with his foot and sipped out of the glass of wine I finally poured.

"I wish I could've done more," Winchester said from the couch. His face was ashen at the mention of the birth. It must have been just as traumatic for him - losing Ana.

"It wasn't your fault, you know that," Jacks turned to me, the need to explain written all over his face. "She started bleeding real bad and it all happened so fast. It doesn't matter how many books you read, you know, there just wasn't enough time. Lily came so fast we didn't even have the birthing suite ready."

"I-I should have been here. I'm so sorry, Jacks." With my hand on his arm, it was easy to feel the tension in his muscles.

Something heavy hung in the room and I knew what it was without asking. The others did too, but no one wanted to discuss it. So I blurted out another question that had been nagging me all evening.

"Where were you?"

"Shit!" Winchester jumped off the couch so fast I sloshed wine down the front of my shirt. Drake, also surprised by Winchester's loud outburst sent a dirty look in my direction.

"Riley, you are *not* going to believe who we found," he said. A buzz of energy began to fill the room as the topic switched from Ana's death to the mystery surrounding their late night return to the cabins.

"Calm down, Win, *shit.* She just got back. You look like hell, by the way. What did you do, throw yourself off another bike?" Jacks teased, nudging me with his elbow.

"No," I rubbed at my face, desperately trying not to scream out the one thing I wanted to know but was too terrified to ask. "It's a long story. I don't even know where to start."

"How about with this?" He reached out and touched the stitches that ran along my shoulder. In my tank top, I forgot how visible my injuries were. Bruises were nothing new, but stitches always had a story behind them.

I pointed to my arm and then to my hip. "Gunshot. Gunshot." I felt around my neck where the imprint of Mariah's hands left raised welts and scratches, "And this was from a brief fight - a minor misunderstanding."

With an involuntary grimace, I remembered the chopped up body parts in the room Mariah was held. I'd forever wonder if it was she or one of the men that killed the woman as Drake stormed the building. It was an answer no one would ever know.

"And...you're okay now?" Skip asked. His voice was a bit hoarser than usual and I chalked it up to having a rather emotional night.

"I'm okay now. Thanks to Drake. Like I said, it's a long story, but he found me, cleaned me up. Saved my life, really."

"And brought you back here," Kris said. Her eyes were rimmed with red, cried out and tired.

"Yes." Setting the glass down carefully on the counter, I took her hand into mine and looked at her collarbone while I said the words everyone seemed to be avoiding. "Where's Connor, Kris? Is he...did he...*not* make it?"

I couldn't look at her, even after she shook her head. "No! Well," she paused to look at Jacks, "I don't really know where he is. He tried to go back but there was so much shooting and Foxy freaked out. Connor and I barely had a chance to climb into the saddle before she took off. And...we went back that night. We did. But you were gone. And there was so much blood...so much blood..." she trailed off in sobs. With my arms wrapped around her, she let me pull her close into my chest. Her sweet pea and pear washed over me again, choking out the smell of new baby.

"You thought I was dead?" I whispered. She nodded once against my shoulder. "And Connor. What happened, how did you get back here?"

"He brought me back. But...but not on Foxy. They shot her in the leg and Connor had to...you know...he had to..." I nodded that I understood so she wouldn't have to say the words out loud. Connor had to put her down. "Anyway," she sniffed, "he had to know what happened to you. So he went back."

"What? When?"

"Weeks ago."

"Weeks? How?"

"He took his motorcycle," she sniffed again.

"Weeks," I repeated.

Where had he been for that long? How did he not find us at the house near the golf course? Connor wasn't dead. I sat stunned, leaning against the kitchen bar counter so hard that the edge dug into the skin of my back. Connor wasn't dead. Connor was alive. At least he was a few weeks ago.

"He'll come back, right? I mean, if he can't find you, he'll come back home?" Kris looked up at me with sad eyes and I nodded because that was the right answer to give her, even if everyone else in the room didn't believe it.

"Of course he'll come back." With a smile, I hugged her slight frame against mine. Kris was okay. Connor didn't die that day, he didn't abandon me - he *saved* Kris. He did the right thing bringing her back to the mountains where she was safe. I told my heart he would give up eventually and return. He'd have to. And I'd be waiting for him.

"So," Drake interrupted, tugging at the collar of his shirt as if it was suddenly too tight around his neck, "You said you found someone else. Who?"

Winchester blurted out the words before anyone else had a chance to answer, "A pilot."

Drake and I stared at each other, confused and waiting for a further explanation. Lily stirred in her seat and we all looked down at her as she sighed and flailed a hand around her face till Jacks moved it close to her mouth. She found her knuckles with her rosy *Betty Boop* lips and the only sound in the room for a full minute was a soft, repetitive suckling.

Skip smiled at Jacks and Lily and then ran a hand over his jaw. He'd aged a good five years in the few months I'd been gone. "His name is Lou and yes, he's a pilot. He's been doing flyovers in the area and spotted our chimney fire a few nights ago. He landed his plane on the freeway can you believe that? Right down there on the 8. We heard the plane fly over and turned one of the radios on. Five minutes later, we were chatting back and forth like old buddies. He came back tonight, brought a few supplies with him and we all drove down the mountain to say hello."

"Tell her the good part, tell her about Arizona." Winchester all but bounced on the arm of the couch. He seemed to be the only one that couldn't hear the wooden frame creaking out a desperate warning - one good bounce and the couch was threatening to break beneath him.

"Arizona?" Drake and I spoke at the same time.

"Yeah, he's from Arizona, from some secret community with a whole underground bunker set-up and everything. They've got enough water and supplies to last one hundred people twenty years," Jacks said.

"Wow."

"Yeah, but there's only thirty or so people there now. Lou's been picking stragglers up in his plane from all over the country. He scouts once a month."

"Really?"

"Riley, they have all kinds of people - they have a Doctor, a real Doctor and water tanks and a greenhouse system and everything you could ever need."

"A Doctor. That would be good for the baby," I said quietly.

It dawned on me why Winchester was so excited and why the others were so somber. They wanted to leave California and go to Arizona. Maybe they were preparing to do that before I came back. *Would they have left?* Something told me they would. Even with Connor out there looking for me.

"Arizona. Do you want to go?" I aimed the question at Jacks but looked around the room. Drake sat quietly with his gaze locked on me but no one else made eye contact.

"We're all alone here. And with winter on the way, how are we going to have enough food? We've got tomatoes and beans growing out back, but that's not enough for all of us. We've got a little one to think about now, too. They have a *Doctor*." Skip leaned back into the couch, looking more harried as the seconds ticked on.

The room began to shrink around me. The browns, greens and blues of the fabrics swirled together into one bright color and the walls pushed inward. I let my head fall down on the counter and pressed my forehead against the coolness of it until the room stopped spinning.

"It's been weeks, Riley. I know you're thinking about Connor, but if he didn't find you and he hasn't come back..." Jacks flinched back from me when I looked up.

"Why do you trust this Lou guy so much? What's the rush, anyway? We have plenty of time before we have to worry about the first snow."

Jacks looked over my head at Skip, who was still leaning into the couch. With a weary nod, he repeated what he already told me, "They have a Doctor, honey."

Of course. How did I miss it? Skip was sick - really sick from the look of his pale skin, sunken eyes and thinner build. He watched me walk across the room and smiled weakly as I sat on the coffee table in front of him.

"How bad is it?" I asked.

"Oh, no need to worry, dear."

"How *bad* is it?"

"Well," he sighed, "I couldn't finish my last round of chemo in December, so I imagine the cancer is having quite a field day in this old body of mine."

"Cancer." We spent so much time worrying about the dangers of our new world that we forgot about the killers of our past. Skip was dying of cancer. "Are you in pain?"

He laughed, "When you get to be my age, something always hurts."

Well, that was true. I was twenty years his junior yet could barely walk after sleeping on the ground. Even climbing out of a real bed in the mornings made my knees creak and complain. He wasn't going to tell me how bad it was - not in front of everyone.

The room did that weird shrinking thing again and I closed my eyes and imagined pushing the walls away from my body until the claustrophobic feeling faded. When I opened my eyes, I saw the glass of wine still sitting on the counter. It was entirely too far away.

"To Arizona we go, then. We're a family - we stick together. We can leave a note here for Connor. Or I can stay and wait for him."

"We won't leave you here alone," Winchester said.

"Okay. Then, I'll leave a note. I've done it before," I smiled. "When is Lou, coming back?"

"Next week," Skip sighed.

"Let's hope Connor makes it back before then."

෨ฺ෧

"Fin…" I said his name softly but the warm breeze still carried my voice into the trees behind his grave. "Are you here?"

Nothing stirred and of course - nothing answered me. With a long sigh, I sat down next to where his body rested and placed my hand on the overgrown bulge of land. A blade of grass tickled my ankle where my jeans lifted; the weeds had grown almost a foot since the last rain. Every few seconds, a gnat would fly around my mouth or nose so my hands were in a constant state of fanning the late afternoon air around my head.

"I need to know you're okay, *wherever* you are," I said. My voice was quiet and hushed. I didn't want the others to hear me talking to the grave. "You know I can't stay here with you, I can't keep seeing you every time the lights go off. I'll never recover - you'll never move on."

The only reply I got was the whistle of the wind in the tree above me. It sailed through the pine canopy like a train and I cocked my head to follow the sound all the way into the woods. Even the birds seemed to be listening to the air flowing around them. That moment when you know a storm is coming, when there is electricity in the air and your joints ache a little - that was what it felt like on top of the hill. Like a storm was building in intensity, waiting for the right moment to split open and unleash its fury on anything and everything in its way. *Was that what things had come to? Fin as the storm and me as the obstacle that was going to be swept up in its wrath?*

With a noisy grunt, I pushed up off the ground and dropped the wildflower I held in my hand on top of where Fin's body rested. "This is all I have left to give you. Move on in peace, my friend."

The wind rushed down the mountains, scattering leaves and dirt across the highway in a frenzied mess. The others had already boarded the plane, each of them with a small bag of personal belongings - two for the baby. But I stood on the shoulder with one foot on the highway asphalt and the other in the soft dirt looking to the east where the stubby manzanitas tapered off as a more desert-like landscape took over. Dawn had come and gone only an hour before and the day held promises of something new.

Lou waited inside the cockpit patiently, assuming the reason for my hesitancy was a fear of flying. It wasn't. Even when the small plane roared to life, I kept my feet planted where they were. The moment both of them were on the highway it meant I was *really* leaving California. I wasn't ready.

"Having second thoughts?" Drake said from behind me.

I shrugged. It was the right thing to do for the group but no matter how many different ways I told myself that, my heart refused to listen. "I'm not sure I'm ready."

"Will you ever be?"

I laughed. It was a hollow sound, a sarcastic laugh. *"No."*

Drake looked back at the plane as the men inside laughed about something. "Win and Jacks…are they like, a couple?"

"What? Why would you think that?" I blinked at him.

He shrugged. "Win follows that man around like a puppy. And he stares at his ass a lot. They aren't gay?"

"Oh my God, no!" I scoffed, considering Drake's words carefully. Jacks was a ladies man. Always had been - always would be. But Winchester - Win being gay made perfect sense. His insistence on living in the cabin with Jacks and Ana, his discomfort with kisses and hugs from Kris or me. His good taste in clothing and knowledge about shoes. His impeccable appearance - *Win was gay*. And he had it bad for Jacks. I suddenly wanted to bolt into the plane and ask him, but obviously, it wasn't something he felt comfortable discussing, otherwise he would have told one of us.

"Wow," I muttered. It didn't bother me in the least, but that I hadn't seen it before shocked me. I wondered if Jacks knew.

"So, are we staying or are we going?"

"I thought you were a loner?" I turned to look at him. He smiled and tugged on my hair.

"I *was*. Maybe I'm rethinking that life."

Rethinking life - wasn't that what I'd been doing every day for the last year? "Okay, let's get on the damn plane."

It was small and cramped inside but with enough seating for our group plus a few more. The empty seats were littered with bags. Lou came back to ensure we were all secured, including Lily in her car seat and Zoey who was leashed to the seat next to me before closing up the hatch and returning to the cockpit. As the plane barreled down the open stretch of highway, I imagined standing on the hill above the lake where Fin and Ana's bodies were buried. I had said goodbye to them with the promise that one day I would return. With my eyes closed, I pictured the note inside the cabin, pinned to the counter under a whiskey glass.

My Dearest Connor,

I know you looked for me. I looked for you too. By now you know the cabins are empty and there's too much to explain in a few sentences. There's an address on the back of this note that I hope you will go to. When you get there, follow the instructions for the CB radio. Someone will be listening. You should know that I found what I was looking for but lost it. Connor, you were right. We shouldn't have gone. I'm so sorry... forgive me. Please be careful - the dead are still watching but it's the living you have to worry about now, because I set the City on fire. They're free now, baby...they're all free. Please hurry up and find me.

I need you to come back to me. I love you. - Riley

The End of Book two

The Story Continues in Book three...

The thin mattress squeaked beneath my body as I rolled from side to side in an attempt to get comfortable, but everything about the small room was foreign to me, including the full-size bed. A pale night-light flushed the lower half of the room, tinting the white walls a yellowish color that reminded me of used toilet water. All of the concrete floors were laid atop heated wiring that kept the hard surface warm, but the coldness of the space still eased its way into every room and reached for me like invisible cold hands. The sleeping quarters didn't have windows and I missed the fluttering of the cabin curtains and creaky windowsill more than I imagined possible.

It was strange sleeping underground. There was always a chilly draft, though the temperature was carefully controlled. It was as if the earth itself leached all warmth from our little concave of man-made tunnels like a thief and didn't stop the crime until it stole the warmed breath from my lungs. The others said we would get used to it, but I doubted that. I came from a place where it was warm even in winter. People weren't meant to live under the dirt like rodents. Only three weeks had passed, and yet I felt as if I had been locked in the dark for years.

With a long groan, I pushed up and swung my clothed legs over the side of the bed, wincing as my bare feet touched the cool ground. The solar power was at its weakest just before five in the morning, which meant the heat system under the poured concrete was slowly losing its power. The socks I kicked off before falling into bed the night before were nowhere to be seen, so I padded across the room, and stood on the small area rug, digging my toes into the plush tuffs of balled cotton while rifling through the dresser. After pulling on thick, white socks with padded soles and an oversized sweater, I quietly opened my door and peeked into the hallway. The only sound was the hum of a generator down the hall and my feet softly padding along the polished floor.

For the third morning in a row, I found myself upstairs in the community library before dawn, cold and alone. Curled into a ball, buried as deep into one of the plush chairs as physically possible, I sat with a book balanced on my knee and blinked wearily at the printed words. After reading the same paragraph twice, I looked up and stared at the windows that lined the round room like the arc of a rainbow. They were ground level and too small for even a child to crawl thru; their only purpose was to allow light into the space during the day, yet still go almost undetected from outside. The wind roused the loose dirt and weeds and I jumped when a tumbleweed blew across the glass, darting in and out of sight as it scratched along the windows and eventually bounced out of view.

"A storm's coming," Jacks said softly from the doorway. He held a wiggling Lily in his arms and itched his scruffy chin with the bottom of her bottle as she sucked greedily from it.

I smiled at the two of them - father and child. After patting the chair next to me, I draped my book over the arm of my own chair and turned my body to face Jacks as he settled into the adjoining seat. With my eyes closed, we listened to the soft sucking sounds that Lily made as she ate. *Such innocence. Such simplicity. Such perfection.*

"Is she sleeping better?"

Jacks contorted his face into a myriad of expressions until I laughed. After a heavy sigh, he leaned down and kissed Lily's forehead. One of her tiny hands flailed above her head until it landed on his nose. She squeezed until Jacks winced and when he pulled away from her grasp, his nose was Rudolph-red.

I laughed. "That's new."

"She just learned how to yank. My nose might not survive her first year," he chuffed.

Even though I was happy for the new addition, my heart ached watching sweet Lily, and it ached for my own children. Before Jacks noticed, I turned away to hide my hot tears. Oblivious to my hurt, Jacks whispered softly to the baby before raising his voice slightly.

"Riley...do you think you'll ever have another one?"

My voice was trapped in my throat so I shrugged my answer. *If I could have another child, would I?* With Connor being lost, there was no one I'd even consider sharing that experience with. After casually swiping my damp cheek, my eyes once again drifted upward to the sand that pelted the heavy-duty windowpanes high above us. *Yeah, a storm was coming all right. A big one from the looks of it...*

ACKNOWLEDGEMENTS

My family is amazing. I thank you for your patience, understanding and excitement for my writing. Without you all, I would not be where I am now in my career. I love you Shane, Rory and Foxx. Big thanks must go out to my supportive extended family and friends. Thank you, Mom for reading my work. It means the world to me.

Liana Mark - thank you for your time editing this book. It has been a pleasure working with you. I appreciate your patience and enthusiasm more than you know. I look forward to our future work together.

Deb Rogers - I love everything you do. Your covers are amazing. Thank you for your artistic work, creative inspiration and patience doing the cover for this book! Much love to you!!

Thank you to the amazing Beta Readers: Erin Lang Enochs, Jessica Bailiff, Jennifer Spell Wedmore, Stacey Taylor and Cat Alley. I appreciate your enthusiasm and interest and am so glad you all enjoyed the book.

M-7 - I love each and every one of you: Kristie Haigwood, Miranda Stork, Tara Wood, Lindsay Avalon and Caroline Levy. You lovely women complete me as a writer. FACT.

Writing is a passion, of course, but it would not be as much fun without the wonderful support of my readers, TMD fans and the M-7 Street Crew. You are ALL amazing and my work is for YOU.

ABOUT the AUTHOR

Trish was born and mostly raised in San Diego, California where she lives now with her family and pets. She's been writing short stories and poetry since high school and began her first book, 'I Hope You Find Me' in December of 2011.

When Trish isn't writing, she's homeschooling her amazing daughter and mildly Autistic son, reading whatever she can get her hands on, or enjoying the Southern California sun. As a strict Vegetarian, Trish holds a special place in her heart for animal rights and dashes into the backyard weekly to rescue lizards and mice from Zoey, the dog.

TRISH'S BOOKS and COLLABORATIONS

FIND ME Series
I Hope You Find Me
Lost and Found

THE STATION Series
Dying to Forget
Dying to Remember
Dying to Return (Coming Soon)

ANTHOLOGIES
Via Moon Rose Publishing: Once Upon A Twisted Time (Hawke &
the Beast)

You Can Follow Trish Here:
Twitter: https://twitter.com/Trish_Dawson
Facebook: https://www.facebook.com/WriterTrishMarieDawson
Trish's Blog: http://writertrishmdawson.wordpress.com

**Trish's work can be found online as well as in print. Please
support your favorite Indie Authors by buying their books and leaving
them honest reviews. Say NO to book piracy!**

www.ingramcontent.com/pod-product-compliance
Lightning Source LLC
Chambersburg PA
CBHW031722170626
46808CB00005B/1849